A Chaotic Courtship

Bethany Swafford

Published by Lilac Petal Press, 2018.

This is a work of fiction. Similarities to real people, places, or events are entirely coincidental.

A CHAOTIC COURTSHIP

First edition. November 13, 2018.

Copyright © 2018 Bethany Swafford.

Written by Bethany Swafford.

For my parents, who taught me to love books and
reading

Chapter One

"Diana?"

My aunt's voice pulled me from my thoughts, and she inclined her head slightly to the right. I followed her gaze to the young lady I'd only known a few short weeks. Her face held an expectant expression.

"Miss Jennings, I was seeking some clever way to say this but I fear I could not find it," I said, attempting to explain away my absentmindedness. "Your Mr. Carister appears to be a handsome man, and you are to be congratulated on your engagement. I wish you both much joy."

Miss Jennings beamed at my words. Similar expressions had no doubt been said since the happy announcement had been made earlier in the evening. She genuinely seemed to be head over heels in love with her new betrothed, something all too rare in our society.

"Thank you, Mrs. Forester, Miss Forester," she said, her tone sweet as she glanced between my aunt and myself. "I believe I see my mother trying to get my attention. Please excuse me."

I was more than happy to allow her to make her way to the other side of the drawing room. Her mother was surrounded by several of the matrons, no doubt expounding on the excellent match her daughter had achieved in such a short of time.

"Diana, my dear, do try to keep your head out of the clouds," my aunt said in a low voice. Her gaze slid past me and she walked away. "Ah, Mrs Richards. How lovely to see you again."

Left to myself, I found a seat apart from the other ladies, tired of the gossip that filled the drawing rooms every time the ladies waited for the gentlemen to finish their port. Part of me wished I had brought my hated needlework. At least it would have been something for me to do, and I knew Mother expected me to actually finish the shawl I had been embroidering for the last year.

"It's Miss Forester, isn't it?"

Surprised, I lifted my gaze to find a young lady standing in front of me. Her pale pink dress, though simple, was elegant. The dark brown eyes and fair hair were familiar, but I couldn't immediately think of her name. Admitting so would be horridly embarrassing.

"Yes, I am." As I acknowledged my identity, I rose to make my curtsy and tried to think quickly. After a moment, I had it: we had been introduced mere moments before we had gone in for dinner. She was the daughter of one of Uncle Forester's business associates. That narrowed it down enough I could remember her name. I gestured to the seat beside me. "Would you like to sit down, Miss Reynolds?"

"Certainly. Thank you," Miss Reynolds said, moving to sit next to me. "I do so dislike this part of the evening. It's dreadfully tedious listen to gossip that has already been shared. Nothing new can ever be learned by this point in the day. Do you not agree, Miss Forester?"

"I can't say I have ever been fond of gossip at any hour of the day."

My honesty made Miss Reynolds frown and tilt her head as she focused on me. "Why have we never met before this, Miss Forester?" she asked, her tone curious. "I have been here with my family since the beginning of the Season. Surely, we would have crossed paths at a ball or a dinner party before this."

"I only came up to London with my aunt and uncle a few weeks ago. My uncle had business to tend to and I was privileged to be allowed to come as well."

"You poor thing! How many delightful events you have missed! Could you not have convinced them to come sooner? Or to have your parents bring you? Everyone knows the most eligible gentlemen have been caught by this time."

"Oh, so you are engaged then, Miss Reynolds?" I asked, avoiding her questions. Forcing her to talk about herself was the only tact I knew would deflect the questioning from myself. It was a skill I had perfected on my younger sister, Sarah, who Miss Reynolds somehow reminded me of.

Immediately, Miss Reynolds stiffened. "No," she said with reluctance. "It is only recently I decided upon a gentleman worth pursuing. The others were quite beneath me, you understand."

"And does this gentleman know of the honor you have granted him?" I asked sweetly. Miss Reynolds frowned again as if sensing my sarcasm but not quite understanding it. "Is he here tonight? You must point him out to me."

"I have no doubt he will approach me the moment he comes in," Miss Reynolds told me.

Her certainty made me curious. Which of the men at the dinner party could she possibly have decided upon?

The silence that followed seemed to stretch on and on. Among strangers, silence has always made me nervous. This was no exception. Just as I was about to offer an excuse to move to Aunt Forester's side, the door of the drawing room opened.

Miss Reynolds swiftly directed a pleased smile at me. I responded with a polite smile of my own as the gentlemen entered. The last of the men walked towards us. My breath caught in my throat and I glanced from him to the young lady at my side. Was this the man she had set her heart on?

Mr. Richfield?

I didn't know what to think as the tall man drew closer. Having first met him at the first soiree Aunt Forester had taken me to, he and I had conversed at nearly every event I had attended since then. He was not titled, which made me wonder why Miss Reynolds, who came from a well to do family, considered him so superior to other men.

He was handsome, of course, with hair the color of sand and blue eyes. And there was the rumor I had heard hinting he was not penniless. Still, was that enough to attract Miss Reynolds' interest? I would have thought she would aim higher.

My interest, on the other hand—well, I never claimed to be holding out for a titled gentleman. Everything about Mr. John Richfield proclaimed him to be a most respectable young man. His kindness and attentiveness whenever we met had set me at ease and then charmed me, especially as I saw him display such care with any lady he came across.

Miss Reynolds was already on her feet and I quickly rose as well. "Mr. Richfield," I said, dropping a slight curtsy.

"Mr. Richfield," Miss Reynolds said at the same time, her tone bright and coy. The expression on her face was one of absolute delight as she held out her hand. "I was hoping we would have the chance to continue our conversation."

"Miss Forester, Miss Reynolds." Mr. Richfield bowed slightly over her hand and then pulled his own hand away. "I hope I'm not interrupting."

Miss Reynolds took a step forward. "Certainly not. Miss Forester and I were merely becoming better acquainted. Could I persuade you to take a turn about the room with me, sir? After sitting so long, it will be refreshing to have a change of scenery and I hear the paintings are exceptional."

Just as I resigned myself to watching Miss Reynolds flirt with him for the rest of the evening, Mr. Richfield said, "I was actually coming to request Miss Forester play the pianoforte for us. I have heard many times she is quite accomplished, but have yet to hear it for myself."

That brought my head up swiftly. Mr. Richfield held his arm out to me, a smile on his face. "Will you allow me to turn the pages for you, Miss Forester?"

"Yes, of course," I said quickly. I put my hand on his arm and let him lead me to the pianoforte. "I should warn you, I am not the master of pianoforte my aunt makes me out to be."

"I never thought Mrs. Forester to be the kind of woman who would exaggerate," my escort said, looking amused.

"No, I think you are being overly modest, Miss Forester It doesn't become you."

I bit my lip as I took my seat at the instrument. Out of the corner of my eye, I could see Miss Reynolds talking to another young lady to whom I had been introduced earlier. From the sour look on both of their faces, I guessed neither of them were pleased with this turn of events.

It wasn't my fault Mr. Richfield preferred my company over her fawning. Since I'd met him, time and again I had seen him ignore any flirtatious behavior directed at him. Clearly, it wasn't the way to get his attention.

Somehow, without trying, I had managed to do that.

"Is there something wrong?"

Realizing I had been staring at Miss Reynolds, I switched my focus to Mr. Richfield's question. "No. I'm afraid my mind has a tendency to wander."

"I am hurt!" he said, holding a hand to his chest dramatically. "Am I such uninteresting company?"

"Of course not! That isn't what I meant!"

He chuckled as he allowed his hand to drop. "I know, Miss Forester. I was simply teasing. Now, have you decided what you will play for us?"

Feeling my cheeks flush with embarrassment, I searched through the sheet music our hostess had made available. I selected a simple piece—*Lavender's Blue*—and spread the sheet music out. With so many young ladies who had undoubtedly had the benefit of a master's training in the company, I was not about to show off in any way. Generally, I left that to Sarah.

Mr. Richfield remained by my side and turned the pages at my nod. I didn't tell him I knew every note and word by heart. An exhalation of relief left my lips once I finished. The gathered party applauded politely, Mr. Richfield the loudest of all.

"Another, Miss Forester?" he asked. He reached for the sheet music to display it for me.

Shaking my head, I left the seat for another, eager young lady to take. "Oh, no. I think I have displayed my meager talent enough for one evening."

Chuckling, Mr. Richfield showed me to a seat and then fetched a cup of tea for me. He sat beside me as music filled the room. "Miss Forester, you were lying to me," he said, leaning closer so that I could hear him.

"I don't think that's true."

"As you wish. You *implied* you were only adequate at the pianoforte, and yet you played exquisitely."

I raised my eyebrow. "I do believe you are trying to flatter me, sir."

"What reason would I have to do that?" he asked, raising his own eyebrow at me.

Blushing, I dropped my gaze to my cup. There was only one reason a girl would think any gentleman would be paying any attention to her, but perhaps I was overthinking the matter. "I didn't mean to embarrass you," Mr. Richfield said quickly as I sought to find something to say. "Perhaps you would prefer to talk about the latest gossip?"

"No!"

A few older members of the group glanced over at me, and I felt my cheeks flush even more. In my horror at the thought of having to maintain the senseless gossip commonly spoken of, I had spoken a trifle louder than necessary. I forced a swift, polite smile and they returned to their conversations.

Why was I constantly embarrassing myself in front of Mr. Richfield?

"Quite honestly, Mr. Richfield, I have no desire to listen to stories that are told merely to spread scandal," I said in a much lower tone. "I do not know those involved, and it could well be that matters have been greatly exaggerated with each person who repeats it. I want no part in that."

"Good," Mr. Richfield said with a smile, seeming not to have noticed I had, just moments before, drawn the attention of others with my improper exclamation. "I suspected you shared my feelings on the matter. However I had to make sure."

"A test, sir?"

"Do you mind?"

I considered the question for a moment. "No," I said slowly, careful to keep my voice low. "But it is hardly fair of you to do something like that to me."

"I promise not to do it again," Mr. Richfield said, gazing at me in a suddenly serious manner. He seemed to hesitate. "Miss Forester, if I were to find my way to your family's home, would I find a welcome?"

My breath caught in my throat. "My home?"

Mr. Richfield nodded. "With your permission, I'd like to meet and speak to your father."

What he was saying, what he was asking, was unmistakable. I felt frozen, not knowing the proper thing to do or say or even think. No one had ever told me how to handle a situation like this. Certainly, I enjoyed the company of Mr. Richfield, but marriage?

"Miss Forester?"

With a start, I realized Mr. Richfield's gaze was still on me, a furrow forming on his brow. I had to say something, and so the first thing that came to mind was what left my lips. "It's always pleasant to have someone new come to the neighborhood. I believe you said you know my neighbors, the Sandwoods?"

Mr. Richfield's frown deepened. "Yes, that's true. And it has been some time since I last saw them. But that wasn't what I meant, Miss Forester."

Right. "My father does enjoy making new acquaintances. I'm sure you will find a warm welcome in my home."

My answer was exactly the vague, flighty response an empty-headed debutante would give. Mr. Richfield's expression was puzzled and opened his mouth to say more. "Diana, Mr. Forester," my aunt said, getting my attention. "We're setting up the card tables. Would you care to help make up a set?"

"I would love to!" Standing, I hurried to join her. Already I regretted my answer to Mr. Richfield. With much effort, I pushed it from my mind until a moment when I could think it over.

A LETTER FROM MY MOTHER waited for me at the breakfast table the next morning. I couldn't help smiling as I picked it up. "Such eagerness! You do realize you will be home in a few days to learn the latest news?" Uncle Forester said, amusement in his voice.

"By then this news," I said, holding my letter up, "will be old news."

"You forget, dear niece, I am from the country as well. News does not grow old so quickly."

"True. May I plead affection for my mother as a reason for my pleasure?"

"I believe we all know the affection you have for your family, Diana."

"My dear Mr. Forester, are you teasing Diana again?" Aunt Forester asked, coming in just then. I breathed a sigh of relief to have escaped anymore of my uncle's teasing. "Diana, what news from home do you have?"

"When I have read my letter, I will tell you what it contains," I said, breaking the seal. I ignored my food in favor of reading my letter. The majority was made up of my mother's greetings to her old school friends. She knew me well enough to guess I had forgotten to visit them. The final paragraph, though, caused me to smile. "Mother wishes me to give her regards to her school friends if they are in town."

"Ah, yes. I do remember her giving you those instructions before we left. But what do you find so amusing about that?"

I glanced up. "It's not that. It is what she has to say from my brother. Listen to this," I said, lifting the letter up to read aloud. *"William requests that I tell you there have been rumors of a highwayman in the area. If you should happen to be stopped, cooperate in every way and your brother swears he will avenge you as soon as he hears of it."*

Aunt Forester chuckled. "You wouldn't dare be accosted by a highwayman without Will, would you, Diana? He will accuse you of doing so just to spite him."

"Highwaymen, indeed," Uncle Forester said, folding up his paper. "The boy is inventing stories now. At sixteen, William is old enough to know better. I will return this evening, my dear."

Smiling, my aunt rose to say goodbye to him. Embarrassed, I gazed steadfastly at the words written on the paper in my hand, looking up only when the door closed. Aunt Forester's smile was pleased when she sat back down, and I couldn't help smiling as well. The affection that existed between my aunt and uncle was sweet, rivaled only by the love I saw between my parents.

"Well, enough about your brother's odd fascination with criminals," Aunt Forester said. "I believe you and Mr. Richfield were having an intimate talk last night."

I felt my cheeks flush as I folded up my letter. "Did we call much attention to ourselves?"

"No one else seemed to remark upon it. But that may be because it is the kind of situation you should expect when you are being courted by such a well respected young man."

"Courted." Perhaps it had been naive of me, but I had never seriously considered Mr. Richfield had been courting me. Though we spoke whenever we attended the same dinner or soirée, I never thought he made a special effort to seek me out. I had simply enjoyed being with him as we shared similar opinions and tastes.

Aunt Forester finished her meal, and pushed her plate away. "I had hoped he would make his intentions known before we left. I even warned Mr. Forester he might be approached by Mr. Richfield."

Oh, dear. I dropped my gaze to my letter. "I don't think you will need to worry about that,"

Even I could hear the misery in my voice. "What's wrong?" Aunt Forester asked. "You two didn't have some sort of quarrel, did you?"

"A quarrel? No." Though a quarrel might have been preferable. At least then I could make amends. How do you go about apologizing for being thoughtless and nervous? I closed my eyes. All my doubts and regrets were giving me a headache.

"Diana?"

Breathing out, I forced myself to look at my aunt. She deserved nothing but the truth. "Last night, Mr. Richfield asked for my permission to speak to my father. And—."

"Oh, Diana!" Aunt Forester reached across the table to grab my hands. "How wonderful! Congratulations! I knew it would do you a world of good to come to London!"

"I didn't give it!" Allowing her continue under the assumption I was as good as engaged was something I could not do.

Aunt Forester became visibly puzzled. "What?"

"I didn't give my permission. Not exactly. Please understand I was surprised by what he said."

"What did you tell him?"

My fingers tightened around my letter, crumpling the paper. I remembered each word with clarity. "I said how enjoyable it was to have new faces in the neighborhood, and my father enjoyed making new acquaintances."

Holding my breath, I waited to be berated by my aunt for being an empty-headed ninny. "Well, that's not as bad as I expected," my aunt said, with a relieved sigh. "We can fix this easily, Diana." She narrowed her eyes at me. "Unless you were merely trying to avoid refusing an offer outright?"

"No!" I relaxed my grip on my letter to clasp my hands together as I tried to explain something I didn't quite understand myself. "I don't want to refuse him—I think. I just do not feel i know him well enough to commit the rest of my life to his care."

"Diana, what more can you wish to know about him?" Aunt Forester said severely. "You cannot live forever with your parents, and you have no inheritance to start up your own household, which would ostracize you from society. You are already twenty years old. How many more offers can you expect to receive before you are considered to be 'on the shelf' as they say?"

I flinched under her bluntness. "I know." I did know. Everything she had said had crossed my mind many times in the past couple years, and especially the recent winter months. "But I cannot accept someone's offer without knowing him. I have not known Mr. Richfield for long, Aunt."

"Have you heard anything to make you think he is anything but a fine gentleman? Has he ever acted in a manner other than completely respectful?" Aunt Forester asked.

"No," I said in answer to both questions.

"Then I fail to see why you are so concerned. Think of Sarah. You know it would not do for anyone to offer for your younger sister's hand while you are still unwed. Do you want her to become an old maid as well?"

"Of course not!"

"Then, you must accept Mr. Richfield's offer. As I said, we can save this situation with no difficulty. When we see him tonight, you can merely explain you were startled and you desire him to speak to your father."

"How do you know we will see him tonight?"

Aunt Forester's expression became pleased. "Because I make sure to be well informed and know every guest attending the soiree. Now, get ready. It won't be long before we have callers."

I left the breakfast room, torn between relief and doubt that the situation could be fixed with only a few words.

Chapter Two

Mr. Richfield didn't come.

I searched for his face among the other guests and barely heard the music. At the interval, I stayed in my seat, twisting my fan in my fingers. When I couldn't bear to search in vain, I closed my eyes. Everything had been ruined!

"Diana? Why are you sitting alone?"

With a start, I glanced up to find a familiar couple in front of me, and slowly I got to my feet. "Anna, Sir Rodger." I offered as sincere a smile as I could. "I'm sorry. I am out of sorts tonight."

"Anna saw you were not paying attention to the program," Sir Rodger Carlyle said with an answering smile. He glanced at his wife with affection. "She insisted something dreadful must have occurred for Miss Diana Forester not to hear the music."

"It's nothing dreadful, I assure you," I said, feeling my smile come quicker this time. Anna Carlyle, née Knighton, had grown up a few short miles from my home, and we had been friends for as long as I could remember. "Merely too many thoughts in my head."

Dramatically, Anna brought her hand to her chest. "It's worse than I thought!" Mock horror laced her tone. "Diana Forester overthinking? What has the world come to now?"

I had to laugh at her antics and sought some way to change the subject. "I am glad to see you tonight for I leave London in two days."

"I thought as much." Anna let her hand drop down to her husband's arm. "And don't think you can avoid the question so easily, my friend. You must tell me everything. How else am I to help you?"

"That is a signal I need to fetch refreshment," Sir Rodger said. He kissed his wife's hand. "I'll be back."

For a moment, Anna watched her husband weave his way out of the room, and I saw the contentment on her face. Yet another happily married couple. I felt my heart clench with a surprising emotion: yearning.

Turning to me, Anna pulled me back down into my seat as she sat on the adjacent chair. "Tell me quickly. What has happened?"

"There is nothing." What point would there be in trying to explain the specifics of the matter in a few short minutes? "You have invented a situation where there is none."

"Do not lie to me, Diana Forester." Anna tapped her chin with her fan, a look of determination on her face I knew all too well. "Fine. I shall simply have to guess."

That would only end badly. "Please don't."

Anna held her hand up, frowning at me. "Don't interrupt me while I am thinking." After a few seconds, her brown eyes lit up. "I have it! It has something to do with the lack of a certain person in attendance tonight, doesn't it?"

"Certain person? Could you possibly be any vaguer?"

Heaving a sigh, Anna shook her head at me. "Diana, everywhere you have been since you arrived in London, Mr.

Richfield has been right by your side. Suddenly though, on one of your last evenings here, he is nowhere to be seen."

"Anna, please, I beg you. Don't."

Looking genuinely concerned, Anna leaned towards me. "Diana, did you quarrel with Mr. Richfield?"

Why did everyone assume I had quarreled with him? "No. I have not." Squeezing my friend's hand, I put it from my mind. "You need to stop worrying about me, Anna. I am a grown woman, capable of solving any problems that come my way. Now, I don't want to spoil our last evening together."

Sitting back in the chair, Anna stared at me. "If you insist, I will say no more about it. But you have to swear you will write and tell me all."

"When I have something to tell you, I will write." I hoped I had managed to convince her. Now I just had to convince myself I had spoken true. Somehow, I would figure this out.

As I looked out over the other guests, a familiar face made me gasp. "What's wrong?" Anna asked, twisting to see what had so obviously startled me. "Is he here? Did you see him?"

"No. Mr. Richfield isn't here," I said, shaking my head. The face I had seen had vanished. "I didn't know your brother was in Town."

"Philip?" Anna frowned. "Mama didn't say he intended to come to London when she wrote me." She heaved a sigh. "But when do young gentlemen, brothers especially, ever keep their families appraised of what they were doing?"

"Perhaps I was mistaken." It had been months since I last saw Philip Knighton and we had parted on such bad terms, I did not want to face him once again in a public setting. "There are a great many people here."

Anna nodded. "Ah, here comes trodger with our refreshments."

"SHE LOOKS AS THOUGH she has never seen the country before."

Three days after the soiree, we were in the carriage. At my Uncle Forester's words, I reluctantly pulled my gaze from the familiar landscape. "We're almost home!" I said, knowing it wasn't necessary. My uncle had grown up in the neighborhood, the same as my father, and knew exactly where we were.

Both Uncle and Aunt Forester's smiles were indulgent. "It's a good thing London society isn't here to see the lovely Miss Forester acting like a child on her first outing," Aunt Forester said, continuing to act as though I was not there. "What happened to the calm young lady who was such a success?"

"Perhaps this is a ploy to become recognizable," Uncle Forester said, mischief glinting in his eyes. "After all, who wants to be known as merely 'lovely' and 'a success' when she could be an oddity or an eccentric and be welcomed wherever she shows her face?"

Even though I knew they were teasing me, I couldn't help feeling a twinge of annoyance and I sought some way of changing the subject. "I wonder if James is home yet." My older brother had spent most of the winter visiting friends from university and I was eager to hear how he'd occupied himself in all that time.

"What?" Aunt Forester said, raising her eyebrows. It was difficult to tell whether this was genuine, or whether part of her was teasing me. "With the constant exchange of letters between you and your sister, not to mention the letters from your mother, and you do not know whether your brother have returned home yet?"

"Mother did not say in her last letter." I determined to act in a way a member of society would. Folding my gloved hands in my lap, I straightened my shoulders. "And my sister would hardly waste her paper space on news concerning our brothers. She had much more important things to share."

"Such as the new song she was composing. It will be a pleasure to hear you two perform together again."

Uncle Forester frowned at me as I struggled to sit straight in the swaying post-chaise. "What are you trying to do, Diana?" he asked.

What was I trying to accomplish? Was there use in trying to be the epitome of a proper young lady? My family wouldn't care if I acted exactly like a London lady; only that I had shown myself a young lady of good upbringing and manners. I sighed and relaxed against the back of my seat. "Nothing," I said, not wanting to attempt to explain myself.

I ran my gloved hand over the cover of the novel on my lap. It was the second volume of *Mansfield Park*. I had spent far to much to acquire the three volumes, but I had so loved reading the previous novel by the same author.

Fixing my attention once more on the passing scenery, I caught sight of an old, large oak we'd just passed. I knew that tree. My siblings and I had spent many a summer day climbing and playing under the branches. It marked the edge of the property surrounding Wisteria House, and I pushed myself to the edge of the seat. "We're home!"

"Diana, for goodness' sake!"

After many, many long weeks away, I finally caught sight of my home. Wisteria House was not the most elegant house in the country, nor the biggest. It was just large enough to hold my family comfortably. The sturdy brick structure was surrounded by a good sized lawn and oak trees. Just beyond stood the small stable. The entire scene hinted at a modest income of the occupants.

What? Where had that thought come from? I shook my head to get rid of the unwelcome line of reasoning. My time in London surely hadn't changed me into a mercenary person, only concerned with the worth of things. At least, I sincerely hoped it had not done such a thing.

My father's estate and tennant's supported the family, and that's all that was needed. When I married, I would have a modest dowry and no need to seek employment, as some unfortunate young ladies did.

"You look worried, Diana. Are you afraid your parents will chastise you over—?"

"Of course not," I said, interrupting shamelessly. Aunt Forester would be the last person to understand my fears of being changed. She had been the strongest advocate for my going to London and getting some 'polish.' "I'm happy to be home, that's all."

"Now, Diana, surely you've taken the time to think about what it will be like when you are married? You won't be able to call this home anymore. Perhaps you will live far away as well."

"I know. But I'm not married yet."

Leaning over, Uncle Forester was able to see ahead as I was not. "I don't see anyone waiting outside. Maybe our letter hasn't arrived yet. That certainly isn't unheard of."

My heart clenched as I thought perhaps my family was out visiting. No! I had waited this long to see my parents again, and I did not want to have to wait a minute longer than necessary!

The chaise slowed as it neared the front door. Impatiently, I acted on an urge I barely took the time to acknowledge. I grasped the door handle and pushed the door open.

"Diana!" Aunt Forester's protest followed me as I sprang to the ground. Gravel crunched under my boots. "What will your parents think?"

Any answer I might have given vanished as I saw the front door open and the person I had missed the most while I was in London stepped outside: my mother. "Mama!" I grasped my skirt and lifted it as I hurried to reach her. "I am so happy to see you! I missed you so much!"

"Diana," was all my mother said as she opened her arms. I clung to her, blinking away the tears in my eyes. How I had missed the comfort and security, my mother had always provided. There was a great deal to tell her, but it could wait until later.

After several moments, when Uncle Forester cleared his throat loudly, Mother untangled herself from me and held me at arm's length as her eyes swept over me. "You look well, Diana. Your time in London doesn't appear to have done you any harm."

"Naturally not!" Aunt Forester protested. "There was hardly any danger of that."

"I had a wonderful time, and I can't wait to tell you about it," I told Mother, reaching for my bonnet's ties. I glanced around. No one else had followed Mother from the house. "Where is everyone else?"

"Your father was asked to help Mr. Sandwood with a matter. Sarah went with him to have a long visit with Miss Sandwood. And your brother—well, whoever knows where Will is?" Mother shook her head. "What happened to your manners in London, Diana? Do you plan on keeping your aunt and uncle out here until dark?"

"Of course not," I said, spinning to face the carriage. "Forgive me."

My aunt and uncle merely seemed amused, though. "Please come in," Mother said to them. "You must be tired from your long journey. I will have the servants bring your things in."

It was good to step into my childhood home. As I made a slow to turn to take it all in, I pulled my gloves off my hands. Everything, as usual, was spotless and appeared exactly as it had when I had left. The wood floors beneath my feet gleamed and there was the faint scent of beeswax in the air.

The only thing missing was the sound of running footsteps, and my siblings calling out. And as much as I wanted to see all of my family, I found myself hoping everyone would stay away long enough for me to have a private conversation with Mother.

"Come, Mary, George, let me show you to your room," Mother said to my aunt and uncle.

I followed them upstairs. When they continued, I slipped into the room I have always shared with my younger sister. A groan left my lips as I saw the interior of the chamber. "Oh, Sarah."

The bed was still unmade, though the blankets had been pulled up as if Sarah had made a half-hearted attempt to straighten things. Her nightgown was thrown over the dressing table chair. There was sheet music on the floor by the window. Our parents had forbidden the maid long ago from touching the room, in the hopes Sarah would mend her bad habit.

"Diana."

My mother's voice pulled me out of my horror at the state of the room. I twisted around to see her in the doorway, shaking her head at the mess. "Your aunt and uncle are getting settled and resting for a while. Tea will be in the sitting room in fifteen minutes."

There was an unspoken command in the last statement. "I will be right down."

Mother's smile was all I saw before she closed the door. I set my gloves on the crowded dressing table, next to the novel I had been reading before I left. Swiftly, I unbuttoned my pelisse and hung it with the other garments for outdoors in the wardrobe. Pouring water into the basin, I washed my hands and face. One of the grooms, someone new I'd never seen before, brought my trunk in while I was checking my hair. For a moment, I considered getting out the gifts I'd purchased while in Town but decided to leave them for later.

Standing in front of the mirror, I checked my appearance and gave an approving nod. The walking gown I had worn for the journey wasn't wrinkled, so tt was not necessary for me to change into a different gown as I would have in town. "Good enough."

The sooner I went downstairs, the more time I would have to talk to Mother alone. And there was one benefit of being in the country: expectations for appearance were entirely different and easier to achieve.

It was good to be home.

MOTHER SAT ALONE IN the sitting room when I entered. "Come have a seat, Diana," she said, gesturing to the space on the settee next to her. "Your aunt hinted you had something you wanted to share with me."

"Yes, I do." I crossed the room. The entire trip from London I had spent thinking of the best way to approach this subject. All of my planning vanished the closer I got to my mother. By the time I sat down, my hands were damp with moisture. "You recall I met a Mr. Richfield in London, shortly after I first arrived?"

"Yes, you mentioned him several times in your letters."

Her tone was matter-of-fact, giving absolutely nothing away, which I should have expected. Mother was an expert at keeping her thoughts to herself. "Well—" I hesitated as I sought the right words. I rubbed my palms against my skirt. "At Aunt Forester's last dinner party, Mr. Richfield asked for my permission to come speak to father."

For a moment, there was silence. "What was your answer?" Mother asked, as calm as ever.

I bit my lip and found I could no longer meet her gaze. "I fear I may have spoken without thinking." Back when I had said the words, I had been surprised. Now though, I realized just how mistaken I had been. "I said it's always pleasant to have someone new visit."

"I see. Do you like him?"

Ah, there was the question. "I think so." I took a deep breath and let it out slowly. "He is respectable, at least as far as Uncle Forester could discover. No one ever had a word to say against him. I think he is a good man."

"And yet, you don't seem enthusiastic about marrying him."

"I have only known him for a few weeks." It felt good to be able to talk this out with my mother, now the awkwardness of saying the words had passed. If anyone could help me untangle my feelings, it was her. "Is that enough time to know a person? You knew Papa your whole life before he proposed."

Mother's hand came over mine. "Diana, look at me." I lifted my eyes to hers. "You are the only one who can make this decision. It is your right to refuse an offer you find distasteful. However, you need to understand it is not likely you will have the opportunity to travel again and meet other people."

"I don't find the offer distasteful. I don't think I know him well enough to accept his hand in marriage." I sighed. "I wish I had had the time to know more about him."

"Perhaps you will."

I shook my head. That seemed an impossibility. "Mama, the look on his face when I pretended I didn't understand. I acted as if I were a senseless, empty-headed child! What kind of man would pursue me in the face of that?"

"A man who would be understanding. Someone who would realize your shy nature."

Pulling my hand away, I reached to pour myself some much-needed tea. "There are other, much prettier girls with better dowries than I," I remarked, adding just the right amount of cream and sugar. "I doubt I will ever see him again."

Of that, I was quite certain. I had spent hours considering what a mess I had made of the situation. Why would he chase after me when Miss Reynolds was on hand to charm and flirt with him? I sipped my tea as I watched my mother's face. Her smile was one I couldn't quite understand. Why did she look so amused?

"Mr. Richfield is already here."

Chapter Three

I choked. Of all the things I expected Mother to say right then, that simple statement had never crossed my mind. It took several moments for me to stop coughing and to recover my composure. "What did you say?" I asked, hoping I had heard her wrong.

"Your Mr. Richfield arrived two days ago," Mother said, her smile widening. "He had dinner with us and then had quite a long conversation with your father afterward. I believe he is staying with the Sandwoods as they are friends of his family."

"Mr. Richfield was here?"

This time my mother laughed out loud. "Diana, did you not hear me? Not only was he here, he is still here now. Must you question me so?"

Amazed, I found I had nothing to say in response. "I was fully prepared to chastise you for not warning us ahead of time, but now I understand that it happened all of a sudden and you didn't think anything would come of it."

Still smiling, Mother poured herself some tea and sipped it. "I cannot believe he came." Happiness swept over me. Perhaps he did in fact like me. But then, I frowned. "Why didn't you say anything before this? You must have known I was anxious about the matter!"

"Certainly." Anything else she might have said was interrupted by the sitting room door opening.

"Diana!" Sarah's bonnet fell to the ground as she danced across the room. "Finally!"

Laughing, I stood up to hug her. At times, I envied my younger sister's bubbly personality, but now I was happy to see her. "What do you mean 'finally'? Aren't you the one who said you never wanted to see me again the day I left?"

"Why would I say something like that?" She pulled away from my embrace to snag a pastry from the tea tray, making Mother tut in disapproval. "Did you bring me anything?"

"Maybe. Did you miss me?"

Sarah waved her hand dismissively, cramming the pastry into her mouth. "That goes without saying, of course," she said, once she swallowed. She pulled a chair over as I returned to my seat. "Charlotte and I have had a wonderful chat. We have decided that since you have returned and can teach us a few new dance steps, we should have a ball."

"What would be the point of having your sister teach you new steps if no one else will be able to dance them with you?" Mother asked, ever practical. "Sarah, please pick up your bonnet."

"Well, Charlotte said her family could invite some of their friends from London," Sarah said as she obediently getting up to collect her bonnet. "Besides, there is Mr. Richfield. He would know the steps. We couldn't have him thinking we are not sophisticated because we don't know the latest dance steps."

I shook my head at that. "I doubt he would care about the dance steps you do or do not know. It's not the most important thing in the world, you know."

"You may not want to impress a prospective husband, but I know better."

My hands clenched around my teacup. "What did you say?"

"Sarah, your sister has only just arrived," Mother said, a weary note in her voice. "Please try to keep from arguing at least for the rest of the day."

"I'm not trying to pick a fight," Sarah said in protest. "She is the one being contrary. It's not my fault if she doesn't like hearing the truth."

Holding up her hands, Mother rose from her chair. "I don't want to hear it, Sarah. Is your father in his study?"

"Yes, Mama, he said he had some papers to take care of." Sarah reached for more pastries, but I snatched the plate out of her reach. "Diana! I wanted that!"

"Diana, why don't you go unpack and rest for awhile?" Mother said, her tone firm. "You've had a long journey."

"Yes, Mama," I said. "Dinner will be at the usual time?"

"Yes."

As Mother walked to the door, I will admit I acted in an appallingly childish way. I took the last pastry and took a big bite from it. Sarah's eyes widened and then narrowed in anger. Setting what was left of the pastry back on the plate, I placed the plate back on the tea tray.

"Diana Forester! How dare you—?!"

I hastened after Mother, unable to hold back a laugh. There was nothing like being home.

THE FIRST CHANCE I had to see my father was right before dinner. He hugged me and asked if I had enjoyed my trip to London. Although I would have liked to learn more about Mr. Richfield's conversation with him, I hesitated to say anything with my sister within earshot. I would have to find a more private occasion to mention it.

My younger brother only question was if I had brought him anything from London. I had, however I had no intentions of telling him so right then. Will was impetuous enough to go in search of it.

Sarah somehow managed to glare at me through the entire meal, but I seemed to be the only one who noticed. Aunt and Uncle Forester had a great deal of gossip to keep the meal lively and frequently appealed to me to verify their statements.

After dinner, while Papa and Uncle Forester talked, I went upstairs and collected the gifts I had brought with me. The moment I stepped into the sitting room, Will tried to relieve me of my burden. Because that is just the caring, selfless younger brother he pretended to be at times.

"I have it," I said, twisting to keep the packages away from him. The fact that he was several inches taller than me and had such long arms made it nearly impossible to get out of reach. "Mama!"

"William, you will get your gift sooner if you leave her alone," Mother said from where she was sewing in front of the fireplace. I don't know how she always managed to sound patient with all of us.

Groaning, Will dropped his arms and retreated to the settee, where he could hang over the back. "Hurry up."

Deliberately, I slowed my steps. "For goodness' sake, Diana, you look ridiculous!" Sarah said, running her fingers across her harp. "Rather like you're walking down the aisle."

"What is so wrong with that?" Though I was determined not to let her pull me into an argument that would only get us both in trouble, I had to know what was going through her mind.

Plucking out a tune, Sarah sent a quick glance over at me. "Well, you're old enough not to play silly pretend games, or at least you should be. You have no prospects of actually walking down the aisle anytime soon."

"Sarah Forester, do not speak of things you know nothing about," Mother said sharply. "You have hardly spent five minutes with Diana without arguing, so how would you know whether she has 'prospects' or not?"

"I think you will find if you did take the time to ask, you will learn your sister does indeed have one prospect, Sarah," Aunt Forester added, sending a smile in my direction.

"You must be joking!" Sarah shifted her gaze, filled with betrayal, to me. "And you haven't told me, Diana?"

There was no way I was going to talk about Mr. Richfield right then. Rushing to the settee, I dropped my packages on the cushion. I focused on handing them out: a book about steam engines for Will, a cashmere shawl for Mother, and new sheet music for Sarah.

It was enough to distract my sister from any thoughts of my prospects. In fact, we spent the rest of the evening re-

viewing the duet together, she on her harp and me on the pianoforte.

I WOKE UP THE NEXT morning and stretched with a
smile. The sun shone in through the window and Sarah was
still asleep next to me. As quietly as I could, I rose, washed
my face, and was dressed in no time. Down to the breakfast
table I went, where Father was reading his newspaper alone.

"Good morning, Papa," I said as I crossed to the table.
I paused next to his chair and bent down to kiss his cheek.
"How are you today?"

"I'm well, Diana. And you're in an unusually good mood
for this hour." Father folded his paper. I hummed happily as
I went to get breakfast from the sideboard. "Surely you were
never up and about at this hour in London."

That was all too true. I doubted Father truly wanted to
know just how late I slept in while I was in the city. "Perhaps
not, but it is good to be home again." After I took a seat at
his right hand, I had taken several bites before I realized Father was looking at me. "Yes?"

"Your mother explained to me how things stood between you and Mr. Richfield."

Just like that, my appetite was gone, and I put my fork
down. "I see. Mama said he came to speak to you."

"He did."

I waited, but he didn't say anything more. "What did
you tell him? Did you like him?"

"I think the more important question is whether you
want me to like him or not?"

"Yes?" I cringed inwardly at the uncertainty my tone betrayed.

Father shook his head at me. "Your Mr. Richfield seemed like an honorable man, and sincere in his interest in you," he told me. "If you don't intend to consider his suit seriously, I think you should tell him before this goes any further."

"You think he genuinely likes me?"

"Diana, when a man such as Richfield comes all the way from London to acquire a father's permission to ask for a girl's hand in marriage, there must be some attraction. And since your dowry is quite modest, I am certain it isn't a mercenary reason he's come. Does that please your vanity?"

The twinkle in Father's eyes reassured me. If he could tease me about the subject, it must not cause him any concern. "Papa, I am not vain."

"No, I know you're not." Father smiled at me. "You and Sarah appeared to be getting on last night."

When he and Uncle Forester had come in, Sarah and I had been working our way through a new duet. "It was a momentary truce. Once we were up in our room, she started complaining about how much space I take up." I heaved a dramatic sigh. "At least I had a room to myself in London, and no sister to intrude upon my space."

"It's amazing how you two can rub each other the wrong way, even now."

Shrugging, I reached for my tea. "Mama says we are too alike in some ways and far too different in all others. Maybe next time I should stay away for much longer, and then we will get along just fine."

"I'm afraid things don't work that way, Diana." Father shook his head. "Now. Do you have plans for today?"

I nodded. "Aunt Forester wants to make a round of visits. It will be good to see everyone again, especially Widow Davison. I have so much to tell her."

"You'll be going to Sandwood Hall first thing, I imagine."

An instant blush burned my cheeks. "Undoubtedly. Sarah and Miss Sandwood appear to be as thick as thieves now."

"Then perhaps while your mother and aunt visit with Mrs. Sandwood and Sarah is whispering with her friend, you will have time to get to know Richfield better." His smile widened. "Be careful how you go about it. Once Will and James find out, you will have no peace."

"I'm afraid of that."

"If anyone should ask, I will be in my study," Father said, rising from his chair. "And make sure Will understands that any more tales of his highwayman do not warrant interrupting me."

Nodding, I sipped my tea. No longer interested in the food in front of me, I leaned back and stared at the opposite wall. Meeting the man I was nearly betrothed to was going to be memorable, to say the least.

AS SANDWOOD HALL WAS not far from us, we all agreed the walk over would be enjoyable. Mother and Aunt Forester kept up a steady stream of light, meaningless news.

Sarah skipped ahead of us until we reached the gate of the Hall, and then she fell into step by my side.

"Diana, wait until you meet Mr. Richfield," she said to me as we neared the front door. Her blue eyes were bright with excitement, and I felt the first stirring of uneasiness. "He's a gentleman from London who is a friend of the Sandwoods. He is ever so pleasant. Perhaps you had a chance to meet some of his acquaintances."

The previous night, I had tried to wait for a good time to tell my sister about Mr. Richfield. First, we were too involved in practicing the new music. Then, when we were undressing in our room, I was too tired to to bring up such an important subject.

"Sarah, I should tell you—."

The front door swung open, interrupting me. Sarah hurried to be at Mother's right hand. I knew then, as I entered the massive entryway, I would regret not having made the time to tell Sarah.

Watkins, the butler, escorted us to the drawing room where the ladies were seated. Greetings were exchanged on all sides. Sarah and Charlotte hurried over to a window seat and started whispering together. I glanced from them to where Mother, Aunt Forester, and Mrs. Sandwood sitting with the tea tray. My choice was to either join the giggling pair or the adults.

"You appear well, Miss Forester," Mrs. Sandwood said as I took a seat beside my mother. Her brown eyes shone with interest. "How did you enjoy London?"

"I enjoyed it greatly, Ma'am." I accepted a cup of tea from her. "But I am even more happy to be home."

The older woman's smile held understanding. "You are one who will not travel far from home, I think," she said, a note of approval in her voice. "We will have to find you an eligible young man in the neighborhood to keep you close to your family."

I was only glad I was not drinking my tea at the moment. Choking on liquid was not an enjoyable experience, and I had done it far too often as of late. As it was, I took a moment to take a deep, calming breath. "Thank you, ma'am," I said, pleased that my tone was calm. "There is no need for you to go to such trouble on my behalf."

"I believe the Knighton's second son is of an age to marry now," she said as though I hadn't spoken. She faced my mother. "He will get a large enough inheritance and the family is a good one. I believe Philip Knighton and Diana would make an attractive couple. After all, didn't Diana get along with one of the daughters?"

"They would look perfect together!" Miss Sandwood said, jumping up from her seat at the window. How had she even overheard the conversation while whispering with Sarah? "He is so tall and light-haired, and you are—well, not tall and your hair is dark. The contract you would make would be striking!"

Horrified, I sent a glance at my mother. She was frowning, so she must not have been any more thrilled with the idea as I was, especially given what had happened. "That is exactly what I was thinking, my dear," Mrs. Sandwood agreed enthusiastically, unknowingly interrupting my train of thought. "Perhaps that ball you've wished for would be the perfect opportunity to throw them together. They can become better acquainted."

This was ridiculous. "Thank you, but no," I said, raising my voice. I got to my feet as they shifted their attention to me. "Your gardens look particularly lovely today, Mrs. Sandwood. May I go take a turn about them?"

"Certainly," Mrs. Sandwood said, surprise tingeing her voice. "You'll find the spring flowers are beginning to bloom."

Forcing what I hoped was a pleasant smile, I curtsied and left the room. "London always has a strange effect on girls like your Diana, my dear Mrs. Forester, but I wouldn't worry too much about her. Once she and Mr. Knighton are courting, she will be herself again, I am sure." Mrs. Sandwood's comment followed me as I walked down the hallway.

I let my breath out slowly and could only hope Mother would squash that particular plot before it went any further than that room. Resigned on that point, I made my way to the garden. Nodding to a gardener at work, I chose a path to go down, breathing in the smell of damp earth and light flowers that were just beginning to fill the air with their scent.

London had no gardens that could even begin to compare with the ones adorning the country. Growing up, Sarah and I were often in the Sandwood's garden, almost as often as we visited the Knightons. I found my favorite place: a small alcove set just off the path. Vines were already growing up the trellis. The quaint, old bench along the wall was cold when I sat. It was the perfect place to think.

Yes, it was my fault no one knew I was close to being engaged to Mr. Richfield. And yes, I hadn't accepted his proposal. Still, no one had the right to get involved with my relationships.

I plucked a tiny bud from a stem and stroked the soft, unopened petals with my fingertip. When had life become so complicated?

"You look like a young lady with the weight of the world on her shoulders."

Startled, I lifted my head as I recognized the voice. "Mr. Richfield."

Chapter Four

The flower bud fell from my fingers as I struggled to get to my feet. Richfield held out his hand to stop me. "There's no need for you to get up, Miss Forester. In fact, I was about to ask if I could join you."

For a moment, I didn't know what to say, and I bit my lip. Sitting alone with him in a garden nook would set the gossips to talking if we were discovered. However, there was much that needed to be said without others around to overhear. "Certainly." I gestured to the seat across from me. Clasping my hands in my lap, I dropped my gaze to the ground.

Now that he was in front of me, I had no idea how to begin the conversation we needed to have.

He took a seat, and we both were silent for several minutes. "I was surprised to hear you had arrived before me," I finally said softly. "You must have left London immediately after my aunt's dinner party."

"There was nothing to keep me in London, and I felt it was important to seek the approval you deemed necessary during our last conversation." He was silent for a second and then made a move to stand. "Perhaps I misunderstood. If my presence here is unwanted—"

"No!" I lifted my head quickly and reached my hand out. Though I may not have been certain of my exact feelings, I did know I wanted the opportunity to discover what they were. I met his dark eyed gaze. "You are not unwanted here. I was merely unsure whether my thoughtless answer had given offense."

"Thoughtless?" He raised his eyebrows as he spoke. "It was hardly that, Miss Forester, and I took no offense. I thought your answer was wise. It would be best if we took some time to get to know each other before we commit to an attachment that would last the rest of our lives. "

"Exactly!" I blushed as he chuckled. "However, I cannot accept I spoke 'wisely' in London. You startled me, and I said the first thing that came to my mind."

Mr. Richfield shook his head. "I cannot fault you for wanting your father's approval before you accept an attachment," he said with a smile. "As we are both in agreement now, what does it matter how it came about?"

He was right. All that mattered right then was he and I intended to become better acquainted. But how to accomplish that? "Are you enjoying your visit to Avonton, Mr. Richfield?" I asked, mentally cringing at the overly formal tone of my voice.

"Yes, I am, Miss Forester," he answered, just as formally; only he somehow managed to sound amused at the same time. "I always admire the picturesque nature of the countryside here."

That, at least, was a subject I could talk about without feeling flustered. "We're proud of it, but we can't take any credit for it," I informed him. It occurred to me then it would undoubtedly be best if we took our conversation out of hiding and into the gardens where we could be seen. "Shall we take a turn about the garden?"

"It would be my pleasure, Miss Forester," Richfield said, getting to his feet. He held his arm out to me. "I assume you visit the Sandwoods often."

"Yes, several times a week," I said as I put my hand on his arm. "Miss Sandwood and my sister are close companions. They are practically inseparable."

"They remind me of my younger sisters, the way they giggle and whisper together."

"I imagine many young ladies behave in such a manner."

Mr. Richfield's attention was on me as we went around a corner. "I've never seen you behave in such a way."

I felt a blush burn my cheeks again. How to respond to that? "I suppose I've always been too busy with my nose in a book," I said. A moment later, I sucked in my breath as I realized how he could take that. "Not that I'm a bluestocking or any such thing."

"There's no need to apologize. I enjoy a good book myself now and again."

"Have you read anything of particular interest, lately?" I asked. I always enjoyed hearing of a new book to read.

"I confess I have not. But I imagine you have a favorite novel?"

My smile widened. "*Sense and Sensibility* is a particular favorite of mine," I said with enthusiasm. "I was pleased to find a copy of the latest book by that author and look forward to reading it now I am home."

"Diana!" I heard my sister's voice call out from nearby.

I could have kicked something. Of course, when the conversation was becoming more interesting, my sister would interrupt. "I'm here, Sarah."

A moment later, she came into view from the direction of the house. She paused for a brief moment when she saw who was with me. "Oh, I didn't know you had company," she said, reaching up to make sure her bonnet was on straight. "Mr. Richfield, it is a pleasure to see you again."

"The pleasure is mine, Miss Sarah," Richfield said, bowing slightly. "You require your sister?"

As if reminded of her errand, Sarah spun to face me. "Mother and Aunt Forester are ready to leave now, Diana. We have several other places to visit."

Then I will escort you both back," Richfield said, holding out his other arm. "Your sister and I were discussing hobbies, Miss Sarah."

Looking pleased, Sarah accepted his arm. "Oh? And what are your hobbies, Mr. Richfield?" she asked.

"Like your sister, I enjoy reading a good book occasionally. I also hunt."

"Every gentleman hunts!"

I glanced between them, feeling a knot of disappointment in my throat. But it was more than disappointment. It took a moment for me to figure it out, but when I felt the small knot become bigger as Richfield laughed at my sister's response, I knew. I was jealous of Sarah!

Did I have reason to be? I didn't think so, but her relaxed manner with Mr. Richfield was something I feared I could never hope to have.

Was I afraid I would lose my maybe-betrothed to my sister?

"Ridiculous."

"What was that, Miss Forester?"

Swiftly, I glanced at my escort, embarrassed my softly spoken rumination had been heard. "I was thinking out loud, I'm sorry," I said, hoping he would not remark on my unwitting statement.

It was a vain sentiment. "What exactly are you thinking is so ridiculous?"

"Hunting," I said, thinking swiftly. A true enough sentiment, though not one I had dwelt on much beyond my distaste listening to hunting tales. "You chase a poor fox around or shoot beautiful birds. How can that be a pleasant way of spending time?"

"How is constantly sitting with a book in your hand a good way of passing the time on every occasion?" Sarah said, her tone sharp. She leaned forward enough to glare at me. "There are times we have meat on our table because someone hunts, Diana."

I did not want to get into a debate with my sister. Not now. "Of course," I said, remembering my social manners. "I should have kept my thoughts to myself. Forgive me. Please."

"No. You're right, Miss Forester," Mr. Richfield said, surprising me. "Some hunting can be cruel. I hope, though, you don't think I hunt merely for the sport of killing something."

"What other reason can you have?"

He paused as we reached the edge of the garden. "The thrill of the chase."

His smile made my cheeks heat up with a blush. I was relieved and slightly disappointed to see Mother and Aunt Forester were coming towards us. "Mr. Richfield," Aunt Forester said, her eyes widening with surprise and delight. "What a pleasant surprise to see you here. How long have you been in Avonton?"

"I left London the day after your dinner party ma'am," Mr. Richfield said, making his slight bow yet again. "Mrs. Forester, it is a pleasure to see you again."

"Which one are you speaking to?" Sarah asked with a laugh. "They are both Mrs. Forester, you know."

Swiftly, Richfield glanced between Mother and Aunt Forester. "Both."

"We are having a small family dinner party ourselves to-morrow evening, Mr. Richfield," Mother said with a pleasant smile. "Does your schedule allow you to join us?"

"Certainly, ma'am. I can think of nothing that would bring me greater pleasure."

Sarah clasped her hands in enthusiasm. "Wonderful. Diana brought me some new music for my harp, and I need someone to be my audience."

"I look forward to hearing you and your sister perform together. Miss Forester can play the piano quite well, I know."

"She ought to," Sarah said before I could respond to his compliment. "You cannot know how many hours she spends on the pianoforte. I'm surprised she didn't mention the pastime as her hobby."

"A lady does not brag about her accomplishments, Sarah," I said, containing a sigh. "And as Mr. Richfield has already heard me play, he has already deduced I enjoy it."

Stepping away from our escort, Sarah regarded me with disbelief written on her face. "Good day, Mr. Richfield," Mother said, putting an end to the conversation. "Girls. Come along."

"Good day, Mrs. Forester. Mrs. Forester. Miss Forester. Miss Sarah," Richfield said, looking torn between amazement there were so many Foresters and amused he had to name us all off as a matter of formality.

Smiling up at him briefly, I hurried to follow my mother. Sarah caught my arm and held me back, keeping us several feet back from Mother. "What was that about?" my sister asked, her voice just above a whisper. I merely shrugged in response. "It was almost like you were—flirting."

I barely kept from sighing. "All girls know how to flirt, Sarah."

She wrinkled her nose. "But you are my sister, and he happens to be someone I think likes me." Sarah gave an exaggerated shudder. "Believe me when I say what I just saw is a sight I never want to have to observe again."

Oh, lord. It was worse than I had feared. "Sarah." I bit my lip, trying to think of the right words. How was I supposed to explain something like this? "Why would you think he likes you?"

"Why else would he stay in the area this long?" Sarah said with confidence. "And Charlotte agrees with me. She says Mr. Richfield has always just stopped for an overnight visit, which explains why we've never met him before. But he's been here for several days now! There must be some-thing that is keeping him here this time."

"I'm surprised she didn't think he was interested in her." My mind raced to find the best way to break the truth to my sister. Every idea I could think of I could see having the same result: Sarah wouldn't speak to me for a week. Maybe longer.

"She did at first, but then he had dinner with us and spent several hours with Papa in the study. Did you bump in-to Mr. Richfield in the garden just now?"

"You might say that."

She hummed a note. "You haven't had a proper introduc-tion then! I will take care of that at the dinner party tomor-row."

"Sarah, I met Mr. Richfield in London," I said, annoyed she thought she had to do the proper thing for her older sis-ter. "He and I are well acquainted. He just told you he heard me play in London."

Sarah stopped smiling. "Oh. He did say that, didn't he."

"I met him at a musical soiree," I said as fast as I could without stumbling over my words. Perhaps if I informed her of the whole situation, she wouldn't be angry? "In fact," I paused to take a deep breath. "At Aunt Forester's last dinner party in London, Mr. Richfield asked me to marry him. In a way."

I hadn't meant to exaggerate, but I knew my sister. It would take something drastic, something blunt, dissuade her.

"He asked you to marry him?" Sarah repeated, looking shocked. Swiftly, though, anger filled her face. "Are you serious? And what do you mean 'in a way'? Either he did, or he did not!"

"Why would I invent such a story?" I asked her, unwilling to go into the details of the situation and she held up her hand like she didn't want to hear another word from me.

"Why did you wait until now to tell me something like this?"

"It's not something that comes up in conversation. It was unexpected, and I wasn't sure of my answer."

My tone was more defensive than I cared for it to be. Grabbing my arm, Sarah jerked me to a stop. "Diana, are you or are you not engaged to Mr. Richfield?"

"I don't know!"

"You don't know." Sarah echoed my words with a sharp laugh. "I should have known you would do this to me."

I frowned at her. "What are you talking about?"

"I was prepared to accept you and Mr. Knighton, but now you're interested in Mr. Richfield?"

At that moment, I honestly did not understand her. "Sarah, you're not making sense. What do you mean?"

"I'm talking about you always pushing me from what I want!"

"How have I done that? Honestly, Sarah. Tell me what I have done to make you so angry."

"Girls?" Looking concerned and slightly annoyed, Mother had faced us. "Is there a problem?"

"We're fine, Mother. We will be visiting the Widow Davison now, are we not?" Sarah said. Before she moved to walk next to Mother, she hissed, "Phillip Knighton chose you, remember that, Diana?"

Chapter Five

I pushed the memory of the situation to the back my mind to deal with later and went through the motions of the following social calls. It was late at night as I prepared for bed when I thought it over, reliving what had happened the month before I went to London. Oh, how I did remember it. Even now, it still caused a tangle of emotions: embarrassment, regret, and shock.

I hadn't seen it coming. Cliché, I know. But it was true. My life changed completely the day I went out for a walk on my own. True, it had been changed for the better, but it took some time for me to see it in that way. Maybe if someone else had gone with me, things would have been different. Perhaps so many people would not have been hurt.

Sarah had refused to accompany me that day because it was so cold. I hadn't thought it an inconvenience at all since she had been an annoyance to us all day. Bundled up, I walked out, determined to enjoy the sun, however cold the air.

I was on my way back when I saw a horse and rider coming towards me. "Miss Forester!" Phillip Knighton, blond and tall, said, reining his mount to a halt next to me. "What are you doing out on a day like this?"

"Good day, Mr. Knighton. I am taking advantage of the sun while it is out." I directed my smile up at the young man I had practically grown up with. "What about you?"

"The same. What is it they say about brilliant minds thinking alike?" He dismounted and offered me his right arm, holding his horse's reins in his left. "Shall we walk together?"

"People will talk if they see," I said teasingly, putting my gloved hand on his arm.

"Let them."

His serious tone should have been my first warning, but I didn't take any notice of it. Chatting as usual, we neared my home. "Thank you," I said, dropping my hand from his arm. "Do you want to come in? The boys are all gone, but my father would be happy to see you. And Sarah has some new compositions she has been working on."

"Not just yet," he said, grabbing my hand. "Diana, I must speak to you."

That was when I became nervous. "Let go of my hand please." I tried to take a step back, glancing at the house in the hopes someone would see us and come to my rescue. If anything, though, he gripped my hand tighter. "We have already been speaking, Mr. Knighton. I must go inside now. The air has chilled me more than I expected it would."

"I know this will seem a bit sudden, but I have been giving it a great deal of thought. You and I rub along fairly well. I believe the best thing for us to do would be to get married."

"What did you say?"

"I want you to be my wife, Diana," Phillip said his tone earnest. "We can make our home here, and nothing would have to change."

Dumbfounded, I stared at him. My older brother's best friend asking me to marry him? "Is this a jest?" That had to be it. He and my brothers so loved to play tricks. Any moment, my brothers would be jumping out of the bushes, laughing their heads off. It was the only sane explanation.

Phillip shook his head, shattering my hope. "I have never been more serious in my life, Diana. We are friends, aren't we?"

"Yes, of course, we are. Friends." I pulled my hand free. "You are like my brother, you know. I cannot marry you."

"You can't?"

I have never seen a look like the one Phillip wore on a person's face, not before or since that day. It was a mix of disbelief and heartbreak, emotions I have seen before. But it was the expression with it, one all too similar to what would usually follow when he and James were too rowdy, and one of them ended up getting punched in the stomach.

"No," I said, using as firm a tone as I could muster.

Seeing that look broke my heart. Phillip stared at me for a moment and then closed his eyes. When he opened them, the look was gone, and he spun on his heel. "Mr. Knighton?" I asked uneasily. He pulled himself up onto his horse and surveyed me expectantly. What could I say? "I—I'm sorry. Please don't be angry."

For a moment, I thought he would say something, but he only rode away. My arms wrapped around my waist, I watched him go, and then, once he was out of sight, I ran to the door I had to tell Mother about what had occurred.

It had taken nearly the rest of the afternoon for Mother to calm me down and tell me it wasn't my fault. And that evening, Father heard my story without interrupting and, once I'd finished, he assured me I had done the right thing. We didn't see Phillip Knighton at our home anymore after that.

It was a week before I had felt calm enough to tell Sarah the whole of it, and her reaction had surprised me.

"I could have told you this would happen," Sarah said, tossing her hairbrush onto the dressing table. I flinched at the loud thud it made on contact. She began to separate her hair into sections to braid. "Anyone could see he was only interested in you."

"I couldn't. If anything, I could have sworn you were the object of his interest, for he would always tease you so."

Rolling her eyes, Sarah stood up and faced me. "Then you are too naive for your own good."

Somehow, Sarah had always seemed to think she knew more than I did. Though that was the last she said on the matter at the time, it was apparent she hadn't forgotten about it.I'd gone all the way to London when the opportunity presented itself so as to avoid Phillip Knighton and any awkwardness between us. Having the situation thrown in my face, after so many months, hurt. It seemed hurting me was an activity Sarah excelled at.

As I lay in bed, staring up at the ceiling, I wondered now if Sarah had ever had an interest in Philip Knighton back then or if she was being petty now.

Turning my head, I glanced over to where Sarah lay at my side; her back was to me. She hadn't said a word to me since her last accusation about Mr. Knighton. The rest of the family hadn't seemed to notice since the two of us not talking was a regular occurrence.

Sighing, I twisted around, so my back was to hers as well. For all the times I would fight with Sarah, once my initial anger was gone, I always regretted my sharp words. When we were children, we had been close as only sisters can be. How was it that we'd grown apart? Was it because I had more interest in reading fictional worlds while she preferred to devote her time to music? Or did the reason lie behind the different companions we had chosen to spend our time with?

As I closed my eyes, I hoped the rift between us would be mended quickly this time.

THE NEXT MORNING I spent with my mother, making sure everything was in order for our dinner party. Mother had an amused smile on her face each time I would begin to worry about the minor details. Would he be offended by the small size of our party? What if the meal itself wasn't quite right? In the afternoon, when I realized how I was behaving, I avoided Mother's gaze when Aunt Forester briefly left the room.

"I'm being ridiculous, aren't I?"

"Just a little bit, Diana," Mother said with a small laugh. "There is no benefit to fret so, my dear. All will be fine."

Breathing out, I ran my gaze over the notes I had made. A great deal too many ink splatters marred my words, hinting at my anxious and distracted thoughts. "Sarah thought Mr. Richfield was interested in her. What if I've completely misunderstood everything?"

"You're becoming more ridiculous." Mother reached over and took the pen from my hand. "What did your father tell you?"

I frowned, thinking back. "He said Mr. Richfield's interest in me seemed sincere. But why would Sarah think she was the object of Mr. Richfield's interest?"

For a moment, Mother frowned, but then she shook her head. "I have no idea, Diana. Did you stop to think that perhaps this is a youthful crush on your sister's part?"

Was it as simple as that? I heaved a sigh. "You're right. I'm overthinking the matter."

When Aunt Forester returned, I held out my hand. Mother returned the pen to me, and I set about rewriting my notes for the dinner. It didn't take too many minutes, and once I was done I picked up the novel I'd purchased in London.

Truthfully, it was a relief when the time came to get ready for dinner. Sarah came in from wherever she'd disappeared to during the day, and we both dressed without speaking a word to each other.

Mr. Richfield arrived at precisely the time Mother had given him. We went into the dining room not five minutes later. I tried to keep a broad smile from my face, which would have been most unladylike, when the gentleman held his arm out to me. He, on the other hand, did not even try to contain his own smile.

Walking in behind us, Sarah muttered something I couldn't understand. In the interest of keeping the peace, I decided to ignore her. Mr. Richfield held out a chair for me, and after I'd been seated, took the chair to my left, which put him at my mother's right hand.

Over soup, the talk remained about general things: the weather, what the crops were looking like, and common gossip from the city. My aunt maintained most of the conversation with a steady stream of issues and opinions. Mr. Richfield kept up with these topics of conversation, while I held my tongue.

"Have you heard about the highwayman, Mr. Richfield?"

Amazed and startled, I glanced across the table at Will, the source of the unusual question. It wasn't often my reserved younger brother spoke up in front of strangers. I supposed him speaking up meant he was comfortable with Mr. Richfield's presence, which meant a great deal to me.

"Oh, not again," Father said good-naturedly. "Are you still thinking about that, Will?"

"What highwayman?" Mr. Richfield asked, his tone mildly interested. "I don't think I've heard any recent tales about highwaymen being a problem once again."

"It's been going on the whole winter!" Will said excitedly. "And just last week there was another robbery! The Knightons were returning from a dinner party, and they were stopped on the road. Mrs. Knighton lost all of her jewels. Mr. Knighton is furious!"

"At least no one has been harmed by this highwayman," Mother said, shaking her head. "Material belongings can be replaced after all."

"Has a search been made for the man?" Richfield asked.

Will nodded, taking a quick bite. Even he wouldn't let a good story get in the way of his need for food. "As soon as they reached Knighton Hall, Mr. Knighton sent out men to search the woods. And this morning they did another search."

"Did they find anything?" Sarah asked, showing the first glimmer of interest in the conversation.

"They thought they found the man's footprints on the road where the carriage was stopped. The search party followed them into the woods but lost them at the stream. Whoever the man is, he is intelligent."

Will sounded as though he admired the man. I couldn't help a shiver. Never would I have thought such crimes would be committed in my small, quiet community. "I imagine people will be more cautious about traveling late at night," I said, looking down at my plate. My appetite was not as strong as it had been only minutes before.

"Gentlemen will be carrying their pistols, I would wager," Uncle Forester said, his tone grave. "One way or another, we'll put an end to this horrible person."

"'Put an end?'" The slightly violent tone that had crept into the conversation surprised me. "I can understand this is a concern, but no one has been hurt. Perhaps he has no other option for surviving. Putting an end to him sounds so extreme, don't you think?"

Never let it be said I didn't try to think the best of people!

"Uncle, you wouldn't truly shoot him, would you?" Sarah asked, sounding every bit as alarmed as I had. Her eyes were wide with horror. For the first time since I had returned, we were on the same side of an issue. It warmed my heart, and I hoped it would last.

"Perhaps not to kill him," Uncle said after a moment of consideration. "But if a wound would keep him from vanishing, I would most certainly not hesitate to shoot the villain."

Aunt Forester sighed heavily. "There have been so many reports of highwaymen. Mr. Richfield, you were in Bath last Season when there was such a to-do over a highwayman in the area, were you not?"

Richfield nodded. "I was indeed, ma'am. As I recall, half of the young ladies of Bath were thrilled at the prospect of getting stopped by the highwayman."

Everyone laughed. "Too many novels, I expect," Father said with a sigh. He glanced between Sarah and me. "I can only hope my girls have more sense in their heads."

Turning to face me, Richfield raised his eyebrows. "Would you like to be caught by a highwayman, Miss Forester?" he asked. The expression in his eyes was teasing, though his tone was perfectly serious. "Are you as sensible as your father hopes?"

"I believe so. Since such a meeting would undoubtedly leave me without what few jewels I do have, I don't think I would find the occasion a pleasurable one," I said honestly, allowing a smile to curve my lips. "And yet, on the other hand, it would be quite a tale to tell after the fact, wouldn't it?"

"I don't think the ladies of Bath had as practical a frame of mind as you, Diana," Uncle said, chuckling. "They were undoubtedly only concerned with having a tale to tell their friends, and perhaps the opportunity to reform a heartless highwayman."

The table rang with laughter. But then I noticed Sarah frowning at Mr. Richfield. A second later, she had shifted her focus to Will and teased him about something. It happened so fast I nearly myself I had imagined it. I knew my sister, though, and could only hope the evening would allow me an opportunity to discover what had crossed her mind.

AFTER DINNER, I FOLLOWED my mother to the sitting room to wait for the men to finish talking. Will had beamed with pride at being allowed to stay. He likely just wanted to know if Father and Uncle Forester had more information about the highwayman that they hadn't wanted to share in front of the ladies.

"Have you ever thought about what it is exactly they always talk about?" I asked, picking up my sewing. "What is so secret they can't speak of it when we are in the room?"

"Topics not to be spoken of in front of females, naturally," Sarah said, sarcasm in her tone. She sat at her harp, running her fingers over the strings. "Surely you would know something so obvious, Diana."

I shot her an annoyed look. "What kind of 'topics', though? Specifically."

"I once asked your uncle the same question," Aunt Forester said, calmly doing her needlework. She chuckled a moment before she continued, "He said they generally discuss community affairs and business. The kind of things we ladies would only find boring."

It was hardly a satisfying answer. Didn't we share local news over the table during the meal? What business details could they want to share? It was obvious, however, the answer would be the only one I would get from my aunt. "I wouldn't find it boring," Sarah said boldly. "Aren't those subjects of which we all should have some knowledge? What would happen to us females if we should happen to be left alone, with no man around to run things?"

Surprised by her words, I glanced at my sister. She had a point. Had she thought about this before? If so, *why* had she done so?

"Sarah, I'm surprised at you," Aunt Forester said sharply, letting her sewing fall to her lap. She frowned at Sarah. Obviously, she did not care to countenance a view such as my sister had offered. "You must not think of such things, or they are bound to happen!"

"But they do happen, whether I speak of it or not. Why are women kept from the knowledge that could only be useful?"

"Such knowledge could be a great burden as well," Mother said, a chiding note in her voice. "Are you arguing with your aunt, Sarah?"

"Never, Mother." A scowl wrinkled Sarah's forehead for the briefest of moments. She played a sharp chord. "I merely presented a possibility. Diana is the one who began this conversation in the first place."

"If you think so bitterly about the future, then you should pray you are not left a widow with no son or your father lives a long life," Aunt Forester said, determined to have the last word on the subject. She focused on Mother, shutting out her nieces, and began to talk of some piece of gossip she had heard in London.

My attention, though, was still on my sister. Setting my needlework aside, I stood up and went to the harp. "Have you come to suggest a song for this evening?" Sarah asked, her tone distant.

"Sarah, I've never heard you talk so," I said, ignoring her question. I kept my voice low so only she would hear as I put the question I had into words. "Are you afraid you will be left alone in this world?"

Her eyes widened as though she was mocking me. "Why would you ask such a question, dear sister?" she asked, taking on the dramatic tone I knew all too well. "Do you presume to think I would live in fear of something that may or may not happen?"

"No, of course not! I want—."

Sarah stood up quickly. "Here are the gentlemen now," she said, interrupting me. "I hope you kept up with your practicing while you were away, Diana, for now you must keep your intended amused. You will need every bit of what little talent you have for that, you know."

As the men came through the door, Sarah walked over to where Mother was sewing, leaving me staring at her back. How dare she imply I needed a musical talent to hold Mr. Richfield's interest! I had only wanted to talk to her; there was no reason to become angry with me for it!

"Shall my nieces be entertaining us this evening?" Uncle Forester asked jovially. "Sarah, I know you have the new music Diana brought you from London."

"We both will be delighted, Uncle," I said.

"As long as Diana isn't the one singing," Sarah added, as she always did.

"I am waiting in eager anticipation to hear you again, Miss Forester," Mr. Richfield said, coming nearer with a smile. "It was a pleasure to hear you in London."

As I returned his smile, I caught the look on Sarah's face. Even though I could still see a hint of jealousy, there was a different emotion in her eyes. The same thoughtfulness I had seen at the table.

There was something on her mind, and I determined one way or another I would learn what it was.

Chapter Six

"So, when were you going to tell me?"

Sarah and I were getting ready for bed, at the same time for once. The evening had been a pleasurable one. Mr. Richfield had made himself agreeable to everyone, which was no small feat considering there were so many of us. Sighing, I set my hairbrush down and twisted away from the dressing table to face her. There was no sign of any anger or resentment in her face. Still, I hesitated to tell her the whole story. "It's only a possibility," I finally said, beginning to braid my hair. "When he hinted at asking for Father's permission, I was startled. I didn't give a definite answer."

"Well, that was stupid," Sarah said, hugging her pillow to her chest. "It's not like there is an abundance of eligible young men in the neighborhood for us to choose from."

While there was a great deal of truth in her words, I was still annoyed by her attitude. "What kind of marriage would I have if I accepted a man I hardly knew?" I flinched as I pulled too hard on my hair. "Look at how unhappy Mother's sister, Aunt Benson, is. Would you have me in the same position?"

"Aunt Benson married beneath her station. It's hardly relevant, and scarcely the same situation." Sarah frowned at me. "Did London make you sentimental, Diana? Are you truly hoping for a love match?"

"Our parents had a love match. I think I would rather be a spinster like Great-Aunt Forester than be trapped in an unhappy marriage." Hesitating for a moment, I decided I had nothing to lose if I was completely honest with her. "All I ask is to marry someone I can respect."

Sarah heaved a sigh. "Mr. Richfield appears to be a respectable man. He would have been a good choice, I think, Diana."

"'Would have been?' It's not quite as dismal as you are implying, Sarah. I have been informed, from the best authority possible, Mr. Richfield still wishes to pursue a match between him and myself."

My sister closed her eyes and leaned back against the head of the bed. "It's been a long time since we had a late night chat like this," she said, changing the subject.

Why did I have the feeling she didn't believe what I said about Mr. Richfield? "Nearly three months."

"I've missed it. And you."

That made me laugh, though I was careful to keep it soft. I wouldn't want to have Will complaining in the morning. "You missed me so much you choose to pick a fight with me minutes after I arrived?"

Sarah shrugged. "It's not my fault you bring out the worst in me."

I finished my braid and stood up, blowing out the candle. Cautiously, I made my way around to my side of the bed. When I tripped over some article of my sister's clothing, I caught myself on the bedpost. "What are you doing? Trying to wake everyone else up?" Sarah asked.

Reluctant to start another argument, I bit back the sharp response that came first to my mind. I followed the side of the bed to the headboard and pushed the blankets aside. "What have you and Miss Sandwood been up to while I was away? Mother told me you'd been over there nearly every day."

"You know Charlotte and I are the best of friend. I don't think I could even begin to tell you everything we have discussed and planned," Sarah said, her voice happy in the dark. She hummed a note. "What are the girls like in London?"

"Silly and self-absorbed. And each one of them desires to gossip about everyone else. I never found anyone with whom I could hold a serious conversation—besides Mr. Richfield, I mean."

"Mr. Richfield." She heaved a loud sigh.

Now was as good a time as any to ask what she'd been thinking at dinner. "Sarah, when we were talking about the highwayman earlier," I said, still trying to figure out the best way to put my question. "I had the feeling you had something on your mind."

"Hmm. Did you?"

"Was there something you wanted to say?"

"If I'd wanted to say something, I would have. Good night, Diana."

As I closed my eyes, I couldn't shake the feeling my sister was still hiding something from me. Hopefully, now that we seemed to be back in accord with each other, it wouldn't be long before she told me.

JUST BECAUSE WE WERE speaking to each other again did not mean I had any desire to sit and listen to Sarah chatter with her friend. So when Sarah invited me to walk with her to the Sandwood's, I politely declined.

Unless I was mistaken, I was reasonably sure she intended to tell Miss Sandwood how their assumption about Mr. Richfield was utterly wrong.

Instead, I set out on a walk with Will. We hadn't had a chance to spend much time together since I had returned. He and I were the most alike out of all of us siblings, so I was glad to have a chance to be with him.

"Are you looking forward to James coming back?" I asked, referring to our older brother.

Will's affirmative answer was brief as his eyes moved across the countryside. I had a good idea why he'd agreed to walk with me. He had taken the lead immediately, and that could only mean one thing. "We're going to where the highwayman robbed the Knightons, aren't we?" I asked in resignation.

"Yes." That was all he said for a moment, and then he scrutinized at me with a wide grin appearing on his face. "Are you scared?"

"Scared? Hardly. We're going in broad daylight. It's something that happened days ago. We're hardly going to be in any danger."

Will shrugged. "It's still going to be exciting though, right?"

His enthusiasm was contagious and I couldn't help being a little interested in where the robbery had happened. "Right," I said, smiling back at him. I was glad I'd worn one of my oldest gowns and my sturdiest boots for this walk. An overnight rain had made the ground muddy. "Do you think you'll find some clue everyone else missed?"

"Maybe."

I laughed at that. We spent the rest of the cross country walk to the woods teasing each other. At one point, we were even shoving each other. It was harder for me now Will had gone through a growth spurt and towered over me. I realized then I had to look up at him.

"When did you get so tall?"

"I've been this tall for a while." He grabbed my arm and pointed ahead of us. "Look! We're here!"

Letting me go, Will ran ahead, and I walked after him at a much slower pace. This particular stretch of the road appeared exactly like the rest. Trees grew on both sides, their branches stretching over the road. I remembered playing Robin Hood in this area with Sarah and my brothers not too many years earlier.

"So, do you see anything?" I asked, going over to where Will was kneeling down, staring at the ground. "Some great sign everyone else missed?"

I'd never seen him look so disappointed. "No," he said, standing up. "There's been too many people walking and riding through here." He brightened a split second later. "But maybe if we look at the trees we'll find something."

He darted off to check his new theory. Deciding to let him have his fun, I wandered along the roadside, picking some of the wildflowers that were blooming. We both spent our time occupied in this way for several minutes before I heard the unmistakable sound of hoofbeats.

"Will, someone is coming." When I didn't get an answer, I groaned. I didn't want to be found alone, so I set off after my brother. "Will, answer me! William! Answer me right now, or I promise I'm going to go straight home and tell Mother!"

With each sentence, my voice rose. Since I couldn't know whether my brother had done something stupid or chose not to answer because he was trying to scare me, I became increasingly angry and worried. "William Forester! Answer me right now!"

"Miss Forester?"

The voice that spoke startled me, even though I recognized it right away. "Mr. Richfield?" I spun around. The man was walking towards me from the road. Had it been his horse's hoofbeats I had heard on the road? Relieved, I hurried to meet him. "I'm trying to find my brother. He took off this way, and now he's not answering me."

"I assumed since I heard you shouting," Mr. Richfield said. He took my gloved hands in his and squeezed them reassuringly. "Don't worry. I'll help you find him. He is undoubtedly completely focused on what he's looking for."

I forced a smile. "Yes, some trail everyone missed that will lead him to the lair of the highwayman."

To my surprise, concern appeared on Mr. Richfield's face. "You two are out here, alone, searching for a criminal?"

"Will is the one who chose to walk this way. You saw for yourself how interested he is in this matter. So, here we are."

"Why didn't you try to stop him? Surely you know this man might be dangerous!"

His sharp tone, though flattering with all its concern, annoyed me. "What possible danger could there be? It was days ago! Any sensible criminal would be long gone, would he not? What harm is there in letting Will explore if that is what he wants to do?"

"Diana?"

My brother's uneasy voice interrupted any reply from Mr. Richfield. I spun around to face my brother, whose appearance was of one who had found a mud puddle and rolled in it. "Will! What happened to you?"

"I tripped," Will said simply. He sent a narrow-eyed look past me. "Are you well?"

The warning and real question in his voice were clear, even to me: 'Don't hurt with my sister' and 'Is this man bothering you?' I was touched by my brother's concern for my well being. "I am perfectly fine, Will. Mr. Richfield and I were discussing the safety of being in the area."

"I can protect my sister," Will said haughtily. It was difficult not to laugh at the incongruity of the situation: him covered in mud but somehow sounding like a titled gentleman. My younger brother walked over to stand next to me, and we faced Mr. Richfield. "Besides, there's no tracks or footprints to show the highwayman came this way."

Breathing out a sigh, Mr. Richfield nodded. "I have no doubt you would defend your sister's honor to the best of your ability. I apologize if I have caused any offense."

"We should start back," I said, glancing up at the sky through the branches. "Mother will be wondering where we've gotten ourselves."

"May I walk with you?"

To my amusement, Will's gaze became expectant. I nodded once. "You may," Will said, with an odd formality that was hilarious to hear coming from him. And as the three of us began walking, Will stayed by my side, as if to make the point clear he was going to protect me even from Mr. Richfield if the occasion arose.

There was silence until we reached the road, and Mr. Richfield crossed to where his horse was tied to a low hanging branch. "I heard you getting angry, and I was worried," Will said in a low voice. "I thought you might have been in trouble."

"Thank you for coming to my rescue, Will, but I was fine," I said, just as quietly. "Mr. Richfield and I were disagreeing about a point. Think nothing of it."

Leading his horse, Mr. Richfield returned to us. "Lead the way."

Glancing once more at me, Will took off in his usual fashion. The only difference this time was how he glanced back to check on me as I walked next to Mr. Richfield. Concern from my brother was heartwarming as I'd never seen him take such an interest in my welfare.

"I've upset you."

"Yes," I said honestly. I kept my eyes forward, on where my brother crouched down examining something on the ground. "Do you think so little of me you believe I would knowingly allow my brother to follow a course of danger?"

"If he chose to follow such a course, would you be able to stop him? Or would you get pulled into the danger yourself?"

I opened my mouth to answer but paused as I gave the matter some thought. "Perhaps he wouldn't listen to me. However, I do hope I would have the sense to avoid danger, Mr. Richfield."

"Or would your sense of duty and affection for your siblings blind you to the danger?"

That was going too far! I glared at him. Before I could speak though, Mr. Richfield raised his hands and said, "I mean nothing by it, Miss Forester, I can assure you! There's no need to glare at me so, otherwise your brother may return to run me through where I stand. And I think he would not hesitate to do so."

At the thought, I couldn't keep from giggling. "True. Though why must you needle me about the bond I have with my siblings? Is it so odd for us to be as close as we are?"

"No. It is refreshing. But it does make me wonder just how far you would follow them or what lengths you would go to protect them."

That was an idea I had never considered before. I loved my brothers, and even Sarah, with my whole heart. Was that a weakness? How far would I go to protect my siblings? What would I be willing to risk for them? My reputation? My well-being?

"I don't know," I said slowly. Sighing, I shook my head. "What would you do for your sisters?"

My words silenced him, and I was mildly pleased to have turned the tables on him. We walked for a short time without saying anything. Annoyance drained away as I took a deep breath of the spring air.

"I'm sorry," I said, blurting the words out when I could not stand the silence a moment longer. Out of the corner of my eye, I say Mr. Richfield turn towards me with a start. "I should not have snapped at you back in the woods as I did. I had no reason to be angry with you, and I apologize."

Mr. Richfield gaped at me. "You are the peacemaker of the family, aren't you?"

I shrugged my shoulders in an unladylike manner I'd picked up from my brothers. "Oh, I don't know about that. But my mother always said I should learn to know when I was in the wrong and have the decency to admit to it."

"Your mother is an uncommonly wise woman."

"The wisest."

Coming to a stop, Mr. Richfield reached out and caught my hand, making me stop walking as well. "I am sorry as well," he said, sincerely. "I shouldn't have berated you as I did. I was merely concerned you did not know what you were about, being in a woods alone when a criminal had been in the area. I know you to be more sensible than that, and should not have let my feelings take over."

He had been worried about me. "You have my full for-giveness," I said, feeling the blush spread across my cheeks. "Although, you know I can't speak for Will. He may not be so forgiving considering you did ruin his adventure."

We both observed Will picking up a rock and was study-ing it. "I think he's probably forgotten all about it," Mr. Rich-field said with amusement.

"Oh, no! Do not let him fool you. He is merely letting you think he has forgotten when in reality he is biding his time to exact his revenge."

"And will it be horrible revenge?"

"The worst!"

Our gazes met, and we both began to laugh. It felt right, the most comfortable thing in the world. "Diana," Will said, sounding annoyed. "We should be getting back home. There's nothing to be found here."

"Coming." I fought to control my amusement. Then, I realized Mr. Richfield was still holding my hand and pulled it free with an embarrassed flush.

"Yes, let's not annoy him any further, else you will find yourself on the receiving end of some horrible revenge," Mr. Richfield said for my ears only. I choked on my laughter. He offered a low bow. "I will leave you here, Miss Forester, and hope to see you again soon."

"Good day, Mr. Richfield," I said in response. I stepped back as he mounted and Will came to my side. Mr. Richfield tipped his hat and took off across the country. I stayed where I was to watch him but shook myself into activity after a few moments. "Mother will not be happy when she sees you, Will."

My brother just shrugged, looking at me quizzically "I'll just distract her by telling her Mr. Richfield was holding your hand."

"Will! You wouldn't dare! It wasn't like that!" Shrugging, Will took off, and I didn't hesitate to dash after him. "Will!"

Chapter Seven

Of course, there was no possible way I could catch him. Our game of chase ended when I finally lost sight of Will. So much for thinking he wished to protect me. Breathing heavily, I slowed to a walk. I plucked the petals off one of the wildflowers I'd gathered as I made my way back home.

I had nearly reached the edge of the gardens when I saw a black horse race across the horizon. I knew it immediately: Phillip Knighton's favorite horse. Pausing to watch the distant figure ride out of sight, I felt a moment of sadness. There was a time, once, when I would have waved to him to catch his attention.

Shaking my head, I hurried around to the front of the house. I bit back a laugh as I saw our father had managed to catch Will by the arm. "Will, what happened this time?" he asked, a note of resignation in his voice as I drew nearer. He inspected my muddy brother with a raised eyebrow. "Were you out looking for the highwayman?"

Will managed to look abashed. "Yes, sir. But—"

"Young man, I want you to go in and clean up before your mother catches you. You can tell me about your adventure when you are not covered in all the mud in the county."

My laugh earned me a glare from Will before he went in the house. "Did the two of you have a good walk?" Father asked, turning to me.

Smiling broadly, I looped my arm around my father's, leaning against him affectionately. "It was informative." Deciding that telling my parents myself what had happened would be the best way to defend myself against Will's plan of attack, I said, "Mr. Richfield was riding today and walked with us."

"Was this an accidental meeting, or a lover's clandestine arrangement?"

I jerked to a stop at my father's overly dramatic tone. "Papa!" I could feel my cheeks burning with embarrassment. "Of course it wasn't! I wouldn't— Why would you—"

Father burst out laughing. "'The lady protests too much, methinks!'" His Shakespeare quote would typically have amused me. I hadn't gotten my love of reading only from Mother.

Pulling my arm free, I shook my head. "Papa! I know better than to do anything that would bring shame to the family!"

"Yes, I know, Diana." Father put his arm around my shoulders for a moment. "And how was this accidental meeting with Mr. Richfield informative?"

His tone was the epitome serious, but I had the feeling he was still teasing me. For a moment, I hesitated to answer. "Well, for one thing, he confessed his concern that Will and I were out chasing a highwayman. In fact, he was more than concerned; he was worried for my safety."

When I focused on my father, I saw his expression become thoughtful. "You're convinced of his affection for you now?"

"I suppose I am."

"And what do you intend to do about it?"

As seemed to be a habit now, I bit my lip as I considered. "Well, he has not spoken about the future. I think perhaps we are taking some time to become better acquainted. To be sure we will get on well enough to make a life together."

"That is a wise decision." He started walking, and I fell into step beside him. "Your mother told me about Sarah and her expectations. Has she recovered yet?"

"She seemed to. But, who knows what her thoughts will be once she gets back from revealing all to Charlotte Sandwood."

That drew a sigh from Father. It was no secret Sarah tended to be influenced a great deal by her friend. "Sarah must learn when some things are best not well known. If she gives you any more trouble on the matter, send her to me."

Smiling, I raised myself up on the tips of my toes to kiss Father's cheek. "Thank you."

"Now run along," Father said as we approached the house. "I have to look over the estate accounts."

Nodding, I reached to take my bonnet off as I moved ahead to enter ahead of him. It was a pleasant feeling knowing I had the approval of both of my parents. Will seemed to accept Mr. Richfield's entrance into my life begrudgingly. Hopefully, Sarah would come to accept the situation as well.

The sound of hoofbeats echoed behind me, and I glanced over my shoulder. It took me a moment to recognize the brown mare Mr. Knighton generally rode. "I didn't know you were meeting with Mr. Knighton today."

"Yes, he has some concerns about the highwayman," Father said, turning to wave a welcome at our approaching neighbor, the father of Phillip Knighton and my dear friend Lady Carlyle. "That there has been no trace of the man suggests he may know our country well."

"I don't believe it!"

Father patted my shoulder. "Knighton, Sandlwood, and I will discover the truth of the matter. Now go on inside and make sure Will got cleaned up."

"Yes, sir." I hurried into the house. I didn't know how Mr. Knighton felt about my refusal of his son, and I wasn't anxious to learn.

TO MY SURPRISE, SARAH was already in our bedroom. I thought she would have been with her friend for most of the day. "You're back early. Did you and Miss Sandwood not have a great deal to discuss?"

"I thought you'd never get here!" Sarah said, ignoring my question completely as she spun to face me. I frowned at her as I put my outside garments away. She wrung her hands together and tapped her foot. Agitation was a state which I had seldom seen her in. "Diana, I must speak with you!"

"About what?" I asked calmly. Sarah took up pacing and seemed disinclined to continue with whatever she wanted to say.

"You must listen to me for once in your life!"

Sinking onto our bed, I tried to hide a smile. "Then come out and tell me what has you in such a state."

"I think Mr. Richfield is the highwayman!"

My smile faded instantly as I stared at her. How had she come up with this ridiculous idea? "You what?" I asked in astonishment.

"There, I've said it!" Sarah collapsed into the chair at the dressing table. "I've considered the matter carefully, Diana, and as your sister, I could not let you become attached to such a black-hearted criminal!"

I couldn't help but laugh in response to that absurd notion. "'Black-hearted criminal'? You cannot be serious, Sarah. I have never heard anything so outlandish. You've been reading too many of those books you are always teasing me about."

"Diana, I am completely serious! Stop laughing!"

"How can I take you seriously when everything you say is utter nonsense? Why would you possibly think Mr. Richfield, a true gentleman if I've ever met one, is a common criminal?"

Sarah leaned forward, her eyes wide. "Don't you remember what Aunt Forester said at dinner yesterday?" she asked, lowering her voice for some reason. She acted like she was about to disclose some deep secret to me, and I found myself leaning closer. "About the highwayman being around the Bath area?"

Thinking back, I did, in fact, remember the conversation and our aunt's comment. "Yes, of course, I remember. What about it?"

"Mr. Richfield was there!"

I failed to follow her line of reasoning. "I'm sure a great many people were in Bath at the same time, Sarah. Aunt and Uncle Forester, for example, were there for two months, I believe."

Shaking her head, Sarah groaned. "Don't be obtuse, Diana! You have to see the connection here. Mr. Richfield was in Bath when a highwayman terrorized innocent people. And now, he's here, where a highwayman has mysteriously appeared to threaten our peaceful home!"

Taken aback, I frowned as I considered her logic. "No, you're taking things far out of context, Sarah. Mother sent me a letter while I was in London and she wrote about the highwayman. And, for another thing, what reason would Mr. Richfield have to rob ladies of their jewels? There is none!"

Crossing her arms, Sarah scowled at me. "Charlotte and I have discussed this in detail, Diana," she told me. Perfect. Now the tale would be spread to everyone we knew. "She has no idea how the Richfield family came by their money, only her father and Mr. Richfield's father were friends at school. Mr. Richfield is posing as a gentleman and supporting himself on ill-gotten gains!"

Again with her over dramatics. "Sarah, this is silly. I don't want to hear another word."

"You just don't want to admit you admire a criminal!"

"That is not the reason I object to this ridiculous theory!"

"You just don't want me to be right!"

"You're making things up that have no basis in fact!" We were both on our feet, and I had my hands on my hips.

"You're still mad Mr. Richfield is interested in me and not you!"

"Hardly! He's a criminal, and I will prove it to you!"

My temper snapped. "Sarah, you will do no such thing! I will not allow you to blacken Mr. Richfield's reputation for no reason!"

"Of course there is a reason. Did you not just hear me? Why do you insist on being such a naïve fool?"

"Diana Katherine Forester! Sarah Elizabeth Forester!"

We both flinched at our mother's appalled voice. Letting my arms drop to my sides, I whirled around to face her. Mother stood in the door, Aunt Forester only a few steps behind her. "Mother," I said, unsure how to explain this latest argument. "Aunt Forester."

Mother held up a hand. "Not a word, Diana." Her tone was stony as she stepped into the room. "I have heard quite enough from you both, and I ashamed of you. You are sisters, and I expect better behavior from my daughters."

I bowed my head as she spoke. "She started it," Sarah said from behind me.

"Sarah, it takes two to maintain a quarrel," Mother said sharply. I dared to look up, relieved I was not the main bearer of Mother's displeasure. "Your aunt and I were taking tea in the sitting room, and we could hear the pair of you shouting at each other across the house."

My head went back down. I hadn't realized my voice had gotten so loud. "Now you will both go up to the schoolroom, and you will write out one hundred lines that will read, 'I will not shout at my sister.' You will not join the family for dinner, and you will not come downstairs until tomorrow morning. At which time, you will both speak to your father."

"But Mother—!"

"If you act like children, you will be punished like children," Mother said, interrupting Sarah's protest. "Now, you heard what I said. Go to the schoolroom."

Her tone of voice made me flinch again. "Yes, Mother," I said, penitently. I had brought this on myself. The thought of being punished as though I were twelve years old again made me flush in humiliation. "I'm sorry."

Sarah echoed my reply, sounding more sullen than repentant to my ears.

Without another word, Mother stepped aside. Keeping my head down, I hurried out of the bedroom. "My apologies, Aunt Forester," I said, glancing swiftly at my aunt. Will gawked at us in the doorway of his room, wearing clean clothes. I walked quickly towards the schoolroom, anxious to carry out the first part of my punishment.

I did my best not to even look in Sarah's direction as I selected my paper. "You know I'm right," Sarah whispered, slamming a jar of ink down with much more force than necessary.

As much as I wanted not to let her have the last word, I bit the side of my cheek to keep quiet. I dipped my quill in ink and began to write. Writing lines would be nothing compared to the talking to I was sure to get in the morning.

"DIANA, WHAT DID I TELL you to do if your sister bothered you?"

Standing in front of my father's desk the next morning, I hung my head. "I was to come to you, and you would deal with Sarah."

"Why did you not do as I instructed?"

I honestly had no clear idea except I had lost my temper in response to her outlandish tale. It was all I could give my father as an answer, and he sighed in response. "Sarah knows exactly how to make you angry, Diana, and I have told you this many times in the past. When will you learn to walk away from her before you shout at each other?"

"I'm sorry, Father," I said, my voice trembling. I sincerely disliked disappointing my parents. "She was saying such absurd things, and then said she would prove it to me she was right."

"Yes, your mother told me Sarah's newest tale. But, whatever your sister said to you, there was no reason to have a shouting match."

"Yes, sir."

"Now, I believe your mother's punishment yesterday was quite sufficient. I do hope you have learned your lesson this time, Diana, and will act more maturely the next time your sister attempts to anger you."

Surprised, I lifted my head. A hundred lines and dinner in my room was the only punishment? "You're not punishing me further?"

"I know you have been berating yourself all night; it's your nature, Diana," Father said with a gentle smile. I could not deny the fact. "And, seeing as you were forced to miss an occasion to get better acquainted with Mr. Richfield last night, I see no reason met out any further consequence."

I stared at him in horror. Mr. Richfield had come last night, and this was the first I heard of it? Why had Mother not told me he would be coming for dinner? And why had Will, who would typically have taken full advantage of such news to tease me out of my doldrums, not said anything about it? "He was here for dinner?"

"He came afterward to spend the evening with us."

"What did you tell Mr. Richfield?" I asked cautiously. How had he reacted when I did not join the family? What reason had he been given the absence of both myself and Sarah? How would I endure it if he knew I had been given a child's punishment for an immature argument?

"I didn't tell him of Sarah foolish belief, so you need not be concerned. I merely informed him you were unable to join us." My father's usual mischievous grin appeared. "He seemed disappointed if that makes you feel any better."

It did, but I was not about to say it out loud. "Thank you, Father."

"Now, I'm sure your mother has things for you to do. Send Sarah in, and try not to antagonize her."

Relieved, I made my escape from my father's study. Sarah had been waiting in the hallway, still looking sullen. "Father wants to—"

"I know. I'm not deaf."

She pushed past me. I flinched as the door shut behind her with unnecessary force. Breathing out, I shook my head and set off to find Mother.

After some searching, I found Mother and Aunt Forester in the garden. Aunt Forester was reading a book, while Mother cut bluebells and daisies. I waited a moment before announcing my presence, taking a deep breath of the fresh, spring air. The entire scene was peaceful, calm, and soothing to one whose life had become such a tangle.

"Do you need any help, Mother?" I finally asked, walking forward.

"No, I'm just about finished here," Mother said with a smile. She handed over a basket already filled with the bright blooms of the season. "But you may take this in and start arranging the flowers for me. I want the sitting room to smell of spring."

"I trust your father has finished with you?" Aunt Forester asked, glancing up at me briefly.

My cheeks flushed with embarrassment. "Yes, he's speaking to Sarah now. I apologize for losing my temper yesterday, Aunt."

"Did your father tell you your Mr. Richfield joined us last night after dinner?" My aunt turned a page of her book, making no acknowledgment of my apology. "As we did not have you or Sarah to entertain us, Mr. Richfield and Will played a rather lively game of piquet."

There was no mistaking the disappointment and censure in my aunt's voice. "I am glad Mr. Richfield and Will get along." What else was there for me to say in answer? "I wasn't sure whether Will would be agreeable to have a new acquaintance."

It doesn't matter whether or not your brother is amiable with Mr. Richfield, Diana," Aunt Forester said rather sharply. I flinched at her tone.

"Mary, Diana's suffered enough," Mother said, coming to my rescue. "I'm sure one evening away from her company will not cause Mr. Richfield to abandon all interest in her."

"Men can be fickle that way. Diana should appreciate the opportunity she has and not throw it away by acting like a foolish child!"

My cheeks burned with embarrassment at the growing criticism. I struggled for some answer to give. Before I could think of a word, Mother caught my eye and nodded for me to leave. Relieved to make my escape, I fled past the hedges of the garden. Satisfied I was out of sight, I came to a halt.

"You would condone your daughter's actions? She will never be suitably married if you allow her to behave like a senseless ninny!"

"Diana has never acted as a 'senseless ninny,' Mary," Mother said, her tone one I'd heard many times when she would scold me or any of my siblings. "She chooses not to behave in the empty-headed way that has become so fashionable for young ladies today. There can be no fault with that. If anything, she has far too much sense for her own good, and I will not hear her browbeaten for it."

I caught my breath at my mother's firm defense of me and my behavior. "But you must agree she will lose Mr. Richfield if she is not careful! Urge her to encourage his attention at once!"

"Pray, allow me to raise and advise my daughters as I see fit. I know them as you cannot. Passing a few months in Diana's company cannot have given you the kind of insight I have as her mother."

Never had I heard her speak so to another person! "There is no need for you to be so angry, Gwendolyn," Aunt Forester said, sounding even more surprised than I felt. "I did not mean to cause offense."

"If you speak so slightingly of one of my children, you should expect me to be offended, Mary. Now, let us not speak of this again. Will you join me inside or do you intend on remaining out in the sun?"

Out of habit, I ducked my head as I hurried to the door. I had no desire to be caught eavesdropping. They say eavesdroppers never hear anything good about themselves, and that was indeed the case with my aunt's words. However, I couldn't have been happier hearing my mother defend me.

At the same time, my heart ached that it had been necessary for her to do so in the first place. I never wished to be a burden on my parents, and for them to have to justify my actions—it made my stomach twist.

I left Mother's basket of flowers in the sitting room for her and went into the drawing room. No one else was there, which was a pleasant surprise. If there was one activity my sister and I shared, it was how we both went to our musical instruments in times of crisis.

Taking a seat at the pianoforte, I breathed out as I placed my fingers on the smooth keys. I didn't have any specific melody in mind as my fingers began to move. As I listened to the familiar notes of one of John Bach's arias fill the room, I closed my eyes.

My mind drifted as it usually did when I was in a mood such as this. I yearned for the times when the only things that concerned me were besting Sarah at some game. Back then, I had been so anxious to grow up and be just like Mother. And now?

In all honesty, I wasn't sure what I wanted.

Mr. Knighton's declaration of love had shaken my once stable world. To know I had been blind to the signs of my friend's growing affection made me question whether I could trust my own senses. Since then, I'd felt little peace. Was Mr. Richfield the man for me? How could I be sure?

I gave a start when a hand came down on my shoulder. Opening my eyes, I lifted my head and found Mother smiling at me. A swift glance at the clock showed I had been playing for nearly half an hour. That's when I realized my fingers were becoming sore. Ruefully, I let my hands fall into my lap.

"Is there something you want to talk about?" Mother asked in the intuitive way she had.

"Am I ready for marriage?" The words left my lips before I even knew I was about to speak them.

Looking severe, Mother pulled her hand back and took a seat on Sarah's stool at the harp. "That's a rather strange question. Why do you ask it?"

"I don't know."

"Well, I would hope I would raise my daughters to be ready for the lives they would lead. You are an accomplished young lady, Diana. And I don't mean in the way many classify accomplished with your musical prowess or any of the other social niceties that are called for. I think you know everything you need to manage a household of your own."

I breathed out. "I'm sure of that." After all, I had spent hours at Mother's side learning what a lady of the house was required to do each day. "It's just that I'm not sure what I should expect in a husband."

Mother's forehead creased in a frown. "Do you mean in his personality? His station in life?"

"How do I know if he is sincere in his affection? How can I be sure we rub along well enough to spend the rest of our lives together?"

"My dear, have you seen anything to doubt Mr. Richfield's intentions?" Mother reached over and clasped my hands. I shook my head. After all, he'd come all the way from london to continue our acquaintance. "Every marriage has it's rough patches. I have never seen a perfect union, not even my own. Love and affection will make those times easier. You are the only one who can be certain of your own emotions and whether Mr. Richfield will make you a good husband."

Of course she was right. "Thank you."

"For what? Speaking the truth?"

Smiling, I shook my head. "For being the most wonderful mother, a girl could ask for, and being generous with your advice when I most have need of it."

With a frown, Mother leaned forward and put her hand on my forehead. "Are you feeling well, Diana? You're acting strangely."

"I'm sorry. Everything has been such a tangled mess these past few days, and I feel like it is all my fault."

"It is absolutely your fault." Mother laughed as I blinked in surprise. "Surely, you didn't expect it to be easy to find a husband."

"Well, no. I wasn't planning on having to overcome claims that my beau is a highwayman, especially not from my own sister."

"Your sister." Mother shook her head with a slight sigh. "No, the thought never came to my mind either. But, you should forget about it. Your father and I will deal with your sister and her foolish ideas."

A sudden thought came to me. "Do you think I should tell Mr. Richfield what she thinks?"

"Of course not!" Mother said in open horror. "Diana, we don't need him to think he would be marrying into a family on its way to Bethlam Hospital!"

"Well then, we'll just have to keep him away from the rest of the family until the wedding is over." I struggled to keep a straight face. But when I caught Mother's eye and saw she was having the same trouble, I couldn't help bursting into laughter, and she did the same.

As I laughed, it occurred to me what I had just said. 'Until the wedding is over.'

I'd decided. I wanted to marry Mr. Richfield.

Chapter Eight

Mother gave me a strange look as my laugh came to an abrupt halt. But before she could say a word, Sarah's voice reached our ears. "Mother! Mother! You won't believe it!"

My younger sister came rushing into the drawing room. In her hand was a sheet of paper. She threw herself onto the settee near our mother. "The Knightons' are having a house party!" Sarah said, all enthusiasm. Her eyes were bright with excitement. "Mrs. Knighton has requested we join the ladies in some of the activities! And then there is to be a ball!"

"And when is this house party to take place?" Mother asked, taking the invitation from Sarah's hand. She raised an eyebrow as she scanned the paper. "This was not addressed to you, Sarah."

"Oh, Will opened it, and I took it from him," Sarah explained carelessly. She grabbed Mother's hand. "The house party is in a week, Mother. Please say I may go! Charlotte will be there, and it will be so much fun!"

"How do you know Miss Sandwood will be there?" I asked with suspicion. If our invitation had just arrived, there was no possible way Sarah could be aware of whether the Sandwoods had also been included or not. This was the first

Mother had heard of it if the surprise on her face was anything to go by, which was odd.

Sarah barely glanced at me. "Charlotte told me about the house party last week." She leaned over enough to be mostly sprawled across the settee as she pointed at the invitation.

Concern filled Mother's face. "The Sandwoods received their invitation last week? You never said anything about a house party, Sarah."

Sarah seemed not to realize the slight of receiving an invitation so close to the date of the house party. "Well, I wasn't sure if I would be invited, given the situation Diana put herself in with Philip Knighton."

"Naturally it's completely my fault the Knightons' would exclude us from their party!" I said, my temper bristling.

"You rejected the advances of their son. Of course they would feel the offense of that! They haven't had us to dinner since then, you know."

"That is completely untrue, Sarah!" I said defensively. "You are exaggerating matters greatly! We have been several times for dinner since then and—"

"Enough, girls," Mother said, interrupting me. She pursed her lips, a look of contemplation on her face. "I shall send Mrs. Knighton a note, accepting her kind invitation. I will be happy to take you both to join the ladies of the party during the day."

Trust Mother to not make a fuss of things. "B-but, surely Diana won't go!" Sarah said, stammering as she sat back. "The invitation says—."

"That Mrs. Knighton will welcome Miss Forester and Miss Sarah Forester to her events, if they are free to do so," Mother said firmly. "I can think of nothing that would keep Diana from accompanying you, Sarah."

I frowned. If we were free to do so? What an odd addendum to the invitation. As Mother said, barring a sudden illness or punishment for another dispute with Sarah, there would be no reason for me not to attend. "People will talk!" Sarah said. "Think of the awkward situation there will be! Philip Knighton will be back!"

Why did she insist on bringing Philip up so often? He'd left a week after he approached me about being his wife and his family said he had gone to visit friends, but I knew he was back, having seen him riding in the distance.

"People always talk, and we will not give them further reason to do so," Mother said as she rose from the stool. "It would cause talk if you were to go alone, leaving your older sister behind. Now, I shall pen our acceptance. Sit up properly before someone sees you acting in such a foolish manner."

Invitation in hand, she swept out of the room with the dignity and grace I so longed to achieve. The drawing room filled with silence. Sullenly, Sarah picked herself up and took a seat at her harp. She plucked at the strings for a moment before she realized I was watching her.

"I am certain Mrs. Knighton does not wish you to come," Sarah said, her tone conversational, though her words were not. "Any mother would understand her feelings in this matter."

My eyes narrowed. "How would you know? You are not a mother."

"Fine. Any female would sympathize with Mrs. Knighton," Sarah said just as quickly. "How would you feel if you were forced to be in the company of a young lady who refused either of our brothers?"

At first, the idea of any young lady interested in James or Will was enough to make me laugh. But then I had to admit, "It would be difficult, certainly. But a lady has the right to refuse a gentleman she has no desire to become attached to."

"Difficult? You would be livid, and you know it!"

Shaking my head, I faced the keys of the pianoforte. "Mother is right, too, you know." I let my fingers play a chord. "There will be more talk if I were not to attend what is sure to be the largest event of the spring."

"Well, don't complain to me if you hear people whisper," Sarah said, standing up abruptly. She left the drawing room, leaving me to think once again.

In truth, I did not look forward to this house party. Meeting new people, especially ones from London, was not enjoyable to me. I'd put on a brave face for London since it meant escaping the troubles I'd found at home. Still, a house party at the Knightons meant my dear friend, Lady Anna Carlyle, would be back.

I could use all the help and support I could get.

THE FOLLOWING EVENING we were invited to dine with the Sandwoods. I was pleased to see the news of the Knighton house party had seemed to drive all thoughts of Mr. Richfield being a highwayman from Sarah's mind. All she seemed to talk of all day was of what she expected the activities of the house party to be: an archery competition, any tournament between the gentlemen, a ball to close the party.

Will, rather impolitely, requested Sarah to stop dreaming out loud on our drive to the Sandwoods. Sarah had something to say in response, and resulting sniping back and forth caused Father to threaten to send them both back home. The ensuing silence was marvelous.

The moment I stepped into the Sandwoods' drawing room, my eyes searched for Mr. Richfield. I found him standing in front of the fireplace, a glass in his hand, which he set down when he noticed me. He came forward, and I felt a smile form on my face. First, he greeted both of my parents before he faced me.

"Good evening, Miss Forester," he said with his polite bow. "You're looking well."

"Good evening, Mr. Richfield, and thank you," I responded. Sarah pushed past me to go to Miss Sandwood. "Are you still enjoying your visit here?"

Out of the corner of my eye, I saw my parents move further into the room. Will, though, stayed near me. It wasn't often he was included to dine with the other families as he was still only sixteen, and even rarer he would stick so close to me when he was.

"I was, Miss Forester, until two evenings ago," Mr. Richfield said, claiming my attention before I could think any more about Will's strange behavior.

I frowned. "Two evenings ago?" It took me a moment before it hit me. He was referring to when he came over after dinner for tea. "Oh!"

"May I say I am pleased to see you no longer indisposed?" Mr. Richfield asked. There was a hint of concern in his eyes. "Nothing serious, was it?"

"Oh, no, not at all," I said quickly. Mother was right. I couldn't tell him what Sarah and I had fought about. Somehow, I had to turn the conversation immediately! "I was told you and Will played piquet together. He doesn't often find anyone enough of a challenge to bother with the game since he was —oh, he must have been twelve when he devoted hours to learning the game."

Mr. Richfield chuckled and sent a glance over his shoulder to where Will was standing nearby. "He did appear disconcerted when I beat him. The second game he paid more attention to the cards being played."

"Did you best him then? I hadn't heard that part of the story yet."

At times, Will was too smart for his own good, and he was well aware of it. It pleased me more than it should have that I had found someone who could challenge my brother. The realization that there were others smarter than he would do Will a world of good.

"I have a few more years of experience than he has, and have had the benefit of playing against some excellent players." Dinner was announced, and he held his arm out to me. "May I escort you, Miss Forester?"

Smiling, I placed my hand on his arm and walked into the dining room with him. I was disappointed to find I was not next to him for the meal. Instead, I was put between Uncle Forester and Will. Mr. Richfield was between Sarah and Aunt Forester on the other side of the table.

"You didn't tell me Mr. Richfield bested you at piquet," I said in a low voice to my brother as the first course was served.

The look Will shot at me was filled with annoyance. "I may have underestimated him."

"Is that so?"

"He beat me. Somehow," Will said, sounding slightly resentful but mostly intrigued. "When he and I have a chance to play again, I'll figure him out."

I couldn't help smiling down at my soup, having no doubt Will would be seeking Mr. Richfield to play piquet as soon as possible. "Mr. Richfield, I don't believe you've told us where you are from." Sarah's rather loud statement brought my head up instantly.

"It's no secret, Miss Sarah," Mr. Richfield said in his easy manner. "My family has a small estate outside of London. The majority of my time, though, has been spent in London."

"A small estate, you say?" Sarah repeated the information as if it was the most interesting thing she had heard so far. "How lovely. And is your family large?"

My hand clenched around my spoon. "I have two sisters, Miss Sarah, both younger than I," Mr. Richfield said. Oddly enough, the conversation had lulled, making my sister and Mr. Richfield's conversation the point of interest. "They are several years younger than I."

"Can we expect your family to visit us at some point?"

This fishing for information could only be for one reason: Sarah wanted to prove her theory. I dearly wished I was close enough to kick her ankle, however much good that would do. Settling for glaring a warning was of no use because she ignored me.

"I cannot say. At the moment, my mother has no plans for travel."

"Surely you cannot spend this much time away from your family's estate," Miss Sandwood said, taking part in the conversation. She was on Will's other side. Why was I not surprised? "Your father must desire your company."

"Charlotte, hold your tongue," Mr. Sandwood said sharply.

"My father is dead, Miss Sandwood," Mr. Richfield said, his tone low.

That heart-breaking fact I had not been aware of before that moment, and it was apparent Charlotte Sandwood hadn't known it either. How had she not known if Mr. Richfield was a friend of the family? Had she simply not taken notice before? Whatever the reason, both she and Sarah became shamefaced. Clearing his throat, Uncle Forester remarked on the weather, and dinner continued.

I spotted Sarah sending a look towards Charlotte, and I narrowed my eyes. The two were conspirators, and I was determined to put an end to it.

BECAUSE OF HIS AGE, Will was sent out of the dining room with the ladies. As always, he was not happy about the situation. He took up a position at one of the windows in the drawing room and rejected Mrs. Sandwood's suggestion of a card game, choosing instead to stare out at the dark scenery.

I took the opportunity to approach my sister and Miss Sandwood where they were huddled together at the pianoforte. I was sure they weren't discussing the music they were going to play. "What were you two thinking?" I asked, making sure to keep my voice low. "I am quite ashamed of you both."

"You're not my sister," Charlotte Sandwood said dismissively. She made a show of spreading out sheet music, though she didn't even glance at it. "Besides, after Sarah and I talked, I realized just how little I know about Mr. Richfield. The questions Sarah and I were asking were perfectly acceptable."

"Then why did your father tell you to stop?"

Charlotte shook her head and sighed. "Sarah is right; you are completely blind to the situation. I am certain if he were to leave the area, we would have no further problems with the highwayman."

That was their way to prove their theory? Attempting to drive him away? Not if I had anything to say about it! "Don't be ridiculous," I said scornfully. "You both have read too many novels and have let them go to your head."

Sarah scoffed. "You don't have to be involved, Diana," she said. "Play cards with Mother and leave it to us to figure this out."

After being in trouble and having Father speak to her, she still was fixated on this? "You will embarrass yourselves and our families!" Maybe that would make one of them think. "This idea you have makes no sense at all."

"I think it makes sense."

Sarah and Charlotte brightened at the sudden support to their cause. I lifted my eyes to my younger brother. "Will! What do you know about this?"

"It wasn't exactly hard to hear you and Sarah talking about it the other day," Will said, pushing away from the window. "And if Mr. Richfield is the highwayman, it makes sense why he was so mad at you and me for investigating."

He was as crazy as Sarah and Charlotte, and I didn't hesitate to tell him so. "And keep your voice down," I said, catching Aunt Forester's glance in our direction. "There's no point in more people knowing about your insane theory than necessary."

"It's not that crazy." Sarah hit the keys on the piano at random. "Charlotte, Will, and I will prove it to you. Go away and let us get on with our planning."

"No! Absolutely not. I don't want you to prove it to me. How many times must I repeat myself before you understand this?"

To my irritation, Sarah and Charlotte exchanged looks again and nodded. "Girls, have you chosen the music for our entertainment?" Mrs. Sandwood asked getting our attention. "It's far too quiet in here."

"In a moment, Mother," Charlotte said over her shoulder. She leaned towards me. "Are you afraid we are right? Because it isn't as if you have an agreement with him, so when we prove he is a highwayman, your reputation will not be harmed in any way."

"That is not the reason I am telling you to forget this scheme," I said, snatching up the closest sheet of music. "Whether or not I have an agreement with him is certainly none of your business, Miss Sandwood. And you should not speculate about a gentleman in such a way. You know not what consequences there will be."

Sarah frowned at me. "Do you have an agreement with him?".

My cheeks flushed, and I chose to ignore the impertinent question. "Please move aside." If I didn't give them any more attention, would they stop? I had little hope that stratagem would work, but if I kept up the conversation, I knew I would lose my temper. "Mrs. Sandwood has asked for music. One of us should comply."

Dangerously close to scowling, Sarah retreated from the pianoforte, pulling her friend along with her. As I took my seat on the stool, I raised an eyebrow at Will. He mimicked my action, giving nothing else away. I dropped my gaze first, and out of the corner of my eye, I watched him return to staring out the window.

At least he wasn't plotting with Sarah and Charlotte. For now.

I was grateful the music I had grabbed so impulsively was a song I had played before, so it wasn't necessary for me to concentrate. As my fingers moved across the keys, I considered the facts I had just learned.

While I had expected Charlotte Sandwood to know, I found it concerning Will had become involved. I had hoped he would not learn of Sarah's insane theory. He was astonishingly determined when it came to figuring things out. With he and Sarah bouncing ideas off each other, neither would back down now.

At least they hadn't already come up with a plan to get the proof they wanted. I would have to keep both eyes on all three of them from now on.

Hopefully, they were the only ones who knew. What would I do if the rumor had already expanded the small circle that started it all?

Now that was a terrifying thought! Someone would end up having their reputation torn to shreds. Sarah, if she was wrong, and by extension the rest of the family. And undoubtedly Mr. Richfield as well, just for being the object of the scrutiny that would come. What would he think of me if he knew my sister's suspicions?

If she were right, though—well, Mr. Richfield would be arrested and, no doubt, hanged for his crimes. And yet, if he *was* guilty, could I stand by and let him get away with it?

Neither option was agreeable. Any way I looked at it, the situation could only end badly.

"Well done, Miss Forester," Mrs. Sandwood said as I came to the end of the melody. "You and your sister have such talent when it comes to music. You must have been all the rage in London."

I rose from my seat to allow Sarah or Miss Sandwood the chance to play. "I played only a few times while I was in London. I would not dare compete with young ladies who have had the benefit of a master's instruction."

"Modest, too," Mrs. Sandwood said, nodding her head. She focused on Mother and Aunt Forester. "A fine thing to see in a young lady of good breeding. Far too often, young ladies have wild ideas these days. Sometimes I don't know what to do with Charlotte. I have already warned her that one more breach of manners and she will not be going to London next year."

My lips curved with a smile. Now that I could use to good advantage. Charlotte Sandwood spent most of her time talking about the prospect of a London Season. All I would have to do is inform her I would tell her parents what she and Sarah were up to, and Sarah would lose her partner in crime.

But how to get Will from Sarah's side?

I was pondering this puzzle when the door opened and the men filed in. Immediately, I saw Charlotte and Sarah exchange pointed looks. Oh, no! Whatever they had planned, I wasn't going to let them get away with it.

"I have my grooms on watch constantly for this highwayman," Mr. Sandwood was saying, his tone serious. "We have to find a way of stopping this."

Had there been another incident over the highwayman? Had someone been hurt this time? Something must have happened for it to have gone from mild irritation to grave concern. I shot a glance at Will. He was too far away to have heard. Given that he hadn't mentioned it earlier, and taking his fascination with the whole thing into consideration, that could only mean he too did not know anything new.

"Mr. Richfield, come and sing with us!" Charlotte Sandwood said from the pianoforte.

For a brief second, my eyes met Mr. Richfield's. He raised his eyebrow at me questioningly. He was asking me if I would join him in the activity? My heart skipped a beat, while my mind searched for something, anything else we could do.

Piquet.

I let my eyes flit to the small table the family used for the game and then brought them back. Mr. Richfield began to smile. "My apologies, Miss Sandwood," he said in answer to Charlotte. "Miss Forester and I have a game of cards to play. Perhaps later this evening, music will be the focus."

"Piquet?"

Smiling at the young lady's shock, I walked over to the table and took a seat on one side. Mr. Richfield was mere seconds behind me. "Is there a particular reason you want to play piquet, Miss Forester?" he asked as he took his seat. "I would never have taken you as one fond of cards."

Out of the corner of my eye, I saw Will glare at me and my smile deepened. I had the perfect excuse and might kill two birds with one stone while I was at it. "I want to be able to beat Will." If he thought I was getting lessons from Mr. Richfield, Will would work even harder to perfect his piquet skills. He'd have no time for plotting with Sarah. "I can think of no one better to instruct me."

The look Mr. Richfield gave me showed clearly he wasn't sure whether to believe me or not. "Well, I suppose we should play a game so I can find out just what you know," he said, apparently deciding not to press the issue.

Nodding, I picked up the cards, inwardly rejoicing I had successfully managed to keep him out of Sarah's plot. I had the feeling next time it wouldn't be so easy.

Chapter Nine

My piquet skills were nowhere near Will's level, so my defeat came within minutes. Mr. Richfield spent the rest of the evening showing me different strategies and often had to remind me of the rules associated with the game. Jealous, Will watched with narrowed eyes, and Sarah sulked at the pianoforte.

I honestly expected Father to say something to Sarah about her questioning on our ride back home. But he didn't, and I should have known better than to think he would in front of the whole family. He merely steered her into the library as soon as we stepped foot in the hall.

She had not returned by the time I changed into my nightgown. I brushed and braided my hair, and still, she hadn't come up. For a moment, I debated leaving the candle on the dressing table for her but decided it wouldn't be wise since at this point I had no idea when she would be joining me. Once I blew the tiny flame out, I dashed over to bed.

I was nearly asleep when Sarah finally stormed in. Blinking in the light from the candle she brought with her, I lifted my head to peer at her. The expression on her face was one of fury, and I knew better than to ask what Father had said to her. Sighing, I closed my eyes and laid my head back on my pillow.

After a restful night of sleep, a small part of me felt sorry for Sarah getting scolded by Father again. Twice in three days had to be some new accomplishment, and not a good one. Still, she had brought it on herself by pursuing her theory.

Feeling generous, I resolved to give her a few days to think better of getting the proof she wanted. If she did not, I had no qualms about relieving her of her chief conspirator. We would see how she fared on her own.

Those were not the most Christian thoughts to be having on a Sunday morning. To distract myself, I asked, over breakfast, "Papa, have you learned anything new about the highwayman?"

"Oh, let's not start that conversation again," Aunt Forester said with a groan. "I've heard quite enough about this highwayman. It's all Mr. Forester would speak of last night."

Will perked up from where he had been glaring at his food. He had been unusually sullen since he watched Mr. Richfield give me a lesson on piquet. "Did the highwayman strike again?" he asked eagerly. "When?"

Looking more severe than I had seen him in some time, Papa lowered his fork. "Yes, the highwayman struck two nights ago," he said. "Shots were fired, and Mr. Sandwood's groom was wounded. Fortunately, there was no one in the carriage at the time."

Someone had been hurt, just as I had wondered. "The poor man! Will he recover?" I asked with concern.

At the same time, Will asked, "Where?"

"The man will recover," Papa said to me. He leveled his gaze on Will. "I know you want to run off and see what you can find, so I will not tell you where it happened. This man is armed and dangerous. I don't want any of you children going off on your own. Is that understood?"

"Yes, sir," the three of us all chorused. Sarah sounded the most annoyed with the situation, though it was difficult to be sure as Will was also reluctant to voice his understanding.

"It's a shame such a terrible person has come to the county," Uncle Forester said, not in the least bit distracted from his breakfast. "It's nearly as bad as the crime in London."

"Mr. Forester, it most certainly is not as bad as that!" Aunt Forester said in protest. "You will give your brother a terrible opinion of London and then I will never get them to join us for a Season!"

Father laughed. "Mary, I can assure you, I would not go to London even if it were the safest place to be."

That sparked a debate between the older members of the family on the advantages and disadvantages of London. I had heard it all before. Every year, Aunt Forester tried to convince Mother and Father a London Season would benefit all of us. And each year, they had refused, saying it was too much expense. I had been beyond shocked when my parents had conceded to allow me to go this year.

The Sunday routine had not changed at all in the time I had been away, and Mother urged us all to be ready on time. And, as always, Sarah was the last to come rushing down the stairs. "Do you suppose we will see Mr. Richfield with the Sandwoods today?" she asked, as she tied her bonnet.

"I imagine so," Mother said absently.

I, on the other hand, glared at my sister. The only reason she could have to be interested in whether or not Mr. Richfield was there would be for some plot she and her friend had devised. To divert another interrogation attempt, I would have to be on my toes.

Sarah may have thought she was being helpful, but in truth, she was doing the exact opposite.

EVEN IF SOMEONE HAD approached me immediately at the conclusion of the service and asked what the sermon was about, I would not have been able to answer. Mr. Richfield had sat with the Sandwoods, near the front of the church, and my attention was not what it should have been.

I searched my brain for some inconspicuous way to keep Sarah from rushing to the Sandwoods after the service. In the end, all I did was loop my arm around hers and spin her around, so we both faced the most gregarious lady we knew: the Widow Davison. "Mrs. Davison!" I said brightly, to get her attention. "How are you?"

"Miss Forester. Miss Sarah." Mrs. Davison focused on us with obvious delight. Beside me, I heard Sarah groan. As much as we adored Mrs. Davison, she could monopolize anyone's time. "How well you two look today. Every time I see you, you both have become more beautiful. You must tell me your secret."

"Thank you," I said, used to her compliments. "May Sarah and I walk you home today? Or do you have a handsome young man to escort you?"

Since I was a small child, Mrs. Davison had always claimed to be waiting for a handsome man to come along and sweep her off her feet. "No handsome gentleman today, I'm afraid," the older woman said. "So I will gladly accept your assistance."

In the past year, it had become harder and harder for Mrs. Davison to get around. She was nearing eighty years of age, and was not as steady on her feet as she once was. I caught Mother's eye and inclined my head towards Mrs. Davison. Understanding, Mother nodded her permission. "Now, we must have a proper chat sometime, girls," Mrs. Davison said as I took her right arm to help support her. "I hardly know what has happened in your lives recently."

To try to beg off now would be rude and would result in another talking to from Father, and Sarah knew it. "Nothing ever happens," my sister said, taking the widow's left side. We began walking towards the Mrs. Davison's home. "But Diana has news you should know."

"Oh? Surely if you had something interesting to tell me, you would have found your way to my cottage already," Mrs. Davison said, looking at me with interest. "Come, tell me all, Diana. I must know. What news do you have?"

On any other day, I would have been furious Sarah would have revealed such a personal detail from my life. But I was giddy from my victory in foiling Sarah's plot and found I didn't mind. "You met the young gentleman who is staying with the Sandwoods?" was all I asked. It was all I would need to say.

Mrs. Davison brightened. "I did. He is such a gentleman. Are you—is he—? Diana Forester! Are you being courted?"

"Please, it's not well known," I felt obliged to tell her. It wouldn't do to have anyone overhear our conversation. "Yes, I do believe I am."

"Well, it's about time a good man discovered you," Mrs. Davison said with no little satisfaction. "I had begun to think the young men of your generation were complete fools. I won't press you for details now, but you must come by soon to tell me everything."

I laughed. It felt so good to speak of it to someone who was not of my family. I ignored the glare Sarah had directed at me was easy to overlook. "You have my word I will do so. And not on a Sunday, either. This kind of conversation shouldn't happen on the Lord's day."

"Oh, my! What kind of thing is that to say, Diana?" Mrs. Davison feigned shock before smiling with satisfaction. "Your heart must have truly been touched, Diana. I am delighted to know it."

I wasn't exactly sure how what I said could tell her that, but I wasn't about to deny it. We reached her doorstep, and she let us go. "Run along," she said, the slightest hint of worry in her eyes. "I wouldn't want you to get caught by that terrible highwayman."

Sarah opened her mouth. Terrified of what she might say, I stepped on her foot. "I hardly think he would attack us in broad daylight," I said, as Sarah yelped in pain. "Good day, Mrs. Davison. We'll come visit this week."

Mrs. Davison waved us on our way as I practically dragged Sarah away. "Let go of me," Sarah finally said, pulling her arm free. "Just what are you trying to do, Diana? Pull my arm off?"

"Sorry." Maybe I had held on too tight. "Let's get home. We don't want to keep Papa from his meal."

"If you're so worried about that, you shouldn't volunteer us to walk Mrs. Davison home. I wanted to talk to Charlotte."

Just as I thought. Only I would wager my best bonnet they would not be chatting about the latest fashions. "We were just there, and nothing new could have happened overnight." I slowed my steps and took a deep breath of the spring air. "Isn't it a gorgeous day? I am so happy winter is behind us."

"You're just trying to change the subject," Sarah said, sounding less grumpy. She sighed. "I wish you would have let me tell Mrs. Davison about Mr. Richfield. Now she's going to think he's such a great catch, and her heart will be broken when she finds out the truth."

"Well, since I highly doubt you will ever prove Mr. Richfield is a highwayman, I hardly think that is something I need to worry about."

The moment the words left my mouth, I knew I had once again said the wrong thing. Sarah's face darkened. "Is that a challenge?" she asked, her tone cold.

"No! Sarah, I just—." I broke off, not knowing how to reach my now angry sister. "I am so tired of you saying you have to prove Mr. Richfield is a highwayman. Don't you understand what would happen if someone outside of our family heard you?"

"You are so concerned with what other people think, Diana!"

"Of course I am! What you and I do reflects on our parents. If we do not act with the utmost propriety, our neighbors will believe we have not been educated as we should have been."

"Being mindful of who we allow into our acquaintance does not mean we were not educated, Diana! And if we discover something unsavory about one of our acquaintances, we have no choice but to make sure others are aware of it!"

"But you don't know for sure Mr. Richfield is 'unsavory' as you put it."

"Because you won't let me find out for sure!"

By this time we were facing each other. We both had our hands on our hips and were glaring at each other. Mother was nowhere near us to intervene in this argument, and since neither of us was about to back down, I had no idea how this impasse would end.

"Give me one good reason why I should let you interrogate and possibly humiliate the man I intend to marry," I said without thinking.

Shock filled Sarah's face, and I realized what I had said. I felt my cheeks burn with embarrassment. "You—you're actually going to marry him? Diana, not long ago you didn't know if you even wanted to know him and now you're in love with him? What do you even know about him?"

My anger faded away as I thought about what I knew. "I know he is an honorable man," I said quietly. "I know he came to talk to Papa when I had given him every reason to think that I had no interest in him. He has two sisters he cares for a great deal, and he has befriended Will, which is no easy feat. Everything I know about him tells me he is a good man."

"And you're just going to ignore what I think?"

Why did she have to question me on everything? "It is not my intention to ignore you, Sarah. But you ignored my wishes. Please, leave Mr. Richfield alone. Don't try to trap him in one of your plots."

For a moment, I wasn't sure Sarah would listen to me. "I swear I will cease trying to interrogate him if that makes you happy," she finally said. "But you have to promise me you will not blindly accept an offer from him without at least considering I might be onto something."

Believing that to be the best I would ever get from her, I nodded. "I promise."

Nodding once, Sarah started walking. "We should get home before Papa sends out a search party."

Breathing out, I quickly caught up with her. "Just out of curiosity, what were you and Miss Sandwood planning?"

Sarah glanced over at me and shook her head. "Diana, if I told you, you wouldn't be happy."

"Why? Sarah, what were you planning to do?" Without answering, Sarah began to hum and she skipped ahead of me. "Sarah Forester! Tell me!" But no matter what I threatened or how much I pleaded, Sarah refused to say a word about it.

Sisters.

THE REST OF THE DAY passed with no other problems. Sarah, as she would do whenever she was thinking about something, had withdrawn into herself. Knowing Aunt and Uncle Forester would be leaving the next day, I spent my time with them. Mr. Richfield crossed my mind on many occasions, as did Philip Knighton.

When Monday dawned, it was a bright, beautiful spring day. With tears in my eyes, I hugged my aunt and uncle just before they climbed into their carriage. Despite the disapproval and disappointment I knew Aunt Forester to have, they both had taken such good care of me in London. I knew I would miss them dearly.

Having no task for me to accomplish, Mother dismissed me to amuse myself. Father was at work in the library, so I knew playing the pianoforte would annoy him. Instead, I picked up the novel I had bought in London that I hadn't had a free moment to begin. I was fully prepared to read for the rest of the day.

Sarah, though, had other ideas. "Let's go for a walk," she said, coming into the sitting room.

I gazed at her over the pages of my book. "Why?"

"Because I want to do something! Sitting around is so—boring."

"I thought you were going to practice your archery, so you could show your skill at the Knighton's house party," I said with a sigh. I uncurled from my seat in the window. "Why didn't you ask Will to take a walk?"

"Will is reviewing everything he knows about piquet, for some odd reason. He's playing against himself and insists he can't leave it. I thought to practice my archery, but somehow I lost all of my arrows over the winter. I can't convince Mother to find them for me."

It never failed when one of us misplaced something, we would run straight to Mother to find it. How she managed always to find the item, I didn't think I would ever know. Maybe it was a skill all mothers developed?

"Why won't Mother help you?"

"She says I need to learn to keep my belongings organized and neat." Sarah grabbed my arm and tugged. "Come on, Diana. You know I can't go for a walk on my own. Not after Father was so insistent about it."

I knew she would never leave me alone if I tried to ignore her or outright refused. "Fine," I said, closing my book with a sigh. "I'll get ready. But I don't see how a walk is going to help you find your bow and arrows."

My sister let out a long sigh. "If I don't think about it, I am sure it will come to me. Now, hurry!"

Briefly, I considered taking my time getting dressed for a walk but decided I did not want to risk annoying Sarah. I feared to do so would bring back her determination to prove Mr. Richfield a highwayman. It was much safer to go along with her today and keep the peace that had settled between us.

Ten minutes later, with my boots laced up, my bonnet on my head, and my spencer jacket buttoned on, I joined Sarah in the foyer. "Finally!" she said impatiently. "I thought you would never be ready."

"Well, I am now. Where shall we walk to?"

"Oh, anywhere."

With that vague answer, she walked out the door, and I followed her. There wasn't a cloud in the sky, and I breathed in the scent of spring carried on the light breeze. It was a beautiful day, and I found myself glad Sarah had pulled me from my book so I could enjoy it.

"Do you think we'll make friends with the ladies who will be at the house party?" Sarah asked minutes into our walk. She had chosen the path we would traverse, going down the lane toward the village. I sincerely hoped we would not be making any visits.

"I should hope so," I said, taking care to step around a fallen branch. "We are to spend several days in their company, and it wouldn't be enjoyable to begin by taking a dislike to someone. Mrs. Knighton's acquaintances are generally pleasant people."

"Must you always speak so positively?" Sarah asked, glancing over her shoulder at me.

I frowned at her. "What do you mean? I don't always speak in a positive manner." These past few weeks of agonizing over my relationship with Mr. Richfield had taught me that. "Is there a problem with me trying to speak about the good in things?"

"It gets annoying."

Forcing myself to breathe out slowly, I didn't respond to her. My attention went to a wildflower growing by the lane. "Look, Sarah!" I said as I plucked one. "We should put flowers in your hair for the ball."

"Everyone does that. I want to be completely original!"

I chuckled, shaking my head. I remembered going through a few months with such an attitude when I was seventeen. "I'm afraid that will be difficult to accomplish. Everything interesting has already been done in society. All you can do is imitate some of the greats and make society think you came up with it on your own.”

“Then I’ll do that.”

“Why, exactly, do you want to stand out so much?”

Thoughtfully, Sarah hummed a note as she considered. “Why not? It is no fun being on the sidelines and watching everything happen. I want to be in the middle of the scene, enjoying what’s going on around me.”

“Well, take care you’re not so busy enjoying yourself you forget to be you.”

Turning to walk backward, Sarah scowled at me. “What do you mean?”

For a moment, I struggled to find the words to explain just what I did mean. “Simply put, I’m afraid you will try so hard to be an original and end up forgetting how to be just plain Sarah Forester who loves to play the harp and play ninepins with her younger brother.”

“You think too much. I can do all that and still be original.”

I decided to allow the matter to rest there. Twirling back around, Sarah bounced ahead a few steps. “When was the last time there was a ball here?” she asked, changing the subject completely. “I can’t even think of having attended a ball before this.”

“Last fall. The Sandwoods gave a ball. You and Miss Sandwood danced every dance, as you pointed out to me for days afterward.”

Sarah laughed merrily. “Oh, of course. Now I remember. That was fun. How many times did you have to sit with Mother?”

"Most of the evening." Even now, it hurt to remember how my outgoing little sister had been more sought after than I had. It hurt even more to remember Philip Knighton had asked me to dance with him twice. I had done so, and only later realized he had taken it as encouragement that I returned his affections.

"Well, maybe this time you will have more fun."

Anticipation made me smile. She was right. This time, I would have Mr. Richfield to dance with. He was an elegant dancer, as I had discovered in London. "Yes, I daresay I will."

"I want to dance and dance!" Sarah said, twirling some more. I laughed as I watched her. "There will finally be something fun to do. Archery, ninepins, Picnics and horse rides! And maybe we can play charades during the evening."

"You have everything planned out." I couldn't help but be amused by her enthusiasm for the coming festivities. "I certainly hope Mrs. Knighton is prepared for you to take over the entertainment for the party!"

The look Sarah shot me over her shoulder said plainly she was not amused. A moment later, her expression changed to one of astonishment. "What is he doing out here?"

"Who do you mean?" I asked, surprised the question. Turning, I caught sight of a tall, familiar figure walking down the lane towards us. A smile parted my lips as excitement bubbled up. "Mr. Richfield!"

Chapter Ten

"Oh, please tell me you're not about to start jumping up and down," I heard Sarah say as I took a few steps forward. "You are positively ridiculous sometimes, Diana."

"Miss Forester. Miss Sarah," Mr. Richfield called out before I could tell Sarah to keep her comments to herself. There was a broad smile on his face. "I wondered if I would find you enjoying this beautiful day."

I laughed. "Well, you nearly did not." I gestured to where I hoped Sarah was still waiting for me. I wouldn't have put it past her to have walked on in protest. Glancing behind and seeing for certain, though, would have required too much courage on my part. "I was happy reading a book until my sister insisted upon dragging me outside."

"Then I am in your debt, Miss Sarah," Mr. Richfield said, making a half bow to my right. I felt a surge of relief Sarah hadn't been rude enough to continue on her way. "Are you walking anywhere in particular? Chasing the highwayman again?"

"We left Will behind, so we have not been searching for a hidden trail today. I don't think we're walking to any specific destination unless Sarah hasn't told me something. Would you like to join us?"

"I can think of nothing I would enjoy more," he said, holding his arm out. Smiling, I looped my arm around his and sent a glance at Sarah. She was already walking away. "Mr. and Mrs. Forester left today, didn't they?" He paused. "I mean your aunt and uncle, of course. Not your parents."

"Yes, they did," I said with a laugh.

"I suppose you are accustomed to others having to clarify which Forester they are speaking to."

I raised an eyebrow at him. "You haven't seen anything yet. My father had two brothers, both of whom married and had children. Any large family event results in an abundance of Mr. Foresters and Mrs. Foresters and Miss Foresters. It must take the county at least a month to recover from such a wedding."

"Are weddings the only family event your entire family attends?"

Why had the word wedding been the first word to leave my lips? Horrified I had used that particular example, I said, "No! Of course not! Well, most of the time, I suppose but—."

There was no telling how long I would have tried to recover from my verbal misstep. I was so caught up in trying to explain myself I failed to watch my step. My foot found a rut in the lane, and I found myself off balance. With a cry, I fell forward, mentally preparing myself to meet the ground face first.

Instead, I found myself with my face against the front of Mr. Richfield's long coat. "I've got you," he said as he helped me regain my balance.

"Oh, thank you. I thought I was about to become intimately acquainted with the ground."

"I would not have let that happen."

My breath caught in my throat as my eyes met his. Mr. Richfield's right hand still grasped my arm, and his other hand was at my waist. I knew I should step back, but I couldn't force my legs to obey that particular command.

"Are you well?" he asked, his voice low.

"What happened?" Sarah's suspicious voice asked, interrupting the moment.

Looking over, I saw my younger sister standing with her hands on her hips, glaring at us. My face flushed red as I moved back. Mr. Richfield let go of me and cleared his throat. "Your sister stepped wrong and nearly fell. I was able to keep that from happening."

"Right," Sarah said, her tone disbelieving. "Diana, I am ready to return home now. I think I know exactly where my arrows were stored."

Why was I not surprised? "That's good," I said, shocking myself with how steady my voice sounded.

"I will walk you both home," Mr. Richfield said.

Her face twisting into a scowl, Sarah strode forward and positioned herself in between he and I. "Wonderful. Let's be on our way. Are you going to be joining the house party at the Knightons', Mr. Richfield?"

That question was not as bad as I had expected. "As a matter of fact, I will," he said to her. "Mr. Philip Knighton extended me an invitation personally."

The feeling of relief that had begun fled when I realized what name he had just spoken. Instead, I felt as though I couldn't breathe at all. "Oh, you have met Mr. Knighton then?" Sarah asked, her tone becoming sincerely interested. "We grew up together, as I am sure you must have realized. We were practically brother and sister."

"I had assumed you grew up together, but did not imagine your families were as close as that. Mr. Knighton didn't mention it."

Once he said that I could breathe again. This was a situation I hadn't considered. How would Mr. Knighton react if he were to find out I was being courted? Since he had ridden away that day and then left for who knew where I had not seen him. I could only hope he would not cause a scene at the house party.

"Oh, look, Diana," Sarah said, getting my attention. "Isn't that Mr. Knighton coming towards us now?"

My head jerked up. Just when I had begun to calm down, I found myself in the middle of the situation I had hoped to avoid. It was Philip Knighton riding towards us, and an unfamiliar man accompanied him.

"Knighton!" Mr. Richfield said, raising his hand in greeting.

I saw my brothers' closest friend hesitate. Holding my breath, I prayed he wouldn't just ride past and ignore us. That would result in a terrible conversation I did not want to have.

"Richfield," Knighton said, slowing his horse to a stop beside us. He nodded once, his eyes moving past me in a second. "Miss Forester. Miss Sarah. How are you today?"

"Well, enough," Sarah said. There was a strange note in her voice, and when I glanced at her, I saw her gaze was on the strange man with Mr. Knighton. "Are your guests arriving for the house party?"

"They will be tomorrow." Knighton gestured to the gentleman on his right. "This is my friend, Mr. John Ward, from London. Ward, Miss Forester, Miss Sarah Forester, and Mr. Richfield."

My eyes widened at the introduction, and I heard Sarah gasp. We should have been given the opportunity to indicate whether we wished to be introduced to this Mr. Ward or not. Mr. Knighton had just forced upon us an acquaintance we had no notion whether would be to our benefit or harm our reputation entirely.

"A pleasure," the man said, nodding once in a bored manner. He did not indicate whether he caught the implied slight to Sarah and I or not.

Mr. Richfield stirred, making no verbal acknowledgment of the introduction. A moment of awkward silence formed. I expected Sarah to have something to say, as she usually did, but she kept quiet. "Kindly give your mother our regards when you see her," I said as it was the only polite thing to come to mind.

Knighton glanced at me. "Certainly, Miss Forester. Good day, ladies. Richfield."

I could not have felt happier they were riding on and we were walking in the opposite direction. "Brother and sister, you said?" Mr. Richfield said to Sarah. "I never would have guessed it."

Oh, perfect. "Well, he has been gone for some time now," I said, hoping it would be enough of an explanation. "And then, of course, I was in Town with Aunt and Uncle."

"You appear flustered. Is something wrong?"

Sarah snorted, seeming to take an interest in the conversation. "Diana is always flustered. It is practically a part of her daily personality."

"Thank you for that, Sarah," I said with a sigh. Happily, though, we seem to have moved on in conversation.

Mr. Richfield laughed. "You never told me your family was this amusing, Miss Forester. I can understand why you would want to return to them."

"Oh, I am so glad we amuse you, sir!" Sarah said, sarcasm lacing her tone. "That was, of course, our whole purpose for existing."

And at that point, I decided I had put up with quite enough of my sister's antagonism. Never mind Mr. Richfield was laughing at her again, taking it all in stride as he did so well. Sarah was taking her odd dislike too far. I reached over and grabbed her arm, answering her glare for glare. All too easily, Sarah shrugged. She stayed between Mr. Richfield and me, and I couldn't think of any plausible reason to make her move.

"So you have an interest in archery, Miss Sarah?" Mr. Richfield asked, attempting to ease the tension.

I held my breath, waiting for Sarah to snap at him. "A lady has to have something to occupy her time."

"That is true, I suppose," Mr. Richfield said, sounding skeptical.

"You suppose?" Sarah's tone became cold. I covered my face with my hand. This afternoon was quickly spiraling out of control. "

"I have heard the men will be having a championship of events during the house party!" I said quickly. I needed something, anything, to redirect the conversation. "Will you be participating in that, Mr. Richfield?"

"I had not given it much thought. I am not much of a sportsman, you know."

"Men have so many other things to think of than whether or not young ladies are entertained, Diana," Sarah said before I could reply.

With relief, I spotted the path Sarah, and I usually took as a shortcut. "You have taken us far enough," I said, pulling Sarah towards the path. "We will see you at the house party then. Enjoy the rest of your day, Mr. Richfield."

"Good day Miss Forester, Miss Sarah," Mr. Richfield called after us, sounding surprised.

"And you think I'm rude," Sarah said, jerking free. "Goodness, Diana. You act so strange sometimes."

It took all my self-control not to retaliate because deep down I knew she was right. He must think me odd now, and it hurt to admit it to myself. How dare she force me into this situation? Why couldn't she have let me walk with Mr. Richfield in peace?

Why was I cursed with a sister who provoked me so much?

MOTHER HAD NOTHING to say when I told her we had crossed paths with Philip Knighton. The only reaction I received from her was when I complained about Sarah's topics of conversation with Mr. Richfield. She promised to speak to Father and then told me to go back to my book.

Whether Father spoke to Sarah again about her attitude, I did not know. But the next day, Sarah became wholly devoted to her archery. She had found her arrows hidden in the corner of the attic, and practiced out on the lawn every hour she was free.

The first day, I joined her in the exercise. My arms ached after only a few shots. It had always been Sarah's hobby, and I was indifferent to it. By that afternoon, I sat on the grass and watched Sarah aim at the multiple targets she had convinced Will to set up for her.

On the second day, I spent the morning making calls with Mother. When we returned, Sarah was still shooting arrows at her targets, growling in frustration whenever she hit slightly off center. Her competitive streak was showing by this point.

"How long do you think she will keep at it?" I asked, walking over to stand by Will to watch our sister.

"I have no idea."

I glanced over at him. "I am surprised to see you outside of your room. Did you finally tire of playing against yourself?"

Will scowled at me. "Yes," he said. I did try not to smirk, but I could not help it. And made my brother's glare deepen. "You planned all of this!"

Laughing, I watched Sarah pulled her arrows out of the targets with too much force. "I can't say I planned exactly for Sarah to do this. But yes. I knew how you would react when you saw Mr. Richfield teaching me some tricks. I had to do something to make you two stop plotting behind my back."

"You're sure he isn't the highwayman?" Will asked, looking less disgruntled.

"Yes, I am."

Frowning, Will tore his gaze away. "Your reaction to it all was so amusing," he said mournfully. "Now what am I supposed to tease you about?"

"Oh, Will," I said, looping my arm around his. He immediately shook me off, giving me a disgusted look. "I cannot tell you how much I look forward to you meeting a girl and I can repay you for everything you plan on doing to me."

"Oh, I will never get married."

That made me laugh again. "Will, you amuse so much. You cannot know at this moment that you will never marry."

"Miss Forester!"

I cringed at the female voice that called to me. Beside me, Will tensed and gave a low groan. "Miss Sandwood," I said, turning to face our visitor. Charlotte Sandwood was crossing the garden, smiling brightly. "How lovely to see you today. Again."

"I came to see Sarah since she has not been over to see me," Charlotte said, looking over towards my sister. "We had so much to plan before the house party, and that begins tomorrow you know."

"Plan?" I asked with suspicion. "What kind of plan do you need?"

Miss Sandwood laughed. "Surely you cannot have forgotten. I am convinced that introducing a potential highwayman into a house party would be disastrous. He will know who will have the most funds for him to steal. We must prevent this at all cost."

So, my sister and brother may have been diverted from their plotting, but Miss Sandwood had not. I could only be glad I knew how to fix this. She feared losing out on her London Season, and all I had to do was maneuver a way to bring it into the conversation.

"Why would it make a difference?" Will asked. "He already knows there is to be a house party, and the invited members are coming from London. He will be able to attack them on the road to the Knightons' manor. What difference does it make if he meets them afterward?"

Have I mentioned just how clever my younger brother is? "Oh," Miss Sandwood said in surprise. "I had not thought of that."

"Do you think your father will approve of this?" I asked, deciding to take advantage of the opportunity that had presented itself.

My question caused a frown to form on her face. "What do you mean, miss Forester? What does my father have to do with it?"

"He was not happy with your questioning of Mr. Richfield the other evening," I said pointedly. "I also know your parents have warned you any outrageous behavior will result in you losing the opportunity to enjoy the next London Season."

Feeling victorious, I watched the younger woman go pale. "I see."

"Don't let Diana bully you, Charlotte," Sarah said. "She has been doing that to Will and I for far too long, and someone should stand up to her."

Annoyed at being called a bully, I glared at my sister. "Miss Forester, I appreciate your concern," Miss Sandwood said, her tone formal. "However, it is misplaced. My father would thank me if I were to uncover a criminal in our midst, especially one who has been residing with my family."

Her chin in the air, she strode over to Sarah. Hopefully, I had said enough to give her a small sliver of doubt. After all, she had said 'if.'

"I suppose you think you have won now," Will said.

"This is not about winning, Will. What else was I to do? Why is it none of you understand the consequences of accusing Mr. Richfield of being a criminal would have been disastrous? I had to stop you somehow!"

"There's no need to get defensive."

Irritating brother! Why couldn't I have been an only child? Even as I asked myself that, I knew I honestly didn't mean it. I could not imagine my life without my siblings, however irritating they could be on most occasions.

"Besides, I don't think it is over just yet," Will said, getting my attention. He nodded to where Sarah and Miss Sandwood were huddled together. As I watched, Sarah glanced over, and her grin made me uneasy. "They will not give up so easily."

What? After my strategy and warnings? Were they still going to continue with their plan? Whatever their plan was? Hadn't Sarah promised to leave it alone? She would keep her word, wouldn't she? Or had she already found a loophole?

"I don't believe this," I said out loud. Leaving Will laughing, I walked towards my sister and Charlotte.

Sarah saw me coming and whispered something to her friend. "Then, it is settled," Charlotte said, just loud enough for me to hear.

"What is settled? What are you two up to?"

They both faced me with broad smiles. "Oh, we aren't going to ambush your Mr. Richfield," Sarah said. She reached over and patted my arm as if to comfort me. "You were right. Proving he is a highwayman would bring some nasty consequences. So you do not have to worry about that at all."

That didn't reassure me at all. "That does not explain what you have planned instead."

"Since we are so adamant we ought not to prove whether he is a highwayman or not, we cannot know for sure whether he is a good man or not," Charlotte said. "And what kind of friend would I be if I let you or Sarah become involved with a man of questionable background?"

Well, this just kept getting better and better. "You should not be concerned. Mr. Richfield is—."

"No, no, no," Charlotte said, interrupting me. "Sarah and I will handle this. I will see you both at the house party."

As she spun on her heel and walked away, Sarah faced me, looking entirely too pleased with herself. "Just what are you going to do?" I asked, to which she shrugged innocently. "You and Miss Sandwood are planning something, and I know I am not going to like it."

"Sister of mine, you worry far too much," Sarah said. "Charlotte and I agreed we couldn't let you marry someone who may be a criminal." She raised her hand to stop me from protesting. "We will not be trying to prove he is just as I promised I wouldn't, remember?"

"Sarah, tell me right now: what do you have planned?" I asked, my voice rising. Why did I have to keep repeating myself? I just wanted a straight answer!

"Well, we just thought with so many beautiful and wealthy young ladies from London being at the house party, we might be able to convince him they are more worth his time."

I stared at her in disbelief. I could see my sister smiling at me, but I felt as though I was back in London with Miss Reynolds chattering about how she intended on pursuing Mr. Richfield. Only this time, my heart felt like it had stopped beating.

"No. Sarah, no!"

How would I bear it if I had to watch Mr. Richfield become interested in another young lady? I knew I was not the most beautiful young lady, simply pretty enough and I did not have a fortune. Mr. Richfield had never made a formal offer. What was there to stop him from being persuaded by Sarah and Miss Sandwood to pursue another?

No. I could not let that happen. "Don't you dare, Sarah! How could you even think of doing that to me?"

Slowly, Sarah's smile faded away. "I am just trying to protect you, Diana. You are always complaining about how I don't understand you, but you never try to see things from my point of view."

"Protect me? Ever since you learned he was interested in me and not you, you have been acting in this insane manner!"

"Are you trying to insinuate I am jealous?"

At this point, we were standing almost nose to nose, but I had the advantage of being slightly taller than my sister. "Girls, I need you." Mother's voice. "What are you doing?"

We exchanged glares one last time before we spun to face Mother with forced smiles. "We are coming, Mother," we said at the same time. As Sarah set down her bow, I walked away from her, my hands clenched tightly. I was sorely tempted to slap her and I knew that would only get myself in trouble with my parents.

"You'll see, I'm right," Sarah said in a low voice as she caught up to me.

"Be careful about what you do now, Sarah," I said in answer, keeping my voice just as low. "I will not be able to forgive you if you do this to me."

Chapter Eleven

Two days later, Mother rode with Sarah and me to Knighton Manor. My sister and I had not exchanged any kind of conversation the whole time, which made Mother annoyed with us both. It did not make for a comfortable existence.

I had thought Mother would be on my side in this. But all she had said when I told her what Sarah had planned was, "I hardly think your sister intends on ruining your marriage prospects. And even if she tries, do you think she will succeed? You must not have a high opinion of Mr. Richfield if you do. If he is lured away by another young lady, then, does he truly deserve you?"

Mother's words had made me think, tand I knew she was right. If Mr. Richfield became interested in another lady, I would not want to marry someone who was so easily distracted. With that in mind, I resolved to let Sarah do what she would and trust I knew Mr. Richfield as well as I thought I did.

"I expect you both to behave yourselves today," Mother said as the carriage rumbled down the lane to the manor. "Mrs. Knighton was kind enough to include you in her activities. I will not have you embarrassing yourselves by quarreling with each other."

"We would never do that, Mother," Sarah said, her tone aghast.

Mother sent her a look that made Sarah squirm beside me. "Do not try my patience because I will not hesitate to deny you time at this house party if either of you disgraces yourselves today, or on any other occasion when we are here," she said. From her tone, I had no doubt she was completely serious.

For the first time in days, I exchanged an uneasy look with Sarah. We were well aware if we were pulled away from the party events, it would be quite some time before we would be allowed to go to anything away from home.

"We understand, Mother," I said meekly.

"Good."

The carriage pulled to a stop in front of the large manor house where the Knighton family resided. A stable hand opened the door, and Mother was the first one out. Sarah and I moved at the same time to follow her. We glared at each other before I sat back and gestured for her to go ahead of me. "Be my guest."

The high road, for the moment, was mine. Rolling her eyes, Sarah climbed out. "Well, isn't this going to be a fun day," I said to myself, pushing myself off the seat.

The manor was a large Elizabethan house that had been home to the Knighton family for over a hundred years. Its stone walls rose high, and the large glass windows sparkled in the sunshine.

Mother led the way up to the front door. The butler opened it for us, and a maid took our bonnets from us. Miss Jenson, Mrs. Knighton's companion, was there to greet us and escort us to the drawing room, where all the women in the party were gathered at the moment.

"I think perhaps you will know a few of the other guests, Miss Forester," Miss Jenson said over her shoulder. "They all spent time in London during this past season."

"Perhaps," I said skeptically. So many people were in town for the London Season that the odds I would know any of the members of this party seemed ridiculous.

Miss Jenson opened the door for us and stepped aside to the side to allow us to enter ahead of her. About ten ladies were sitting in the drawing room. Half of them already had bored expressions on their face, while the other half was huddled together talking excitedly. The first person I saw clearly as I stepped up beside Mother made my heart sink.

Miss Reynolds.

Of course she would be here. The one lady in London who had professed an interest in Mr. Richfield was here. I had no doubt she would not hesitate to pursue Mr. Richfield's attention. Sarah may not have to do a single thing!

"Mrs. Forester! Miss Forester, Miss Sarah," Mrs. Knighton said, rising from her seat. "Welcome. Let me introduce you to my guests. I am sure we will have a wonderful time these coming weeks."

As Mrs. Knighton led us further into the room, I plastered a smile on my face. I couldn't ignore how Miss Reynolds and the young blonde lady next to her stared at us with disdainful expressions on their faces. My hands were full dealing with Sarah, and now two other people disliked me? Wasn't this going make a lovely addition to my life.

"Mrs. Reynolds, Miss Reynolds," I said in as pleasant a manner as I could muster.

"Oh, you are acquainted then?" Mrs. Knighton asked in surprise. She proceeded to introduce us all to Mrs. Delan and her daughter Cassandra. Then, there was Mrs. Carter and her two daughters, Mary the young lady next to Miss Reynolds, and Elizabeth. Mother and Sarah were introduced to Mrs. Reynolds and Miss Reynolds. All of them murmured it was a pleasure to meet us.

Mother joined the older ladies, leaving Sarah and me to face the younger girls. "It is lovely to see you again, Miss Reynolds," I said, breaking the awkward silence. "Did you enjoy the rest of the Season?"

"Of course, Miss Forester," Miss Reynolds said, her tone cool. "Mrs. Knighton tells me Mr. Richfield is in the area, staying with one of the other families. I had wondered why I did not see him these past few weeks in London."

She had gone straight to the point, and I nodded, seeing no reason to deny the fact. "Yes, that is true." Sarah glanced over at me with a slight frown on her face. I opened my mouth to continue, but couldn't figure out what to say on this particular subject. So, instead, I asked, "What has Mrs. Knighton planned for today?"

"Oh, we felt the need to recover from our journey here," Miss Carter answered, yawning said with a large yawn. "Someone suggested playing ninepins earlier, but no one cared to do so. It is a foolish game anyway."

When Miss Carter mentioned ninepins, Sarah's face brightened with delight, as it was one of her favorite games to play. It angered me to see Sarah's disappointment written on her face that the game had been so quickly dismissed.

"Well, that's not exactly true," Miss Delan said shyly. She appeared to be about Sarah's age and had a pleasant smile. "I would be more than willing to play. The weather looks rather fine, and it would be a shame not to enjoy it while we can."

Sarah became delighted once again. "I will speak to Mrs. Knighton about getting the game set up." She bounced away to do just that, leaving me alone with the other ladies.

"Have a seat, Miss Forester," Miss Delan said, gesturing to the chair next to her. "We were discussing the latest fashions before you arrived."

"Yes, it looks as though you could learn quite a bit, Miss Forester," Miss Carter said as I sat.

My smile was frozen on my face at this point. Self consciously, I smoothed my green lawn dress. It was one of my favorites and not even a year old. There was no possible way it was out of style. "I hardly think so," I said as pleasantly as possible. I was not about to listen to such insults spoken to my face. "Thank you for your concern, though."

Miss Carter nodded towards me, her manner condescending. "Have you considered a different color? I think maybe pink would be a much better color for you."

Her younger sister flinched, and Miss Delan glanced at the door as though she wanted to leave the room. I stared at Miss Carter, unsure what to do. We'd never met before this and she had no reason to wish me ill unless she knew of Miss Reynolds' disappointment.

"You must allow me to recommend my mother's modiste in London," Miss Carter continued. "When next you are in London, Madame Devereaux will be able to assist you." She gave a slight gasp, her hand flying to her lips. "Oh, how silly of me. Forgive me for assuming you will be able to visit London again. Georgina told me you relied on your aunt and uncle to come this year."

The implication that my family would not have the means to go to London was clear. Lifting my chin, I met her gaze. "You are correct," I said with as much confidence as I could muster. "My aunt and uncle were kind enough to take me. However, I cannot tell you for certain whether I will return next spring or not. That, Miss Carter, will be entirely dependent on how this year ends."

"Oh? You expect many changes this year?" Miss Carter asked, raising an eyebrow.

"Not many. Just one important change." Leaving her to make what she would of my deliberately cryptic words, I shifted my focus. "Did you have an enjoyable journey here, Miss Delan?" I asked.

"Oh, yes," Miss Delan said in relief. "I was afraid, with the rumors going around, we might have trouble. Papa had his pistol so we would have been well protected. But nothing happened."

"The highwayman no doubt knew you had nothing of value," Miss Carter said, just loud enough for us to hear.

Miss Delan flushed, and my hands clenched on the arms of my chair. If this was her attitude now, I could clearly see this party would only become more difficult. "Mrs. Knighton has ordered the game be set up," Sarah said as she joined us again. She glanced around and seemed to sense she had missed something. "Who will play?"

"As I said before, I would be happy to," Miss Delan said, getting to her feet quickly. "Miss Elizabeth, will you join us?"

The youngest Miss Carter glanced at her sister before nodding. "Happily."

"Diana, are you coming?" Sarah asked.

"What kind of question is that, Sarah? You know Diana only plays ninepins to be as ridiculous as possible."

I lifted my gaze to find my dearest friend, Lady Carlyle, coming into the room. "Anna!" I said, happy to find some support in the room. I got to my feet and held my hands out. "I wondered where you were."

"Oh, I needed to pen a letter to my husband to let him know I had arrived safely. He will not join us until next week. He had business to see to. But I am pleased to see you again, Diana."

Laughing, I hugged her. "You have no idea how glad I am to see you," I whispered in her ear. "I have so much to tell you."

"Let's go play ninepins," Anna said, pulling me towards the door. "We shall see the rest of you out there. Hello, Mrs. Forester. How are you? It's good to see you. We will catch up later, shall we?"

Used to Anna's impetuous nature, Mother just nodded with a smile as we went past. Anna looped her arm around mine and leaned against me. "Finally, we can have some quiet," she said as we walked towards the garden. "I cannot believe Mother invited the Reynolds and the Carters. She only did it because Philip asked her to, you know."

I did not know that, and the last thing I wanted was to talk about her brother. "Miss Reynolds and I weren't exactly friends in London as you might remember. You interrupted at just the right time. I was about to disgrace myself horribly."

"I am not even sure how Philip knows them." She glanced around and then pulled me in the opposite direction of the gardens. "Now. Tell me quickly. Mother says Mr. Richfield has been here this whole time."

"Are you kidnapping me?"

"If you do not tell me everything I want to know this instant, then yes. And I will not release you until you tell me all."

Sighing, I gave in and told her everything that had happened since I had left London. I tried to keep it as simple and straightforward as possible, which didn't work well when I tried to explain some of the more complicated points like how Sarah wished to direct Mr. Richfield's attention in another direction. Anna remained silent the whole time, and I had to wait a few moments after I finished for her to show any reaction.

"You definitely want to marry Mr. Richfield?"

Surprised that out of everything I had just said Anna focused on that, I stared at her. "Yes, but Sarah—."

"Forget about what Sarah intends to do for a moment. You have nothing to worry about Diana. I knew in London you, and he would make a perfect pair, and I happen to know your Mr. Richfield spoke to Rodger about you. His intentions cannot be any clearer, and it will take more than a jealous little sister to make him change his mind."

"He spoke to your husband about me?" That came as a surprise. Why had Anna not told me this in London?

Anna nodded. "Rodger learned everything he could about Mr. Richfield after that. I had to be certain this man was worthy of my dearest friend."

"He may be worthy, but what am I supposed to do now?"

"I am here now, Diana," she said pragmatically. "I will help you, and I have the perfect situation for you to be in each other's company. Mother is having a picnic in two days. What better time for you and he to take a walk together without the presence of your siblings? I could not have planned things better if I had tried."

Excitement bubbled up, and I tried to shove it down. "But propriety—!" Though I had been alone for a few minutes with Mr. Richfield already, I had never planned it. To be caught would be disastrous for us both!

"You will be in full view of everyone else, or close enough to it there can be no objection. If he does not request to speak to your father afterward, I will—." She paused, apparently struggling to think of what she would do in response. "I will figure what I will do when it happens. Which it will not for he will propose to you on the spot."

"I have the strangest feeling you will get me into trouble." While I had been eager to tell my dear friend everything, I had not forgotten her tendency to brush accepted rules aside to suit her own plans. When Anna wished to make sure Sir Rodger didn't leave her family estate without knowing how she felt, she'd ridden astride to catch up to his carriage. Two years before that, when she'd been fascinated with a different man, she'd danced with him three times and then decided he was not the husband she wanted.

A look of mock hurt crossed Anna's face. "I would never get you into anything I couldn't just as easily get you out of—if it was necessary!"

"That, of course, makes me feel so much better."

It didn't, but Anna took my words at face value. "Good," she said, retaking my arm. "Now, we must go defeat some annoying young ladies at ninepins."

WHEN WE ARRIVED ON the lawn, the game had been set up. Miss Reynolds and Miss Carter had deigned to come down and were sitting on the sidelines. Anna and I joined the other three girls who had decided to play. The five of us laughed while the other two young ladies watched with judgemental expressions on their faces.

We were nearing the end of the game when the gentlemen of the house party arrived. Miss Reynolds was the first to see them, and her insipid giggle warned the rest of us. "Oh, isn't that just adorable," Anna said as the other ladies all began smoothing their dresses and checking their hair. I resisted the impulse also check my appearance. "Yes, let's all stop playing and make sure we look good, ladies."

I frowned as I realized Sarah also checked her gown and even went so far as to put her hands behind her back, looking for all the world like an innocent young lady. One who would never play ninepins in as rowdy a manner as she had just been doing.

There were six men with Mr. Knighton and his son. Which one had caught Sarah's attention? Mr. Richfield was among them, and when he caught my eye, his face brightened with a smile and, his eyes lighting up with delight. I felt my cheeks flush and I promptly forgot about figuring out who Sarah could be interested in. Anna snickered beside me. "You are well and truly caught, Diana."

"Ah, ladies," Mr. Knighton, a pleasant gray-haired man, said, calling out first. "Enjoying the fine weather while it lasts?"

"What else is a lady to do in the country, sir?" Miss Reynolds said, her tone coy. I was startled until I realized her eyes were on Mr. Richfield. "Have you gentlemen had a good morning?"

"We had a fine ride around the estate," the elder Mr. Knighton said. His gaze landed on Sarah and me, and his smile broadened. "The Misses Forester! It has been far too long since you have graced this lawn. Have you been staying out of trouble?"

"I see there are some introductions to be made," Philip Knighton said before Sarah or I could make a reply. "Miss Forester, Miss Sarah, may I introduce you to Mr. Carter, Mr. Aaron Carter, Mr. Delan, and Mr. Regan."

Each man made a slight bow in our direction. I breathed a sigh of relief that at least this time, he had made the introductions, phrasing it in such a way we could have refused the introduction if we felt there was reason to do so. Mr. Ward, the gentleman Sarah and I had already met, had a bored expression on his face, his brown eyes scanning us. "Miss Carter, Miss Elizabeth Carter, Miss Delan, Miss Reynolds, and Lady Carlyle, this is Mr. Richfield," Philip said, finishing the introductions.

"Oh, Mr. Richfield and I are acquainted already," Miss Reynolds said quickly. "It is a pleasure to see you once again, Mr. Richfield. London seemed bleak without you there to amuse us."

Politely, Mr. Richfield nodded towards her. "Lady Carlyle, I didn't know you would be here," he said, turning to my best friend. "Is Sir Rodger here as well?"

Smiling in triumph, as Miss Reynolds' smile became brittle, Anna said, "Not yet, Mr. Richfield. But he intends on arriving in time for the ball if not sooner. He will be pleased to see you."

"Well, don't let us interrupt your game, ladies," the older Mr. Knighton father said jovially. He sent a glance at the sky where gray clouds had begun to gather. "It looks as though it may rain, so you may want to finish quickly."

"Come, Mary, we should go inside now," Miss Reynolds said to Miss Carter. "Perhaps one of you gentlemen would care to escort us?"

Her eyes were on Mr. Richfield, and my grip on my ball tightened. "Certainly, Miss Reynolds," Mr. Knighton said, holding out his arm. "I understand some young ladies are not as adventurous as my daughter and her friends."

Anna laughed out loud at Miss Reynolds' look of aggravation. Miss Reynolds had no choice but to accept her host's arm, and Miss Carter took Mr. Ward's arm. I saw annoyance fill Sarah's face, and my sister glared at the backs of Miss Carter and Mr. Ward.

"I hope you won't mind an audience," Mr. Richfield said, gaining my attention before I could think about my sister's apparent interest in Mr. Ward any further. "I believe the rain will hold off long enough for you to reach the end of your game."

"We don't mind at all," Anna said. "We only have a few more rounds to go. Miss Delan, I believe it is your turn."

Mr. Regan and Mr. Aaron Carter, both younger men, also chose to stay while the rest of the men moved on. I stepped to the sidelines to wait for my turn, and Mr. Richfield sidestepped as well so he was right next to me.

"Lady Carlyle is a force to be reckoned with."

I had to smile. "She is that. But I am always glad to see her. She was, and still is, my dearest friend."

Mr. Richfield nodded. "I had guessed as much when I saw her with you in London."

We watched Sarah knock all of her pins down, and then Miss Elizabeth Carter entirely missed her targets. There was a low rumble of thunder as I stepped up to take my turn. The clouds had darkened quickly above us.

"This will be the last round. If you knock down all of your pins, Diana, you will win this game," Sarah said, raising her voice to be heard by all. "Miss one, and Miss Delan will be our victor."

I had failed to keep track of the points, so was surprised to hear I was so close to the top. "One crown says she misses," Mr. Regan said with a laugh.

"A crown says she will strike true," Mr. Richfield said instantly. "In fact, I wager she will knock them all down."

Oh, dear. I hadn't knocked all nine of the pins down this entire game, so could not hold out any hope I would manage to do so this time. Taking a deep breath and conscious of all the eyes on me, I sent the ball spinning towards the pins. Hoping, I held my breath as I watched the ball strike the pins. They tumbled over, knocking into each other. The last teetered for a moment before it joined the others on the ground.

"I did it," I said in shock.

"You did it!" Anna squealed with joy. She hugged me, laughing as the other girls cheered. A shrill whistle joined the applause, and I glanced at Mr. Richfield. He shrugged and applauded the loudest of all.

"You have nothing to worry about," Anna said in my ear as the footmen began to gather up the game. "He has eyes only for you."

Sarah and Miss Delan joined us. I spotted Mr. Regan handing over the bet to Mr. Richfield. "You didn't completely mess up," was all Sarah said, her expression one of mild surprise.

In the middle of my celebration, a fat raindrop landed on my nose. Anna let out a gasp. "Rain! Everyone inside!"

There was a mad dash for the manor as the raindrops began to fall around us in increasing frequency. Holding their hands over their heads, Miss Delan and Miss Elizabeth squealed about their hair being ruined. Sarah and Anna were laughing with delight, while Mr. Carter and Mr. Regan were competing to be the first to make it to the door.

I caught myself when I tripped on a stone. Mr. Richfield's hand came around mine, and he stayed beside me, making sure I stayed on my feet. We were the last to make it through the door, and he let go of my hand once we were through the doorway.

"Well, you were right. The rain held off long enough for the game to end," I said with a laugh.

"A mere guess," he said with a shrug. He leaned forward and brushed a wet lock of hair out of my face.

A smile curved my lips as I lifted my gaze to his. "Congratulations on winning your bet."

"Oh, I couldn't stand to think someone would bet against you. I knew you wouldn't let me down."

His calm confidence made me blush. "You would have been the only one, as most people know ninepins is not my forte," I said, fighting to keep my tone light. Miss Jenson appeared in the hallway, clucking her tongue in distress at our wet clothes.

"You don't give yourself enough credit. You play for the fun of it, not to win, and that makes your victory so much sweeter. I admire that in you."

My cheeks burned even hotter. "Come, ladies," Miss Jenson said, clapping her hands to get our attention. "We must get you warm and dry."

Offering one last smile, I moved to join Sarah and Anna. I was undoubtedly the wettest out of the group. Where the spring air had been warm in the sun, now it was chilly, and I found myself shivering.

"Come to my room," Anna said. "I'm sure I have something warm you can put on." She lowered her voice conspiratorially. "And we can talk some more."

I allowed myself be pulled along with her. Miss Carter and Miss Reynolds were snickering together in the doorway of the drawing-room when we went by them. This time, I didn't let it affect me. They only saw our wet, bedraggled appearance and could have no idea I had never felt prettier.

Chapter Twelve

The rest of the day passed in a blur. Once dry, and dressed in one of Anna's gowns, I joined the other ladies in the drawing room. Miss Reynolds and Miss Carter continued being unfriendly, though the younger Miss Carter and Sarah were getting on well with their conversation primarily on music. With Miss Delan, I suggested new trimmings for a bonnet Anna had grown tired of.

Mother asked how we had enjoyed ourselves on our ride back home. "Oh, it was pleasant to do something with someone new," Sarah said, her tone absent. "I think Miss Elizabeth Carter and I will be great friends. Charlotte will adore her."

"What of Miss Reynolds and Miss Mary Carter?" Mother asked, glancing at me. "I noticed they, as well as Mrs. Reynolds, were not inclined to be friendly, which I found to be odd."

"Miss Reynolds and I met in London, Mother," I said honestly. "She did not take kindly to Mr. Richfield giving his attention to me and not to her."

There was no other way of saying it. Miss Reynolds had not found another gentleman to occupy her interest and was jealous I had gained Mr. Richfield's affection.

Thoughtfully, Mother nodded. "I wondered if was the case. I will remind you that however she treats you, you must remember to be polite. Don't think I didn't hear your remarks to her earlier, Diana. What you said was not kind."

I cringed. I had hoped my comments had gone unheard by her. "I'm sorry, Mother. It won't happen again."

"See it does not. You are old enough I "

Sarah seemed preoccupied the entire ride, and although Mother tried to engage her in conversation, my sister's responses were only a few words at a time. By the time we reached home, Mother had given up entirely.

There was a change in the hall when we entered. Small cases were stacked up in the middle of the room, and I knew them on sight; I had helped pack them myself months ago. "James is home!" I said, pulling at the ribbons on my bonnet.

That pulled Sarah out of her thoughts. "James!"

My older brother came out of the library. "Sarah," he said as our sister threw herself at him. He lifted her up and set her down easily. "Have you gained weight?"

"James! How can you say that?" Sarah hit his shoulder with her hand, but not hard enough to cause pain. James just grinned at her.

"You're home," Mother said, moving forward. She hugged James and kissed his cheek, though he towered six inches above her. "Did you enjoy your travels?"

James had spent most of the winter traveling with some friends around the country. "I had a wonderful time." He put his arm around my shoulders for a one-armed hug. "But I am glad to be back now."

"Will must be thrilled to have you back," I said, smiling up at him. "He has had to put up with Sarah and me all by himself these past few months."

"He didn't stop talking for half an hour," James said with a laugh. "Father finally sent him upstairs to finish his lessons." He sent a knowing grin in my direction. "He had much to say about you and a Mr. Richfield." I had no doubt Will had told him everything, from his point of view. "My little sister is being courted by a highwayman."

Every little detail. "I am not! You must not believe a word he or Sarah says on the matter."

"You're in time for the house party at the Knightons', James!" Sarah said, pulling on James' arm to get his attention. "I have been practicing my archery so I can best everyone!"

"Well, I suppose you must have something to distinguish yourself from the other ladies," James reached over to tug on her hair.

"Let's not stand here in the hall," Mother said, ever practical. "We will go to the sitting room, and I shall ring for some tea."

JAMES HAD MUCH TO TELL us about his travels with his two school friends, and he didn't stop talking for the rest of the day. We all hung on his every word as he spoke about the families he had visited. Dinner was lively that night, and we all laughed louder than we had in a long time. We were up well past midnight as we each tried to relay the details of an event that had happened while James had been gone.

It felt good to have everyone back in one place again.

Come morning, I felt the effects of the late night and was reminded of how I had often felt in London. Due to that experience, I seemed to cope with the fatigue better than my two younger siblings. Sarah behaved as though she was about to fall asleep on her plate, her head dipping lower and lower, and Will kept staring at his breakfast in confusion. Mother and Father had eaten earlier, leaving just the siblings.

"Poor little country children," James said, exchanging looks with me. "How would they ever survive in the big city?"

Will and Sarah were awake enough to understand the insult, and they both sent glares at their older brother. "Oh, I'm sure they will be grown up enough by the time they get the chance to go up to Town," I said, unable to keep the patronizing tone out of my voice.

The glares were aimed at me next. "Do you plan on visiting the Manor?" James asked, changing the subject.

"There's going to be a small archery competition today for the ladies, as I'm sure you recall Sarah mentioning yesterday," I said when Sarah didn't seem inclined to answer. "She and I are going to walk over at ten o'clock."

That brought Sarah's head up again. "Walk? Diana! I refuse to walk the whole way there."

"Since Mother has arrangements to visit Mrs. Davison, she needs the carriage. So either we walk, or we don't go at all. That's the way it is, I'm afraid."

Groaning, Sarah pushed her plate away and put her head on her arms. "Since Will has his studies this morning, I can go with you," James said. "I haven't seen the Knightons since

I left. I thought I would run into Philip at some point but our paths never crossed."

"He probably wouldn't have wanted to talk to you, you know," Sarah said, her words mumbled.

James frowned. "Why do you say that?"

Oh, perfect. I had never written him about what had happened between Philip Knighton and I. It wasn't the kind of thing you put in a letter, after all. Well, perhaps someone could but I hadn't been able to face the words in black and white. "Philip Knighton asked to marry me," I said quietly, "and I refused."

Silence filled the table. I had never put it quite so bluntly before. "Philip wanted to marry you," James said slowly. "I see. Did you know he had formed an attachment to you?"

"I knew," Sarah said, louder than was necessary.

"No! What kind of a question is that?" I said at the same time. I glared at my sister. "No one asked you, Sarah. James' question was for me."

Shrugging, Sarah sat up. "I'm going to get ready." She pushed her chair back and stood up. "Just explain it all, Diana. I don't want to have to hear this all the way to the Knightons. It's become tiresome, you know."

Will raised his hand. "Agreed."

I threw my napkin at him. "I'm not the one who always brings it up. Do you think I like having to remember what happened? It breaks my heart every time because I lost a good friend."

James frowned at me. "You don't mean Phillip refuses to associate with us anymore. He didn't say a word when we crossed paths earlier this year."

For a moment, hope fluttered in my heart. If Phillip hadn't mentioned it and had been as he usually was with my brother, perhaps he had moved on and things could be normal again? That hope shattered as I remembered how he had behaved to me. No, Phillip had not forgiven me and I couldn't be sure he would.

"There's no need to get worked up about it," Sarah said, her tone impatient. "You are so annoying when you get like this."

"No more than you are."

"Diana, Sarah, I've only been home one evening. Please don't start quarreling," James said, his tone placating. "Let me believe for a short time my sisters get along, and there are no troubles at home."

Sarah stuck her tongue out at him as she left the room. "But there is trouble," Will said. "The highwayman hasn't been caught yet, and he attacked the Reynolds on their way here. Mrs. Reynolds lost what jewels she had."

"She did?" I asked in interest. "Miss Reynolds didn't say anything about that. The only thing she mentioned was Miss Delan had not been a worthy target for the highwayman."

"Well, it wasn't exactly a hold up of the Reynolds' themselves," Will said with relish. "It was the wagon with their belongings that was stopped. For some reason, that's where the ladies' jewels were being kept."

Ah, I see. She didn't have the experience herself, and no lady wants to bring her maid up in polite conversation. "I don't think being held up and losing your jewels makes for a good conversation," James said pointedly. "You can see how it would be embarrassing."

I laughed. "That shows how little you understand young ladies. Embarrassing or not, such a tale would give us something to talk about beyond the latest gossip or fashion or which handsome gentleman we fancy."

Although, Miss Reynolds only wanted to discuss was gossip and fashion, so perhaps James was right on that point.

"Anyway," Will said loudly, inserting himself back into the conversation. "We need to find the highwayman before someone else gets hurt."

"You think we could succeed where Father and all the other men in the county have failed?" James asked with a laugh. There was a note of interest in his tone, though. "How do you plan on doing that?"

"We already know who it could be. Diana just doesn't want me to prove it."

"Because it's ridiculous!" I said quickly. "I refuse to allow you to embarrass yourself or Mr. Richfield."

James raised his eyebrows, a habit I never realized we all shared until that moment. "I don't think I have ever seen you look so serious, Diana," he said in amazement. "You would do everything you could to try stopping Sarah and Will, wouldn't you?"

"Try?" I repeated. "Oh, brother of mine, I wouldn't just try. I would stop them."

Never let it be said I was not confident. When I had a reason for confidence, at least.

I got to my feet. "Sarah and I will be in the foyer at ten o'clock. If you're not there, we will leave without you."

Both of my brothers just waved me away. Shaking my head, I left the room and headed up the stairs. An awkward conversation I'd been dreading was finally over, and I was determined not to bring up the subject again.

Instead, I was in anticipation of the day ahead of me, maybe for the wrong reason. Miss Carter had been bragging about her skill at archery, and I could not wait to see the look on her face when Sarah beat her.

RIGHT AT TEN O'CLOCK, I was the only one standing near the front door. Tapping my foot, I checked the clock again and watched the minute hand move slightly. Father walked into the foyer, dressed to ride around the estate. "Waiting for someone?" he asked with a smile.

"Well, I thought we were going to be walking to the Knightons, but I appear to be the only one who intends on going," I said as I leaned against the wall in an unladylike way. "Are you sure I cannot walk there on my own? It would serve James and Sarah right if I just left them."

"That is not an option, Diana. I meant it when I said none of my children are allowed to walk on their own. The others will be along soon. You will simply have to wait for them."

"Is the situation so bad I cannot walk to the neighbors like I used to?"

Father put his hand on my shoulder. "Yes, it is. You've heard one of the visiting families was stopped? Fortunately, no one was hurt this time. Each time we search for this man, we find no trace of him. He must have a hiding place nearby, and that makes it all the more dangerous."

That was what I had been afraid of. "Just so you know, Will has tried to convince James to help him figure this out," I said in a low voice.

"Yes, I thought that might happen. I will handle it," Father said, chuckling as he patted my shoulder. He glanced over to the stairs. "Here they are right now. Have a good day."

When I twisted around, I observed Sarah swiping at James' head, getting him back for something that had happened upstairs. "What happened to 'anyone who isn't here right at ten o'clock will be left behind?'" our older brother asked with a grin.

"Since no one was here, I couldn't leave," I said sharply. "We are not allowed to go out alone, James."

"What? Why?"

I rolled my eyes as Father said, "The highwayman. He has shown he will not hesitate to harm someone. I want you to look after your sisters, James."

"We have nothing to worry about," Sarah said, sounding cheerful and more awake. "It's broad daylight. What could happen?"

Father waved us all out and shut the door behind us. Energetic, the three of us set off on our long walk. We had made this same walk hundreds of times in the past. The only difference between now and then was now we were all taller and older.

Apparently inspired by the news of the highwayman, James spent the walk throwing around ideas on where the highwayman would be hiding in our neighborhood. Sarah just laughed at him, egging him on to more and more ridiculous ideas. I was left to walk behind the two of them, shaking my head at their antics.

"I bet he lives under the bridge," Sarah said as we reached the creek that bordered the edge of the Knightons' property. She led the way onto the stone bridge.

"Under the bridge?" I said derisively. What made her suggest such a thing? We'd crossed it several times in the past week, and as far as I knew, no one gave it a moment's thought. "Where it is wet and cold? That would be a horrible place to hide, Sarah."

James, though, came to a stop and considered the bridge we were standing on. "No, she may have a point. Has Father said anything about checking under the bridges? It would the perfect place to hide. If anyone were riding over, the highwayman wouldn't be seen. Hold on a moment. Let me see if anyone has been under there. We could suggest it t Father when we get back."

"You're not serious, are you?" Sarah asked in disbelief. "I was just joking."

Grinning, James darted to the end of the bridge and scrambled down the bank. "It won't take long. Just a few minutes. I will be right back."

"You cannot be serious!" I said, impatient to be on our way. "James, don't you think Father or Mr. Sandwood would have already checked there? It is the most obvious place to hide!"

With that, he vanished underneath the bridge. A moment later, he reappeared on the other side and hurried into the trees. Sarah crossed her arms. "James, we have to keep going," she said, leaning against the side of the bridge. "I don't want to be late for the competition!"

It did not come as a surprise James didn't have an answer for her as he disappeared among the trees growing along the stream. "We may as well keep going," I said. "I don't think he's going to listen to us for awhile."

"How is that supposed to work?" Sarah asked, frustrated. "None of us are supposed to be alone out here. If we keep walking, we're going to be the ones in trouble with Father."

"Hey, I found some footprints!" James' excited proclamation reached us from the trees.

"Did you really?" Sarah rushed to the side. She lifted her skirt up and hurried off the bridge. "James, wait a moment! I want to see!"

Breathing out, I walked to the side and leaned against the railing in time to get one last glimpse of Sarah's blue dress before she too vanished among the trees. I had no desire to get my feet muddy and stayed where I was. "We should tell Father," I said, raising my voice so they would hear me. Neither answered me, and I groaned, knowing I couldn't stay where I was by myself.

Stepping carefully, I kept my eyes on the ground as I tried to follow in the direction my siblings had gone. As I did so, I spotted something glittering in the sunlight. "Hey, what is this?" I wondered, bending down to pick it up. I frowned at it, holding the small piece of gold in my hand. It was oddly familiar, but I couldn't quite place it. "Where have I seen this before?"

There was a noise behind me, and I started to turn. Something smashed against my head, and I felt myself falling. Then, everything went black.

"DIANA! DIANA!"

"Miss Forester? Diana, can you hear me?"

My head was pounding. Someone kept patting my cheeks, and a hand was holding mine. A blade of grass tickled my ear. Why was I on the ground? There was a hairpin poking into my head, not helping my headache in the least.

"Diana, wake up."

That voice sounded like James,' and I forced my eyes open just to make sure. I had to blink several times because everything was blurry. Once my vision cleared, I had to squint in the bright sunlight that shone through the branches and leaves. My older brother leaned over Sarah's head. On my other side was Mr. Richfield, who was holding my hand.

"Oh, Diana," Sarah said in relief. She brushed at her face. Were those tears I saw? "I didn't think you were going to wake up."

"W-what happened?" It took so much energy to speak, and it made my head pound even harder. I closed my eyes again, hoping they would all just leave me alone.

"No, don't go back asleep," Mr. Richfield said. He sounded so worried. "You need to stay awake, Miss Forester."

Odd. I could have sworn just a moment ago he had used my Christian name. Whatever had happened must have been serious. I felt like as though I had forgotten something important and I struggled to remember it as I lifted my free hand to my head.

"I don't feel so well."

There was a slight laugh. "I would imagine not," Mr. Richfield said. "It looks as though you took quite a blow to the head. We need to get you home and send for a physician. Open your eyes for me, and your sister and I will help you sit up."

He asked so nicely, and I didn't want to disappoint him. "Fine," I managed to say, making my eyes open again. The sun was still bright, and I flinched in pain.

"Do you remember what happened?" James asked as Sarah and Mr. Richfield sat me up. Everything spun for a moment, and I felt sick to my stomach. "Diana, we found you unconscious on the ground. Did you see who attacked you?"

I decided to ignore him as I fought to keep from losing my last meal in an unladylike way. Feeling dizzy, I had to close my eyes again and hoped Mr. Richfield would forgive me for it. I curled the fingers of my right hand, feeling like something was missing I had been holding. What was it?

"I will take Diana on my horse and get her to your home faster," Mr. Richfield said. "Will you two find your way?"

"We will be fine," James said sharply, sounding highly offended. He sounded funny when he was upset. "We will be right behind you, sir. I'll carry her to your horse."

Oh, no. I did not trust my brother to carry me. The last time he had done that he had complained about was how much I weighed. "I can walk." I had no desire to let them decide what happened to me. "Just help me up. Please."

"Are you sure?" Mr. Richfield asked as Sarah protested.

Not feeling up to repeating myself, I forced my eyes open and nodded. Doing so made my head spin and I vowed not to do it again in the foreseeable future. Mr. Richfield nodded to James, and my brother replaced Sarah at my side. With Mr. Richfield on one side and James on the other, I managed to get to my feet. I wobbled as I tried to get my balance under control.

"Come on," Mr. Richfield said, putting his arm around my waist. "I'll help you."

Leaning against him as I walked to where his horse stood, I felt safe as he guided me. Sarah, for some reason, tried to straighten my bonnet as Mr. Richfield mounted ahead of me. My bonnet rubbed against an incredibly sore spot on my head. "Sarah, don't. Please."

"I'm just trying to make you look less like you've been dragged through the mud," Sarah said impatiently.

Right, because having my bonnet on straight would make everything better. I was too tired to argue with her James lifted me up in front of Mr. Richfield. "We won't be far behind," my brother said as Mr. Richfield's arms came around me.

"Just relax," Mr. Richfield said to me as he kicked his mount into action. "I've got you.

Sighing, I closed my eyes and leaned my head against his chest. I would worry about whatever had happened later. And hopefully, I would remember what I had lost too.

Chapter Thirteen

I'm reasonably sure Mr. Richfield kept up a steady stream of conversation. The sound of his voice was comforting even though I was just far too tired to listen with any degree of attentiveness. The movement of the horse made my head pound more, and my stomach wasn't feeling well either. I couldn't even distract myself by thinking about what had happened for my head ached something terrible.

Who had attacked me? Why? What threat could I be?

I may have drifted off because the next thing I knew he shouted at someone. "Get Mr. Forester!"

Father. Oh, I was about to be in so much trouble. Not only had I been alone on the bridge, but I was also now on a horse with a man's arms around me. My reputation was so—wait. Had I been alone on a bridge? Why had I done that? I wasn't supposed to have been, so that didn't make any sense. What had happened? Why couldn't I remember any-thing?

"Diana!" Mother. Just hearing her voice made feel more at ease. She would take care of me, and everything would be just fine.

At the same time, though, I didn't want to worry her. I opened my eyes and forced a sort-of-smile. "Mother," I said, holding out my hand. She hurried toward us from the carriage; we must have just caught her before she left.

"Mr. Richfield, what happened?" Mother asked, reaching us. "Diana, are you well? Where are Sarah and James?"

"They are on their way on foot," Mr. Richfield said. He then hesitated, possibly trying to decide how much to tell Mother. "Diana was hit on the head."

Squeezing my hand, Mother frowned. "Hit her head? How?"

"We're not exactly sure what happened. Miss Forester, do you think you can hold yourself steady while I get down?" Mr. Richfield said, turning his attention back to me. I think I liked it better when he used my Christian name. Managing a brief nod, I entwined my fingers in the horse's mane to be on the safe side. Doing a rather excellent job of keeping myself upright, I waited until I felt Mr. Richfield's hands at my waist.

I slid to the ground and immediately stumbled when my ankle tried to twist the wrong way. Quickly, Mr. Richfield swept me off my feet, one arm under my knees and the other supporting my back. "I will carry her in, if that's agreeable with you, Mrs. Forester," he said. "She is not steady on her feet at the moment."

"Yes, of course," Mother said. "Come this way."

"I can ride for a physician, or you may wish to send someone," Mr. Richfield said, striding towards the house. "I know blows to the head can be tricky things."

"When I see how bad it is, and know what happened, I will know better what to do."

As she led the way through the house to the bedroom I shared with Sarah, I wondered if Sarah had cleaned her side of the room this morning. I wouldn't be the only one embarrassed if Mr. Richfield saw Sarah's undergarments strewn across the floor.

Mother seemed to have the same idea because she walked much faster than Mr. Richfield. I saw her vanish into the bedroom and then come out a moment later. "Bring her in here," she said. The room was free of any of Sarah's usual mess when we entered.

Turning sideways to get through the door, Mr. Richfield carried me into the bedroom and set me down on the bed. He immediately stepped back as Mother reached for my bonnet. Remembering the pain when Sarah had tried to straighten it, I winced in anticipation, but Mother was much gentler as she untied the ribbons.

"Tilt your head forward, Diana." I obeyed Mother's command, closing my eyes. She unpinned my hair, and I felt some relief. "Where does it hurt?"

"Here," I said, lifting my hand to the general area. I flinched as she checked the back of my head with her fingers.

"You have quite the lump forming there," she said, kneeling in front of me. "However, it doesn't look too bad. I shall send Mary to help you settle in while I see Mr. Richfield out. I will be back."

I hadn't realized he was still in the room and I lifted my head. For the first time, I saw the concern on his face. "Thank you," I said. Somehow, the words felt inadequate, but I couldn't think of anything else to say.

"It was my pleasure, Miss Forester," he said, stepping forward. He took my hand and brought it to his lips as he bowed, but froze for a moment. "Not that you were injured. That I was able to help. I return to see how you are feeling tomorrow."

I managed a smile as Mother shooed him out. I moved to unlace my boots but decided bending over was not a good idea when my head pounded. Instead, I waited for the maid to help me. Thankfully, I only had to wait a few moments.

"Oh, Miss Diana!" Mary, a maid who had worked in our home for as long as I could remember, exclaimed as she bustled into the room. "Let's get you tucked away. The mistress said you hit your head, and what you need is some rest and a great deal of quiet."

She kept talking as she unlaced my boots and pulled them off my feet. Apparently peace and quiet did not include her. I couldn't complain, though, because she helped me undress. In a matter of minutes, she had me in bed, the drapes pulled tightly closed, and the room thankfully dim.

"Thank you, Mary," Mother said as she came in, interrupting a story about what the cook had planned for dinner. Mary bobbed a curtsy and left the room. Mother took a seat on the edge of the bed. "How do you feel?"

"I have the worst headache imaginable. And I feel like a fool."

"A fool? Why?"

I shouldn't have said anything. Now I had to think about the reason. "This is my fault, right? I slipped on something and fell, didn't I?" That was the only thing that made any sense. Far too often, I tripped over my own feet. But Mother was frowning, so that must not have been what happened. "Mother? What is it?"

"Don't worry about it, Diana," Mother said, avoiding my question. She leaned over and kissed my forehead. "I will keep Sarah out of here. You get some rest, and I will check on you later."

Sleep sounded wonderful. I closed my eyes and pulled the blanket up closer to my chin. Maybe all of this would make sense when I had some rest.

THERE WAS NO WAY OF knowing how long I had been sleeping. I could recall having some strange dreams, the content of which I did not remember. The sound of Will and Sarah's voices was what woke me up. "Mother says we're not supposed to be in here," Will said softly.

Sarah's slightly louder response soon followed. "It's my room too! I can be in here if I want!"

Thankfully, my head was no longer pounding; however, it still was one of the worst headaches I had ever had. I knew if I didn't open my eyes Sarah and Will would keep arguing. And their whispers were becoming louder and louder.

"Would you two stop?" I asked, peeking open one eye. The room was still dim, but I could see the flicker of a candle on the dressing table.

"Oh, good, you're awake!" Sarah exclaimed, bouncing on the bed. "I thought you were going to sleep all day."

Will snorted. "She did sleep all day. It's well past dinner time. And Mother will not be happy you woke her up."

"She woke herself up!"

"Sarah, what happened?" I asked as I pushed myself upright. I still couldn't remember, and it was annoying not knowing what everyone was talking about.

Sarah became serious in an instant. "You honestly don't remember anything? Mother said you didn't, but I didn't believe her. How could you forget?"

"I remember being on the bridge at the creek," I said slowly. That was the one thing I did know for certain. There was something about a competition. The archery competition. "We were walking to the Manor, weren't we? But we didn't get there?"

"The highwayman hit you on the head. Why is it you get to have all the adventures?" Will said, sounding disappointed and jealous.

I twisted my head to stare at him. Was he serious? It must have happened; otherwise, he wouldn't be so put out about the whole thing. "The highwayman?" I said with a frowning. My headache still made it hard to think straight. "Why would he have attacked me? What did I do?"

"Will, we weren't supposed to tell her," Sarah said, throwing a pillow at our younger brother. "We don't know what happened. James and I followed the footprints for a short time and then came back. You were unconscious on the ground, and there was no one else in sight. Mr. Richfield found us a few minutes later while we were trying to wake you up."

I vaguely remembered Sarah hurrying into the trees after James. What had they been following? Footprints, Sarah had said. "Why were you following footprints?" I asked in confusion. "I thought we weren't supposed to be alone."

"I thought you would be smart enough to follow me!"

Will leaned closer. "She and James are in so much trouble," he said in a mock whisper. "James more than Sarah. He and Father haven't come out of the library yet."

"I thought she would follow instead of standing on the bridge like an idiot! It's not my fault!" Sarah objected defensively.

An idiot? Me? "We were supposed to stay together. Why would I want to go sliding around in the mud when I was about to attend a house party?"

Sarah grabbed my shoulders. "You remember the mud? That's a start! What else do you remember?"

"Sarah, stop. Shaking me will make my headache worse."

"Sarah, Will, I thought I told you to stay out of here," Mother said, coming into the room with a tray in her hands. Sarah immediately scrambled off the bed, and Will jerked away as well. "Leave Diana alone, do you hear me?"

"Yes, Mother," Sarah and Will said in unison. They bolted for the door, leaving me alone with Mother.

Smiling, Mother set the tray on my lap. I was happy to see it was all light food: soup and toast. "How do you feel not?" Mother asked as I picked up my spoon. "You have an appetite, so that's good."

"I'm feeling a bit better. My head isn't throbbing like before, but I am tired" I said honestly. I sipped my soup and then continued, "Will said I was attacked. Byt the highwayman. Is that true?"

Sighing, Mother shook her head. "We're not sure," she said firmly. "That's why you weren't to be told. It's only a suspicion at the moment, given how James and Sarah were poking around where they shouldn't have been. Your father has met with some of the other men of the community, and they have offered a reward for the capture of the highwayman."

I continued swallowing my soup slowly as I tried to think. "Sarah said she and James followed some footprints. I didn't want to follow because of the mud. Were they following the highwayman's tracks?"

"They were following footprints. There's no way to know exactly who made them. Mr. Sandwood took his dogs out there, but they lost whatever scent they were following in the water."

Dogs? They were taking the situation more in earnest now. I felt fatigue overtake me as I finished my soup and pushed the toast aside. Mother picked up the tray. "I should have just dealt with the mud and followed them on their wild goose chase," I said as I slid down my pillow. "Then, none of this would have happened."

Mother raised an eyebrow at me. "Then you didn't enjoy Mr. Richfield carrying you?"

My cheeks burned. "Mother!" I said, groping for another pillow to cover my face. I would expect such teasing from Father, but Mother? "Why would you—? Mother!"

She laughed and then kissed the top of my head. "I think you've found a good man, Diana. He was anxious about you. He even returned this afternoon to ask about you and left you some flowers. I'm sure he will be back in the morning."

Flowers? I lifted my head to search the room. "Where are they?"

"I left them in the sitting room," Mother said, laughing again. "I thought they might be an added incentive to get you out of bed tomorrow."

I wrinkled my nose as she left, the sound of her laughter lingering. I had been struck on the head, possibly attacked by a highwayman, and she laughed at me? I gave a huff and snuggled down to sleep again. There was a smile on my lips as I closed my eyes.

No one had ever brought me flowers before.

TWO DAYS LATER, I PULLED myself out of bed later than I usually would have risen. My headache had kept me in bed the entire day before, though I had attempted to rise. The flowers awaiting me downstairs were a strong motivator, but my head disagreed. Sarah's complaining about being kept out of our shared room had not helped the situation in any way. And every time I tried to think about what had happened, I immediately regretted it.

The hole in my memory was unsettling, and the effort I put into trying to remember made my head ache even more. Why had I been singled out to be attacked? Because I had been alone? Why did I feel as though I had forgotten something important?

When I got up that morning, my headache had abated some, and I was able to pull the curtains open. I squinted in anticipation of the bright sunlight but was surprised to find it gray and cloudy.

Was I a terrible person to be pleased the picnic was sure to have been canceled? It would have been nice to spend more time with Mr. Richfield, and I knew how much Sarah was looking forward to it. At least with the poor weather, there was a chance I could still attend if Mother deemed me well enough.

Moving slowly, I washed my face and got dressed. I tried brushing my hair as carefully as possible but still winced when my brush even came close to the rather large lump on my head. At that moment, my biggest concern was what I could do with my hair, and finally just tied it back with a ribbon. Finding my shawl, I wrapped it around my shoulders.

Finally, I was ready to face the world. Or my family, at least.

I left the bedroom and went down the stairs, already hearing James and Will yelling at each other in the sitting room. I did not want to have to listen to that. But my flowers were in there! Standing in the hallway, I debated what I should do. Find somewhere quiet, like the dining room, and eat? Or see my flowers and get pulled into one of my brothers' fights?

"Diana."

Startled, I spun to see Father in the doorway of the library. "Good morning, Papa," I said with a smile.

"Did your mother say you could come downstairs?" he asked, coming towards me. There were lines of worry on his face I'd never seen before.

"I'm feeling much better." He had come to my room for a few moments the evening before to see how I was. "Mother said she had an incentive for me to come down as soon as possible." I paused. Why did I have to say that?

Father laughed, looking a more at ease. "Yes, I heard," he said, leaning in to kiss my forehead. "Have you eaten?" I shook my head. I could do so without getting dizzy, which I felt was a large improvement. "Go into the sitting room and have Sarah get you something."

He patted my arm and hurried on his way. I faced the door to the sitting room. Taking a deep breath, I walked to it and opened the door, flinching at the onslaught of noise that hit my ears. Stepping inside, I surveyed my family.

Sarah played her harp in the corner. Will and James appeared to be playing piquet in front of the window, and each of them was accusing the other of cheating. Mother had needlework in her hand, looking like the calm in the middle of the storm.

"Diana!" Sarah noticed me first. She jumped up and rushed over with sheet music in her hand. "Come hear the song I wrote."

"Diana, tell James I don't cheat!" Will said immediately. "He thinks I am."

Setting aside her sewing, Mother stood up and walked to me. "You're looking much better, my dear," she said, hugging me. "Come and sit down on the lounge. Sarah, run to the kitchen and get your sister some breakfast. James, Will, take yourselves off, or I will insist you remain with us this afternoon."

The threat of being kept inside was enough for my brothers to hastily leave the room, though they continued their debate as they left. "They left in a hurry," I said as I stretched out on the chaise longue. I was eager to see my flowers, it was true, but I didn't want to be too eager.

"Diana, I have no doubt everyone in the county knows what happened to you two days ago, and will continue visiting until they have the story from your lips," Mother said, returning to her seat. She picked up her mending, which resembled a pair of Will's trousers with yet another hole in them. "I am sure we will have many visitors this morning."

The notion of all the ladies in our acquaintance coming made me want to flee back to my bed. I hadn't even thought how I would be the center of conversation for what had happened. "Don't look so frightened," Mother said with a smile. "Just look at your flowers."

Promptly forgetting about the idea of so many callers, I lifted myself up to see the vase she indicated. The wildflowers had been chosen with care, all of them bright with color. I laughed in delight. "They're beautiful!"

Sarah entered in time to hear me. "They look like the flowers that grow by the road," she said with a grimace.

"Sarah Forester, don't ruin my moment! They are the first flowers anyone has ever given me! They. Are. Beautiful!"

Sarah shook her head. "Don't expect this to happen often," she said, holding the tray out to me. "You're welcome."

Life was back to normal in the Forester household, and it felt good.

I had just finished my breakfast when the bell rang. "Give me that," Sarah said, snatching the tray off my lap. "If you could, try to look sickly. Otherwise, everyone might think we made it all up."

What? I stared after her as she vanished from the room. Mother calmly folded the trousers she had been mending and stored them in her work basket. She pulled out her fancy needlework and began sewing as if she had been working on it all along.

Sarah came flying back in and snatched a book up off the table. Was that my book? It bore a suspicious resemblance to my book.

The door opened. "Mrs. Sandwood and Miss Sandwood."

At the maid's announcement, Mother and Sarah rose gracefully to greet our visitors. "My dear Mrs. Forester!" Mrs. Sandwood said as she rushed in. "How is Diana? Oh, Miss Forester, there you are! I feared you would still be in your bed. That such a thing would happen here is horrible!"

She collapsed into the closest chair and began to fan herself. "Calm yourself, Mrs. Sandwood," Mother said, looking anxious. "As you can see, Diana is nearly herself already. She had plenty of rest yesterday. No permanent harm has been done."

"How do you manage to stay so calm?" Mrs. Sandwood asked. "My nerves would be in such a state if anything like this had happened to my Charlotte!"

"Sarah, ring for some tea. Please, sit down, Miss Sandwood."

Obediently, Sarah pulled the bell cord and then sat next to her friend. Miss Sandwood stared at me in fascination. "How are you feeling, Miss Forester?" she asked. "You must tell me all about it! As Mama said, it's shocking this happened here."

But not, apparently, too shocking to be spoken of. I could see how this day would proceed. All our visitors would want a word for word account of what had happened. For a second, I wondered if I could plead a headache and be allowed to return to my room, where it was quiet. "I don't remember much about it," I said honestly. "So, I'm afraid I cannot tell you anything at all."

"Papa said Mr. Richfield brought you home on his horse." Charlotte's eyes widened with each word.

The bell rang again before I could form a response to her observation. "Sarah!" Charlotte said in a low voice as she turned to my sister. "Is it a coincidence Mr. Richfield was the one to come upon you minutes after it all happened?"

Wait. What? "Coincidence?" Sarah repeated, frowning. "What do you mean, Charlotte?"

"Mrs. Davison," the maid announced.

"The highwayman attacked Miss Forester," Charlotte said in a quick whisper. "Mr. Richfield was closest in the area. This may be the evidence we need to prove he is the highwayman."

No. Not this again! "Mrs. Forester! Miss Forester! Miss Sarah!" Mrs. Davison exclaimed, holding out her hands as she swept in. "My dear friends! Tell me it isn't true! This awful rumor I've heard so much of since yesterday!"

Sarah's expression became thoughtful as she bent her head closer to Miss Sandwood's. They were plotting again! And there was nothing I could do about it. I fumed as I watched them. This was swiftly turning into one of the worst mornings I had ever had to endure.

Chapter Fourteen

As morning changed to afternoon, Mary began to look more and more frazzled as she announced visitor after visitor. I saw Mother's expression become stressed. Sarah's smile had become false after an hour, and I feared she would lose her manners altogether. At least I wasn't suffering through it alone.

"Mrs. Knighton. Lady Anna. Mrs. Carter, Miss Carter, Miss Elizabeth Carter, Mrs. Reynolds, Miss Reynolds, Mrs. Delan, and Miss Delan."

Mother's eyes widened at Mary's announcement. All the ladies of the house party had come? Well, with the picnic canceled, as it must have been, what else would they have to amuse themselves? How would they all even fit in the sitting room? We didn't have enough chairs to accommodate so many! I couldn't help a small giggle as I realized this kind of crush would have been considered a good thing in London!

"If another one says 'My poor Mrs. Forester' and so on, I swear I will scream," Sarah said through her teeth.

"You just want to get sent to your room," I said in a low voice. I could sympathise with my sister's feelings on the matter. "Well, I ask that you do not disgrace Mama by doing so."

For the first time in many weeks, we exchanged understanding looks. It felt good to be in harmony with my sister. The room began to feel extremely small as all of the ladies entered. Anna wove her way around several ladies to reach where I was.

"You look terrible, Diana," she said as she took a seat on the edge of the chaise.

"Thank you for telling me something I already knew," I said with a smile. "Having non-stop visitors does take its toll, you know. Especially when I have to repeat the same thing over and over again."

An answering smile appeared on her face, and she glanced around. "Are those flowers I see over there? Can I assume a certain person brought them?"

She would be the first one to notice the flowers. "You are allowed to assume whatever you want. Whatever goes on in your own mind is your business."

Anna laughed at that. "Getting hit on the head has made you grumpy, my friend." Her attention went to where the other ladies were still surrounding Mother. "I could try to keep them away for you, but there's only so much I can do."

"Why did they all come?" I asked with a groan. The cacophony of voices bordered on deafening.

"Well, I wasn't going to stay away a moment longer than I had to, and Miss Delan wanted to see how you were feeling. So Mrs. Delan had to come along as well. The Carters didn't want to be left out, so they joined our party next. Miss Reynolds was sure the whole story was a hoax, so she and her mother were added to the number. Only Miss Jenson thought it might be too much company all at once."

"A hoax?" Sarah repeated, stepping closer. Anger flashed in my sister's eyes. "Exactly what part of what happened does she think is a hoax?"

Anna and I both regarded her with surprise. "What unusual flowers!" Miss Reynolds said before I could comprehend what had Sarah so mad. A brief lull in conversation allowed her words to be heard clearly by all. "I believe I have seen the same weeds—I mean, flowers— growing along the road. Did one of your brothers give you these? How sweet of them."

How dare she? What did she know about my brothers? "They were a gift, but not from one of our brothers," Sarah said, her voice surprisingly polite. "How kind of you to take notice of them, Miss Reynolds. Diana is proud of them."

Miss Reynolds' eyes narrowed. "A suitor, then? You poor dear! You must tell me who it is, and I will set him straight on the kind of flowers a lady wishes to receive!"

Standing up, Anna put one hand on Sarah's arm, presumably to keep my sister from reacting in an unladylike way. "Have you had much experience with suitors then, Miss Reynolds?" Sarah asked, nevertheless. "I had no idea!"

I could see how this would spiral out of control. Anna inhaled sharply, catching my attention. Frowning, I peered around her to see what had shocked her so. My heart nearly stopped as saw Mr. Richfield standing in the doorway. His hat was in his hand, and his expression resembled one who had been punched.

Why hadn't he been announced? The only reason I could think of was he must have been met by one of my brothers or perhaps even Father, and had been sent up.

I had to resolve the situation.

In an instant, I knew exactly how to do so. "Maybe you know what the ladies of London prefer, Miss Reynolds, but I don't think you know the mind of a country lady," I said, raising my voice. "Who would want a fragile hothouse flower? They are beautiful to be sure, but a single variable out of place and they fade away in an instant. Wildflowers, though, can survive anything. I would much rather have them to brighten my room."

A relieved smile curved Mr. Richfield's lips as Miss Reynolds scowled. He nodded his head at me and stepped back. 'Help,' I mouthed since he seemed to be leaving. Didn't he understand I wanted to talk to him and not any of these other ladies? Well, except for Anna and Miss Delan.

He shook his head and vanished from sight by stepping to the side. Mr. Richfield had just abandoned me! How could he ignore my plea for help? The next time I saw him—Words failed me as Miss Reynolds twisted around to see who was there. "Who are you talking to, Miss Forester?" she asked when she saw no one.

"Pardon?" I asked in mock innocence.

Giving me a suspicious look, Miss Reynolds stepped away to speak to her friend, the elder Miss Carter. Miss Delan and Miss Elizabeth Carter moved closer to talk to me, both asking how I was and what had happened.

I was more than ready for the day to end.

THANKFULLY, MRS. KNIGHTON kept the visit short and soon shooed all the ladies away. Mother held a hand to her forehead. "Well, that was worse than I expected," she said as she sank into her chair. "You held up marvelously, Diana."

"How long will it last?" I asked tiredly. "Is it over with?"

"Diana, in a community as small as ours, it will be weeks, perhaps months, before this is forgotten. You're looking tired. Go on up to your room and get some sleep. You don't have to come down for dinner tonight."

"No, I will," I said as I stood up. The sooner things were back to normal the better I would feel. I took a few steps over and bent to breathe in the light scent of the flowers. "I do love them."

Mother laughed softly. "I believe you would love them even if they truly were weeds."

"Oh, I wouldn't let her get away with that," Sarah said, collapsing onto the window seat in her dramatic way. "Some things just should not be allowed. Fawning over weeds is one of them."

Shaking my head, I made my way to the door. Pausing, I remembered how Sarah and Miss Sandwood had been plotting earlier. I had to find out what they had been up to. "Sarah, may I lean on your arm going upstairs?" I asked.

"Tell me you're not serious."

"Sarah, do as your sister asks," Mother said sternly. "She has had a hard day."

Groaning, Sarah pulled herself up. "Oh, fine. After today, this isn't going to happen again. I do hope you understand that."

"Then, I would be wise to take advantage of it today, while I still can," I said, taking her arm with a smile. Managing to wait until we were alone, going up the stairs, I asked,

"Sarah, Miss Sandwood wasn't serious earlier when she tried to imply Mr. Richfield was the one who hit me, was she?"

Instantly, Sarah pulled away. "Is that all this was? An opportunity to question me away from Mother?" she asked. She spun to go back down the stairs. "You don't need my help."

"Sarah, please."

Sighing, Sarah paused and faced me. "It would be a huge coincidence is all she meant. Why was he even out there? He wasn't coming from the Sandwoods'; he was on his way there."

"He doesn't have to stay at the Sandwood's the entire time he is not in our company," I told her, feeling uneasy for the first time. "Please tell me you and Miss Sandwood are not planning something."

"I don't know what you're talking about," Sarah said haughtily. She paused for one moment, and I waited to hear the bad news. "All Charlotte will do is find out what Mr. Richfield has been doing."

Of course she was, and there was no way for me to stop her. Sighing, I went up the rest of the steps on my own. I had every reason to fear Mr. Richfield would find out what Miss Sandwood and Sarah were up to and develop an aversion to everyone even remotely connected with the situation. He would leave this county as soon as possible. Who wouldn't if he or she was believed to be a criminal?

And then my heart would break.

Even now, my heart felt heavy as I walked into my room. I tried to convince myself I couldn't try to control everything, but my head just wasn't in the listening mood. There must have been something I could have done to prevent this.

Trying to think of what, exactly, that something could have been, only made my head ache even more. Curling up on my bed, I closed my eyes and put aside the problem with Sarah and Charlotte until another time.

JUST AS I SAID I WOULD, once I had slept for a few hours, I was able to join the rest of the family for dinner. My headache had abated, and I was able to join in on the lively family discussions.

After dinner, Father asked to see me in the library alone. Initially, I was worried, but as it happened my concern was for no reason. All he wanted to know was if I had seen anything when I had been attacked. I was sorry to disappoint him by telling him I still couldn't remember what had happened. He nodded his understanding and sent me on my way.

Another night's rest did wonders, and I felt more myself. The lump on my head had gone down but remained sore. To be on the safe side, Mother decreed I should stay at home for a few more days before risking the strain of going out.

Sarah, on the other hand, was delighted to be allowed to visit the Knightons and spend the day with the ladies there. Mrs. Sandwood sent her carriage for my sister, and Sarah went off arm in arm with her friend. I watched them go, feeling a twinge of anxiety over what they would attempt out of my sight.

But, I was hardly given time to think about it. The number of visits Mother and I received that day competed with the day before. Several of the visits were from the same ladies, who had the same thing to say and the same questions to ask. Unsurprisingly, the only visitors we did not see were the ladies at Knighton Manor, though Anna did drop in on us for an hour. She claimed to want to escape the crowd at her parent's home.

And Mr. Richfield did not come. I had expected —hoped— he would because if he was with me, he was nowhere near Sarah's scheming. And I missed his company. Had the crowd the day before—or what he had overheard—frightened him away?

When Sarah returned, flushed with triumph from a win at an archery competition, I couldn't get a word from her. She was more than happy to detail the particulars of the afternoon she had spent at the Manor, but she wouldn't say a word on any other topic. I was afraid of what she was thinking about and dumbfounded when I couldn't get a rise out of her.

What was she up to?

I was eager to get back to the house party myself and cover over any damage she may have done while Mother and I were not with her. A personal invitation from Mrs. Knighton for Mother and myself to attend the rescheduled picnic was just the opportunity to do that, though it took some convincing before Mother agreed I could go.

Will and James were going along for the picnic as well, making it tight in the carriage as both of my brothers had a habit of stretching all of their limbs out. When we crossed the creek, I found myself the target of everyone's attention as though they expected a reaction from me. But there was no sudden rush of memory, and indeed, I had nothing to say about what had happened four days previous.

Several black barouches were out and they gleamed in the sun, having been shined for the occasion. Servants were rushing to and fro, gathering the needed items for the picnic. Mr. Knighton himself was on hand to help me to the ground. "I can't tell you how relieved I am to see you on your feet, Miss Forester," he said as he patted my gloved hand. "We shall have the villain in custody soon enough, don't you worry."

"I have no worries." Well, I did. Just none that had to do with a highwayman. Most of my worries had to do with the tall gentleman striding towards me.

"Miss Forester," he said, bowing to mother and me. Sarah had already scurried off, while Will and James were speaking to our hostess. "Mrs. Forester, might I be able to persuade you to allow your daughter to ride with me to the picnic site? I shall see her safely there. You have my word as a gentleman."

Mother nodded as I shifted to face her eagerly, amusement making her eyes sparkle. "Of course. Only I must insist you wait until all of the carriages leave."

"Naturally," Mr. Richfield said, holding his arm out to me. He guided me to a rather handsome looking gig. A single brown horse was in place to pull the light, two wheeled vehicle. "I believe we are waiting for the Sandwoods to make their appearance and then we shall all be off."

From the barouche a few yards from Mr. Richfield's gig, Anna waved to me from where she sat next to Miss Delan.

It was difficult to tell from the distance, but I believe she winked as Mr. Richfield helped me up into the curricle. Unable to hide my blush, I settled myself in my seat as my escort hurried around to climb up beside me.

"Comfortable?" he asked.

"Yes, thank you," I said, smiling at him. Was my imagination playing tricks on me, or did he blush? No, I couldn't possibly have seen that. "And thank you for the flowers you left for me. They were beautiful."

"You're kind to say so. I'm pleased you liked them." He seemed nervous for some reason. "I should have thought to find something better, but they seemed like you, so that's what I picked—."

He was rambling, and that was not like him at all. "They were perfect," I said, impulsively reaching over to put my hand on his. I jerked my hand back the instant I realized what I had done, but I had his attention now. "No one has ever given me flowers before."

I hadn't meant to say that, and my cheeks burned with embarrassment.

"Then, I am glad to have been the first," Mr. Richfield said sincerely. I lifted my gaze and met his eyes. For some reason, I giggled. Which made him laugh, and then we were both laughing as though one of us had told a hilarious joke.

What was wrong with me? And him?

"Richfield!"

Our laughter broke off as Miss Reynolds approached. My forehead creased in a frown at the informal way she addressed Mr. Richfield. "Miss Reynolds," he said pleasantly. "Are you ready to enjoy the picnic?"

"I thought I was to ride with you today," Miss Reynolds said with a pout. "It was agreed yesterday, was it not?"

My breath caught in my throat. What was she saying? How could she make up such a story and then proclaim it so rudely? Surely, she knew as well as I that Mr. Richfield was not the sort of gentleman to offer a ride to one lady only to take another.

Mr. Richfield put his hand on my arm, as if to keep me in place though I hadn't made a move to leave. "I am sorry there was a misunderstanding, Miss Reynolds. I have set arrangements to escort Miss Forester today. I'm sure one of the other carriages will have a place for you."

I waited for her to protest and try to get her way. For a moment, she stared at me with narrowed eyes. Then, she spun on her heel and stalked away. The Sandwoods, fortunately, came rolling into the yard then. Miss Sandwood didn't even wait for the carriage to come to a complete stop before she leaned out of the window. "We are here!"

"I'm so glad you decided to announce it to us all," Miss Reynolds said loudly, over her shoulder. "Otherwise, how would we have ever known?"

Miss Sandwood didn't give any indication that she had heard, but several of us had. Anna's head had come around, and there was a dangerous look of annoyance on her face. Beside me, Mr. Richfield became tense, losing the look of merriment on his face. I bit my lip in an attempt to keep from snapping something that would result in Mother sending me home.

Why was Miss Reynolds so unpleasant? She went out of her way to behave in such a way, and I couldn't understand it.

Her jealousy of me, I could comprehend, but what had Miss Sandwood done to earn Miss Reynolds' dislike?

"Charlotte! Come sit with me!" Sarah said. I flinched at the sharp note in her tone.

As Charlotte hurried to where Sarah was, Miss Reynolds was climbing up to sit with her mother and her close companion, Miss Carter. None of those ladies behaved as if they wanted to be there. "A shame the other ladies are not as enthused about this picnic as your sister," Mr. Richfield said, shaking his head.

"Perhaps Miss Reynolds is not feeling quite the thing."

Shaking his head, Mr. Richfield glanced at me. "If that is the case, she has not been 'feeling quite the thing' for as long as I have known her. And it's a shame for her father is an entertaining companion to have."

Was he? I had sudden desire to become better acquainted with Mr. Reynolds, to know how different he was from his daughter. I watched as everyone split up into the open carriages. In no time at all, we were moving, with Mr. Richfield and I leading the way.

Finally, the picnic could begin.

AS IF TO COVER OVER the negativity Miss Reynolds had brought up, Mr. Richfield spoke as soon as we were on the road. "I suppose the proper thing now would be to discuss the weather."

"Oh?" I glanced at him. Why would we need to discuss the weather? Previous days had rainy but had since cleared, allowing for the picnic to happen. "To what end?"

"Is it not the accepted topic of conversation?"

"I suppose," I said slowly. Surely we knew each other well enough we could find something else to talk of. "What exactly would you like to say about the weather?"

He glanced over at me, his eyes twinkling with amusement. "Only that I am delighted the weather is fine today," he said a mock note of seriousness in his voice. "I would have lodged a formal complaint if it had not."

I wasn't sure where he was taking the conversation but I decided to play along. "Oh? And to whom would you have taken your complaint?"

"You're right. I had not thought it through." Mr. Richfield glanced over at me. "Who would you recommend?"

A giggle at the ridiculousness of our conversation bubbled up, and I struggled to keep a serious expression on my face. "Well, on the one hand, it is Mrs. Knighton's party, but I'm afraid even she does not have control of the weather." I tapped my chin with my finger. "She would have taken her complaint to her husband, but I fear even he would not have been able to do a thing about it."

"Indeed." Mr. Richfield nodded. "I suppose you mean to tell me it would have been a useless endeavor then." He heaved a large, dramatic sigh. "And, it would seem we have taken the topic of weather as far as we can."

"It seems that is the only conclusion we can come to." I nodded, biting my lip to keep from grinning. "What do you propose we discuss next?"

"Now that is the question. Your health, I'm afraid, would be a dangerous topic to consider. Local events seems to be focused on your recent...encounter with the highwayman, which connects back to your health, so I'm afraid that is another subject off the list." He glanced once more at me. "What are your opinions of the trees we are passing?"

I couldn't help but burst out laughing at that. A delighted smile appeared on Mr. Richfield's face, proving he intended for me to laugh. I didn't dare glance back at the other carriages, for I was sure everyone's focus was on him and me. It felt like no time at all and we had arrived at our destination.

The site of the picnic was one we had been to many, many times, so I knew it well. Servants had already been there, and blankets were spread out, along with food and equipment for games like cricket and shuttlecock. There was a pond with a path that wound around and through the trees.

I heard the loud chatter of the others as they came towards the site. It wouldn't be long before I would be asked yet again about the attack. "Shall we take a stroll around the pond?" Mr. Richfield asked. "I swear I shall not leave you to be bait for a highwayman."

"Is that what James did? Will is such a bad influence on him," I said with a laugh.

"If you're not feeling up to it—."

"I am more than ready for a walk." I had no doubt it wouldn't be long before others joined us on the trail, and sure enough, by the time we reached the edge of the pond, the others were spreading out around the bank of the water.

"Your father is anxious there has been no news concerning the highwayman."

Startled by the sudden change of subject, I glanced up at him. When had he spoken to Father about it? "I thought as much, though he hasn't said anything to us concerning the matter. I've never seen him so furious with James about leaving me alone. I tried to convince him it was partly my fault, but—."

"That isn't true, of course!" Mr. Richfield exclaimed, interrupting me. "You mustn't think that."

"That may be. But if I didn't at least try to take some of the blame, my siblings would never forgive me."

Mr. Richfield chuckled. "I see." He fell silent for a few steps. "Are you looking forward to the ball?"

"Yes, of course," I said sincerely. What an odd question! "It has been some months since we last had a ball. Sarah, naturally, is in raptures over the idea. She is always a popular partner for all the dances. She scarcely sits down or catches her breath."

"Is that jealousy I hear?"

How could he possibly have known I had been jealous? "No!" He raised an eyebrow at me, clearly not believing my protest. "I confess I used to be jealous of her, but no longer. We are different individuals. Therefore we cannot expect the same things in life."

He shook his head. "I have the feeling I'm hearing more of your mother's wisdom."

"What better person could I have to repeat?" I asked with a soft laugh "She truly is the wisest and most patient person I have ever known."

"Do you enjoy dancing, Miss Forester?"

Again, a sudden subject change. Why did he want to know about dancing? I was sure there was a purpose to his words. After all, he had danced with me on several occasions in London. "Yes. Why do you ask?"

"Do you waltz?"

The question caused my cheeks bright red, I'm sure. Some of my fondest memories were of having dancing lessons with a master at the Knighton's home. I had learned the dance, as I'm sure most ladies did, whether their parents approved or not. It was not performed in our little community, but no doubt every young lady hoped for the opportunity to go to London where it was more accepted.

Clearing my throat, I said, "I learned a few years ago, yes. I have not had the opportunity to practice of late."

"I think I would like to waltz with you, Miss Forester."

I stumbled, and Mr. Richfield steadied me. "This appears to have become a habit between you and me, Miss Forester," he said with a smile.

"I'm sorry."

"I'm not." He lifted his hand and mine to the correct position. His other hand moved to my waist. He took one step, and I moved on instinct, bringing my left hand up to his shoulder. He drew me closer, making my breath catch in my throat.

Barring the time when he'd caught me and when he had carried me in his arms, I had never been so close to a man before. He was holding me closer than the danced necessitated, but I wasn't about to object. Smiling down at me, Mr. Richfield began to lead me through the waltz, spinning me through the trees.

Heaven help me if anyone were to catch us now! My reputation would be a thing of the past! And I found I didn't care.

Chapter Fifteen

A few minutes of dancing left me feeling completely out of breath. "For someone who has the habit of tripping over her feet, you dance with great elegance," Mr. Richfield said, slowing to a stop. "You will grace the dance floor of the Knighton Ball many times, or the other gentlemen are fools."

I wasn't sure whether to feel the insult that he assumed I was clumsy. It was only on a few occasions my feet moved of their own accord. Instead, I focused on the compliment he'd offered to me. "Are you prepared to see so many fools in one place?" I asked lightly. "It may sound as though it will be amusing, but I can assure you it will be tedious."

Mr. Richfield laughed. "Your sharp mind is one of the things I admire about you."

At least he seemed amused. Most gentlemen didn't wish for a lady to use her mind for anything serious. I appreciated more than ever I had caught the attention of such an honorable man.

"We should return to the others," I said, glancing over to pond. My attention was caught by Will, who was at the edge of the water and reaching for something out of sight. Seeing him crouched down reminded me of something I couldn't quite place, and I felt a sharp stab of anxiety.

"Diana, are you well? Are you tired?"

"I'm—I'm fine," I said, trying to convince myself more than him. Will It took a second before it hit me what Mr. Richfield had said: my Christian name, just as he had done when he'd helped wake me up after the attack. Startled, I brought my gaze back to him.

He still held my hand in his. "Diana. I approached your father, and he gave permission for me to speak to you. I've just been waiting for the right opportunity."

Oh.

"Diana Forester, when I first met you in London, I was struck by how you were unlike other young ladies," Mr. Richfield continued, his eyes meeting mine. "You keep to yourself. You do not get involved in other people's affairs, but you are a caring person at the same time. Mrs. Davison has told me how much time you spend reading to her and helping her home. Beneath your quiet demeanor is an intelligent young lady whom other people appear to overlook at times."

Was this truly happening? How different this was from when Philip had asked if I would marry me. He had simply said we would rub along well together, but here Mr. Richfield had detailed what he appreciated about me. A warm glow began to fill my heart.

"You are a devoted daughter and sister. You trip over your feet when you are flustered, which I find charming."

My cheeks heated up, and I couldn't be sure if it was because I was embarrassed to be hearing this or because I wasn't breathing.

"Will you do me the honor of becoming my wife?"

An incredulous laugh left my lips, and for a moment, his expression filled with horror. "Yes! Yes, of course, I will!"

Smiling broadly, he kissed the back of my hand and then stepped forward. My breath caught in my throat as I realized he intended on kissing me properly. "Richfield!" Philip Knighton's voice reached us. "We need you for a game."

Mr. Richfield—John—groaned as he tucked my hand in his elbow. "Please, let me tell my family first," I said as he escorted me back to the rest of the party. "Before anyone else is told, I mean."

The last thing I wanted was to have it announced to the picnic, in front of Miss Reynolds, who I was sure would cause a scene. Thankfully, my now betrothed was in complete agreement. "Yes, of course. I will write a letter to my mother tonight."

He guided me back to the other ladies and saw I was seated comfortably. Then, he squeezed my hand before he went to join the game that was being started, though he kept glancing back to make sure I was still well.

At that moment, I could not have been happier.

"YOUR MIND IS FAR AWAY."

Looking up from the wooden letters I had been studying carefully, I frowned at Anna. She had a coy smile on her face. "I'm trying to figure out the word you've put before me," I said defensively. She, Miss Elizabeth Carter, Miss Delan, and I were playing a word game where we had to figure out the word based on the letters we were given. "That requires some thought, you know."

"That's not what I'm talking about. You are behaving in a distracted manner this afternoon."

She stared pointedly at where the men of the house party were shooting at targets. Mr. Richfield glanced over at the same moment, and his smile widened as his gaze met mine. My cheeks flushed, and I ducked my head. "That is what I'm talking about," Anna whispered, leaning close to me. "Is there something you want to tell me?"

"Not here, Anna."

I hoped our low voices would go unnoticed. "What are you whispering about over there?" Miss Reynolds asked. Even hours into the picnic, she hadn't lost the pout.

Anna rolled her eyes as she sat back. "I gave Diana a hint for her word. She has been giving it such diligent attention I thought she could use some help."

Returning from playing Graces, a game I had never enjoyed where the participants caught a small hoop with small sticks, Sarah came to have a look at my letters. She leaned over my shoulder and said instantly, "Highwayman."

"Thank you, Sarah," I said in annoyance. I frowned down at the letters and saw that, of course, she was right. Wait. 'Highwayman'? I moved my gaze to Anna. Why, after everything that had happened, would she use that word?

"So, tell us about your run in with the highwayman, Miss Forester," Miss Carter said, spinning her umbrella on her shoulder. "You haven't said a word about it. Surely you must remember *something* by now."

I had hoped to avoid any mention of it. "There's nothing I can say that hasn't already been said. It happened, and I don't remember anything about it."

"Honestly, Miss Forester, I begin to think it didn't truly happen," Miss Reynolds said pointedly. "There have been no details, and only your siblings' word it must have happened as they say it did."

"Perhaps she merely tripped and fell, and is far too embarrassed to say so," Miss Carter said with a laugh.

That was when I knew they had planned this. Mother had a look of pure horror on her face, and Mrs. Knighton's countenance became appalled. Mrs. Reynolds wasn't even paying attention, her entire focus on the men shooting. Mrs. Carter, though, laughed with her daughter as though she had heard a great joke.

Sarah was livid. "Perhaps, Miss Carter, you could explain to me how would be possible," she said sharply. "James and I found Sarah on her back. If she had tripped, as you just suggested, she would have landed on her face."

Miss Carter seemed more than happy to debate with Sarah. "Well, then perhaps she slipped going down the bank and fell backward. Mr. Knighton has said how woefully clumsy she is."

My breath caught in my throat, and I could only stare at her. Anna shook her head. "My dear Miss Carter, that cannot be true. My brother would never say such a thing."

I wished I could have had her confidence. Philip Knighton had been behaving strangely since I had declined to marry him. He could have proclaimed my failings to these ladies. "Perhaps she the whole situation," Miss Reynolds said, ignoring Anna.

And I promptly forgot about how my former friend did or did not speak of me. "I beg your pardon?" I said, my tone shifting one of controlled fury. My fingers curled around the abandoned letters of the game we had been playing. I had the feeling this is what they had been trying to get to this entire time.

"Diana, why don't you see what Will is up to," Mother said. 'I'm afraid if he gets any closer to the pond, he's going to be in it."

She wanted me to walk away, and I knew to do so would be the best course. I couldn't lower myself to their level. "I was merely pointing out you would have been seeking attention, Miss Forester," Miss Reynolds said. "It's common enough in large families I understand. No one would blame you for wanting some acknowledgment."

My plan of walking away from the conversation came to a sudden halt. She had just insulted my entire family, in particular my parents, and I could not let her get away with it. I opened my mouth to give her a piece of my mind. "Shuttlecock!" Mrs. Knighton said, her tone desperate. "Girls, you should play a game of shuttlecock!"

My mouth snapped shut. I wouldn't stoop to Miss Reynolds' level. She had just embarrassed our hostess, and I would not do the same. "I will go see what Will has found," I said, moving to get up.

"Miss Reynolds, take a turn with me," Mother said, getting to her feet. There was a command in her tone Miss Reynolds obeyed without question.

A pleased smile curved my lips. As one who had been on the receiving end of one of Mother's scolds, I knew precisely what Miss Reynolds was about to hear. It was the perfect revenge.

If only I could be there to hear what Mother was about to say.

"A fabrication, indeed," Sarah said in a low tone as Mother firmly steered Miss Reynolds out of earshot. "She has a completely wrong idea."

"Poor Miss Reynolds. She is simply mad because she has lost Mr. Richfield and cannot get Philip to even glance in her direction now." Anna frowned at Sarah as though she realized what my sister had said. "And just what would the right idea be?

Cringing, I realized I had never warned Anna about my sister's theory. "Why, that Mr. Richfield is the highwayman, of course," Sarah said readily. I covered my face with my hand.

Mrs. Knighton laughed. "You girls and your wild tales," she said. She focused on Mrs. Carter and began speaking about the weather. The Carter girls started whispering together, and Miss Delan, caught in the middle of this, had an expression of abject misery.

"Sarah, not another word. Please," I said. My head had begun to ache, and I longed for the happiness I had been feeling no more than ten minutes before.

"Diana being courted by a criminal?" Anna asked, latching onto the idea with her usual vigor. She laughed like it was a joke. "How wonderful that would be if it were true."

Miss Delan had a thoughtful expression on her face, and she glanced towards the men. "Sarah is well known for her imagination," I said quickly, trying to minimize the damage. "Can you truly imagine a gentleman like Mr. Richfield being a criminal?"

"Oh, no," Miss Elizabeth Carter said quickly. "He is quite the nicest man I've ever met."

"Well, it would have made things more exciting, don't you think?" Anna said with disappointment in her voice. She leaned back. "Diana, sit back down. I don't think Will needs you checking over his shoulder. If he falls in the pond, he knows how to swim."

Reminded of why I had gotten up in the first place, I glanced at where I had last seen my younger brother and didn't see any sign of him. Sighing, I settled back down next to Anna as she gathered up the letters to continue our game.

BY THE TIME THE PICNIC was over, I was exhausted. At one point, I'm relatively sure Will let several frogs lose among the ladies. I couldn't prove it, but I saw the mischievous grin on his face while the other ladies screamed at the hopping amphibians. The men all came to catch the creatures with Mr. Ward, of all people, capturing most of the frogs.

Who would have imagined the well dressed, aloof gentleman was skilled at catching frogs?

At the time, I expected Sarah to take off after Will with a frog in hand to get revenge, but she didn't. She had squealed and giggled like the other young ladies. It was odd and I wasn't sure what to make of it.

Anna's husband, Sir Rodger, arrived in time for the last hour of the picnic. My dear friend was openly delighted to have her husband by her side and hung on his arm. Seeing them together made me smile.

Still, I was ready to be back at home where it was peaceful and there was something I had to announce. As Father came out of his office when we entered the house, I blurted out the words. "I have something I need to tell you all."

"Is something wrong?" Mother asked in concern as everyone else fell silent.

After everything that had happened recently, it was a valid question. "No, not at all. It's a good thing, I promise." I took a deep breath. It wasn't every day a young lady made this kind of announcement to her family, and I wanted to say it just right. "Mr. Richfield made an offer of marriage to me, and I accepted."

Holding my breath, I waited for my family's reaction. "You're not serious," James said. "The highwayman?"

"Does he know what he's getting himself into?" was Will's question.

I sent a glare at them. "Congratulations, my dear," Mother said, coming to hug me. "You and he will do well together, I believe. I cannot think of a better match for you."

There was the reaction I had hoped for. "Thank you, Mother."

Father had a pleased smile on his face. "It took him long enough to speak to you," he said, hugging me after Mother released me. "I have been expecting you to announce this for days."

"No, seriously, does he know what he's willingly getting himself into?" Will asked again. "Does he know what a grump you can be in the morning? Or how you fall on your face when you get distracted while you're walking?"

Leave it to Will to bring those things up. "You can ask him the next time you see him," James said to Will. "But think on the bright side, now we don't have to deal with her."

The only person who hadn't said anything was Sarah. I focused my attention on her and waited for to bring up her theory yet again. She merely shrugged and walked upstairs. Frowning, I glanced at Mother, hoping for some explanation.

But Mother only shook her head. "It will be a big change for us all, Diana," was all she said.

Honestly, I hadn't thought about that. If I had thought my life had been shaken before, now it was about be set on its head. The thought frightened me a little as I contemplated the enormity of what my decision.

"You didn't say anything earlier," Will said

"Of course not." I lightly hit his arm. "He and I agreed to keep it quiet until we informed our families. He will write a letter to his mother tonight."

Mother nodded. "A wise decision."

"We won't keep it quiet long," Father said decisively. "We shall have a dinner party, and announce it to our friends then."

"When do you think we shall have time to plan such a dinner party?" Mother asked. She didn't fool any of us. Likely, she had already begun planning the details in her mind. "With the house party going on, we shall all be occupied for many weeks."

A long engagement was not what I had in mind, but I didn't know what Mr. Richfield —John—thought on the matter. It was so hard to think of him by his Christian name! I had referred to him in person and my mind as 'Mr. Richfield' for our entire acquaintance. He, on the other hand, had fallen into using my Christian name with apparently no trouble at all.

"You look exhausted, Diana," Mother said with some concern. I'd missed whatever response Father had given her. Will and James had taken off to who knows where. "You should get some rest before dinner. You're still not quite yourself yet."

Nodding, I pulled my bonnet off and went upstairs. I heard the sound of Sarah playing her harp in the sitting room. The music she played sounded thoughtful, as though she was working things through her mind.

I sincerely hoped she would get used to the idea of having a new brother and abandon her idea of him being a highwayman. If she didn't...I shook my head. Having to choose between supporting my sister or supporting my husband would be a terrible choice to make and I didn't want to lose my sister.

DINNER THAT NIGHT SEEMED especially lively, even with Sarah sulking across the table. James and Will were delightedly coming up with a list of my 'quirks', as they called them, they felt my betrothed needed to be made aware of. Included was my habit of tapping my pen while in thought, causing ink droplets everywhere, and also my tendency to fall over my feet if I was not careful. My father kept suggesting things encouraged them to the point where Will offered to get pen and paper to write it all down.

Just as I defended my habit of playing one song over and over until I had it perfect, a note arrived for Father. We all fell silent as he read the message, watching as his face became more serious than I'd ever seen before. He finally folded the letter and raised his hand to his face with a sigh.

"What has happened?" Mother asked.

"Mr. Sandwood was riding over to join his family at the Knightons' for dinner," Father said, dropping his hand to include us all in his gaze. "He was accosted by the highwayman."

I gasped in horror as my siblings expressed their dismay. "Is he unharmed?" I asked, thinking of the groom who had been harmed a week ago.

"A bullet grazed his arm, but he will recover in no time."

"Did Mr. Sandwood not have a way of defending himself?" James asked. "I thought he planned on carrying his pistol whenever he went riding."

"He did, but he missed when his horse spooked," Father said. "That tells me this ruffian is aware of the safety measures we have in place and has taken steps to counteract them. He is more dangerous than I had thought."

Sarah, I noticed then, had leaned forward, her eyes bright with interest. "Do you mean to say the highwayman is someone who has been party to your discussions?" she asked.

"I refuse to think such a thing about our neighbors," Mother said as I stared at my sister. I knew exactly what Sarah's words implied. "Anyone would know about the precautions we have taken. Surely it has been talked of in town and in front of the servants."

Rising from his seat, Father walked to the end of the table to kiss Mother's cheek. "I must go to Sandwood. I will return later tonight."

"Don't go alone."

Father offered a reassuring smile. "Of course not." As he walked out of the dining room, I heard him call for his horse to be made ready and for our groom, Jimmy, to be told what had happened.

We all heard the front door close a few moments later. Mother cast a glance at us, seeing no one had made a move since Father had walked out. "Well, finish eating. We don't want any of this to go cold and have cook furious with us all."

My brothers returned to their plates with no apparent decrease in appetite. Sarah caught my eye, and there was no mistaking the expression of triumph on her face. She dropped her gaze and made a remark about something Miss Delan had told her.

James responded to her, but my mind stayed on the matter at hand. As much as I hated to admit it, Sarah was absolutely convinced John was the highwayman and her certainty concerned me. His affection for me was evident enough, and I didn't doubt that.

As I picked up my fork, I had a flash of inspiration. I knew what I had to do. Whatever it took, I had to prove he wasn't the highwayman. Sarah and Will already had plots designed and worked out. What better people to help me establish my betrothed was not a criminal?

Filled with determination and a clear goal in mind, I brought my focus back to my family. All I had to do was convince Will and Sarah to help me.

Chapter Sixteen

First thing after breakfast the next day, I followed Will out to the stables. I had to get him away from James because I knew my older brother wanted nothing more to do with the situation. Given what had happened, I could understand and respect his decision, but it wasn't going to stop me from enlisting Will's help.

"What do you want?" Will asked when I stepped in. He was in one of the stalls where a cat had given birth to a litter of kittens several weeks ago.

"I want you to help me prove Mr. Richfield isn't the highwayman."

Nothing like putting things simply and to the point. "Shouldn't you have worried about that before you became engaged to the man?" Will asked, raising an eyebrow at me. "I thought you were certain he wasn't the highwayman."

"I was! I am!" I hesitated and decided to be completely honest with Will. "All I want is to find a way to silence Sarah once and for all. The only way to do that is for me to have irrefutable evidence."

He laughed. My brother laughed at me. If I hadn't wanted him to help me, I might have gotten mad at him. "Sarah finally got to you, didn't she?" he asked in delight. He set a kitten back with its littermates and got to his feet. "What do I get out of this?"

"An adventure. Maybe the prestige of learning the highwayman's true identity."

Dragging the decision out as long as possible, Will considered my answer with a frown. "I suppose that will have to be good enough," he finally said. "So, how do you want to prove who the highwayman is?"

"Well, you and Sarah had plots and plans to prove the opposite not so long ago. What were you going to do?"

Shrugging, Will started walking towards the stable doors. "You're talking to the wrong person, Diana," he said. "Sarah was the one with the big plans, not me. She worked them all out with Miss Sandwood, you know. She never told me what they were going to do."

That was what I was afraid of. I knew getting Sarah to agree to my scheme would not be easy. "Would you help me get her on my side? Please?"

"No."

What? Why not? After all, you agreed to help Sarah. Why won't you help me?"

Will shrugged his shoulders again. "After what happened to you, I don't want to be part of any plan that our parents could get angry about."

"Convenient excuse." I breathed out a sigh and started back to the house. Will fell into step next to me. I decided it was a good opportunity to find out what he thought on something else. "Are you surprised I'm engaged?"

The look my brother gave me was filled with sarcasm and disdain. "Diana, anyone who didn't know you would have guessed you and Richfield would be getting married sooner rather than later. I'm with Father. It took you two long enough to get around to it."

"Sarah wanted to make him interested in another lady."

"Sometimes I wonder if our sister thinks," Will said with a sigh. "I could have told her there was no possible way any other lady would have Richfield's attention."

Will's casual use of my betrothed's last name amused me. "You just want him to teach you more piquet tricks."

Will didn't deny it, and we parted company just inside the house. He went to his studies in the library, and I went to find my sister. She was out in the garden, reading and not practicing her archery as I had expected.

I spent a moment just watching her. She seemed completely relaxed, and again, she had my book. As often as it was missing when I went to find it, I still hadn't finished reading it.

"Is there something you want?" Sarah asked without looking up. How had she known I was here?

"Can we talk for a minute?" She shrugged. I walked over to her chair and crouched down by her. "Sarah, I wanted to talk to you about John. You are so certain he's the one robbing our friends and relatives—."

"Are you still on that?" Sarah asked, turning a page. "I'm not going to say another word about it. I'm sorry I said anything about it yesterday. He's your betrothed now. You're going to marry him. He's going to be part of the family. What more do you want me to say?"

Why did she have to be so frustrating? "I appreciate that, Sarah. But that's not what I was trying to get at. Just a few days ago, you wanted to prove John is the highwayman. How exactly were you going to do it?"

For the first time, Sarah lifted her head. "Why do you ask?" she asked suspiciously.

"Because I want to know."

"Not until you tell me why you want to know all of a sudden. You always want to know things for specific reasons. There is always something. So, why do you want to know this now."

I groaned, leaning my head against my arm for a moment. "I want to prove he isn't the highwayman." When I lifted my head, Sarah was staring at me, and I couldn't read her expression. "I want there to be no doubt in your mind."

"My mind? Why do you care what I think? If you're so certain he is innocent, why would it matter what I thought? Do you doubt your betrothed now?"

"No! It just matters. Will said you were the one with the plans."

Sarah let out a laugh. "I hate to disappoint you. but there was no plan." My jaw dropped. After everything they had put me through? It had been nothing more than talk? "I meant to come up with something, and then it just wasn't worth the effort."

After everything? There was no elaborate plan?

"It was so much fun watching you get nervous and try to keep us in control. I decided I would tell you eventually, but then there never seemed to be a good time," Sarah said, closing the book in her hand. "And then...well, there were other things to think of."

I had spent hours worrying about what she and Will were going to do. And for nothing? What 'other things' could she have been concerned with?

My sister cleared her throat. "Diana, you're starting to scare me. Say something."

"You had nothing?" I managed to say. I could not believe what I had just heard. Sarah sounded sincere, so I had to believe it, but I didn't want to. "You put me through—I thought you had plans you weren't telling me because you knew I would get mad!"

Clearly relieved to hear me speak, Sarah shrugged. "It was fun," she said as if it explained everything. "It was the best entertainment I've had in a long time."

It explained nothing. I had spent days nearly out of my mind with worry, and she thought it was 'fun' to watch it happen?

"I can't believe you did that to me!" It had been a long time since I'd last felt such anger with my only sister.

Visibly, Sarah flinched at my outrage. "Diana, calm down," she said, her voice betraying her nervousness. "You know what Mother says about raising your voice."

She wasn't going to bring Mother into this. Though she may not have realized it, she had just given me the perfect way to get her to help me. "You owe me, Sarah," I said, forcing my voice into a calm, even tone. "For this, you owe me."

Suddenly wary, Sarah eyed me. "What are you talking about?"

"You and Will have put me through—." I struggled to find the words to describe the anxiety I had been feeling the past few weeks. Failing that, I moved on. "You both are going to pay me back by helping me with this now. If you give me any trouble or try to get out of doing this for me, I promise you I will—."

"Let me guess, you'll tell Father and Mother," Sarah said, rolling her eyes as she interrupted me. She stood up. "Say no more. But let's just be clear on one thing. I'm helping you because I want to, not because you threatened me."

Having expected more resistance from her, I shook my head as I straightened up. "I'll go get, Will," I said. There was no chance I would give her time to back out.

It was time to figure out the truth behind this highwayman problem.

WILL NEEDED NO CONVINCING to abandon his studies and James firmly refused to have anything to do with it. In a matter of minutes, the three of us were walking to the creek, following the same path James, Sarah and I had taken the day I was attacked. The idea was maybe I would remember something that would be of use to us.

"What if we just asked him?" Will asked. "And the rest of us will watch him to see if there is any suspicious reaction."

"Since he is in the business of robbing travelers, the odds are he can lie," Sarah said, shaking her head. "He would have to be extremely good at it since he was so concerned about Diana that day. I was convinced."

"Of course, we are all assuming the highwayman is the one who attacked me," I said logically. "What if it wasn't?"

Sarah and Will exchanged glances. "Let's just work out this problem first," my sister said. "Besides, who would have a big enough grudge against you to hit you over the head? I don't think miss Reynolds is motivated enough."

"So, why do we think Richfield is doing this?" Will asked, getting us back on topic. "What reason does he have?"

"Money; to support himself and his family. He only has a small estate, right?"

I shook my head. "He would need to be robbing more and richer people than our neighbors if that were true," I said. "Have you any idea the cost of supporting a family, Sarah?"

"Well, he could have been the one doing it in Bath. But, if money is the motivating force here, why would he want to marry you, Diana? You don't have that much. We all know that. If it were money he was after, he would be engaged to Miss Reynolds right now."

There was the blunt honesty I knew to expect from my only sister. On my other side, Will kicked a stone from the lane. "So he does it for the adventure," he said. "Which doesn't explain why he would have knocked you out, Diana. That makes no sense. Whoever it is, I don't understand why he would do that to you."

That was the question no one had answered for me yet. Why had the highwayman attacked me in broad daylight? What threat was I? Or, as I had suggested, it had been someone else who took offense to my presence on the bridge.

"You must have seen something," Will said, poking my arm to get my attention. "That's the only reason it could be."

"But she doesn't remember, so that's no help," Sarah said, leaning around me to look at Will. "So should we do? If we keep talking, all we will do is go around and around and not get anywhere."

Honestly, there were much better places to be than in between my two younger siblings when they argued. "Has anyone heard anything new about the highwayman, besides last night's attack?" I asked to distract them. I knew if they kept bickering, they would both end up walking away from me and I would be on my own.

My question made them both pause and look at each other. "No," Will finally said. "He didn't do anything until last night."

I had wondered if no one brought the subject up around me because they didn't want to upset me. But nothing? Between when I had been attacked and last night, some six days, and there had been not one single act of highway robbery? Weeks of terrorising our neighbors, and all of the sudden nothing? Why? Because he'd hurt me? Or had the highwayman paused for another reason?

So many questions and not a single answer to one of them.

"That's odd," Sarah said, unconsciously echoing my thoughts. "But, in all honesty, he's hit the wealthy families in our county, more than once in some cases. Who else would be left?"

The more I thought about the situation, the less sense it made.

"Maybe you'll have a sudden recovery from your amnesia, like in one of those stupid novels you read, and all will be revealed," Will said with a grin. "We will be able to return home, tell everyone what happened, and then we'll all live happily ever after."

"Things like that don't happen in real life." He may have been just teasing me about my love for the written word, but there was no need to exaggerate matters.

"Well, we'll find out now," Sarah said, nodding ahead of us.

We had reached the creek. My steps slowed, and I fell behind the other two. I couldn't hide I was nervous to be here. The other times we had crossed the bridge, I had been safe in the confines of the carriage, where no harm could come for me. And now? I was nearing the spot where I had been knocked out of my senses. I was approaching in the same way as it had happened before. My heart raced in my chest.

"It's not going anywhere, Diana! No matter how slowly you walk, it's still going to be here. You may as well get it over with."

How had Sarah known my feelings? Sighing, I brought my steps back up to speed. Will had already scrambled down to the water's edge, and Sarah stood in the middle of the bridge, looking around. I stepped onto the bridge, but my sister came flying at me.

"No," she said, grabbing my arm. She started pushing me towards the bank where Will was. "It didn't happen here. You have to go where it happened. Maybe Will is right, and you'll remember once you're in the exact spot it happened."

"Stop rushing me!" I said, pulling out of her grasp. "Let me do this at my own pace. I need to think."

Throwing up her hands, Sarah slid down the bank to catch up to our brother, who searched for clues in the mud.

I felt a moment of panic at being left behind. "Wait for me!" I said, lifting my skirt, so I didn't trip and fall, a scenario that seemed all too likely given my habit of doing so as of late.

I had a strange feeling of having done this, and I jerked to a stop. "I did this," I said out loud. As I gave my attention to where I was stepping, making sure my feet were on level ground, I remembered looking down before. "I saw something."

As if it would help me remember, I knelt down and put my gloved hand on the ground. I remembered the feeling of something missing when I first woke up. "I picked something up," I whispered. It was more of a guess, but I had the strong feeling I had it right.

"Diana!" Sarah said, shaking my shoulder. Shaken out of my musings, I lifted my gaze. My sister's expression was concerned. "Don't do that to me! Did you remember something?"

"I'm not sure. I think so," I said, curling my hand into a fist. What had I lost? "I remember hurrying to catch up with you and James. I tried not to slip and happened to look down." I dropped my gaze back to the ground. "There was something, and I picked it up. But then, when I woke up, I didn't have it anymore."

"What was it?"

I shook my head as I straightened. "If I'd remembered, I would have told you. It was important, though. I do know that much."

"Maybe it's still here," Will said, climbing the bank to join us. "Let's look around."

Sarah scoffed. "Well, it's not going to be here. That's why the highwayman hit Diana. Whatever it was she found would have identified him, so he had to get it away from her. And that's why he was out here! He had come to find it himself."

Well, that was one part of the mystery solved. "But who is he?" I asked. That was the vital question.

"No one has been down there," Will said, gesturing towards the bridge. "I think he must have found a new hiding spot."

"But he hasn't been doing anything, so why would he need a hiding spot?" Sarah asked. "And if it is Mr. Richfield, what better hiding place than his room with his Sandwoods?"

"I don't care about that! And it *isn't* Mr. Richfield" I said sharply, completely frustrated. I scowled at the bank that had reminded me of just enough to create more questions. "I care about who he is." As long as he wasn't my betrothed. "I hate having this hanging over us."

Crossing her arms, Sarah frowned. "Well, I don't know how we're going to figure this out." Oh, that was so helpful, and I told her exactly that. She shrugged. "Diana, I don't know what you were expecting, but there isn't anything else we can do."

"That's why I'm saying we need to ask Richfield," Will said. "I do not see another way to go about it."

"That would not be an enjoyable conversation," I said with a sigh. If only I could remember what I had found that day. That would solve everything so quickly.

"Well, there's nothing else we can do here. Let's go." We climbed back up to level ground. "So, when will you talk to Richfield?"

At that point, I wasn't even sure whether I would or not. Since he and Sarah were watching me as though they were expecting an answer, I shook my head and walked ahead of them. "You're both not off the hook yet," I said over my shoulder. "You still have a long way to go to make up for making me panic about you wanting to prove Mr. Richfield is a highwayman."

"Well, I don't know what you want us to do," Sarah complained.

I wasn't too sure about that either.

MR. RICHFIELD HAD A private conference with my parents and I that afternoon and agreed to the plan of a dinner party to announce our engagement. He had sent the letter to his mother and was waiting for a reply. A short engagement was what he desired if I was agreeable. Once his mother arrived, any day would do for him.

As soon as I heard that, nervousness plagued my mind. How long would it be before I met Mrs. Richfield? Would she like me? What if I disliked her? And what of John's sisters? How would we get on?

A date of four days later was set for the dinner party, and I was immediately caught up in the planning of the dinner. I wanted everything to be perfect, and I wanted it to be a dinner everyone would remember.

There would be no going back after the announcement.

I should have realized from the start my betrothed would prove to be a distraction to my accomplishing everything before the dinner party. He interrupted me while I wrote out the invitations, and when I sorted through the linens that would be needed, he appeared. When Mother and I discussed with the cook what items would be served, the maid announced he was asking for me.

Most of me was delighted to have him underfoot. His suggestions and comments were sure to make me laugh. Any attempt of his at assisting me with the invitations ended in disaster, with a bottle of ink being spilled on the desk.

He slowed all activity to the point it became a mad dash to finish on time. Amused though she was, Mother had to urge me to see to my tasks constantly. Sarah was outright annoyed because she was forced to pick up where I had not gotten to my assignments.

"Why is he always here?" she finally asked after three days of holding her tongue on the matter. "Every time I turn around, there he is!"

"Where else would you expect him to be?" I asked. We were in the attic, where the little-used dishware was stored. I opened one chest and began to check its contents. "Hanging on the words of another lady?"

"You're going to spend the rest of your lives together as it is."

Smiling, I brushed at a lock of hair hanging in my face. "If I didn't know better, I would say you were jealous."

"Yes, so jealous my sister is engaged to a highwayman," Sarah said, pulling at a chest. "I may just throw myself off a cliff as a sign of my protest and a broken heart."

Laughing, I shook my head. "Don't be ridiculous. There aren't any cliffs nearby."

Sarah rolled her eyes. Despite the uncertainty about the identity of the highwayman, I was happy. And I wanted to stay that way. Not even my sister's complaints could dim my mood.

Chapter Seventeen

The one thing Sarah was enthusiastic about was our trip to to the dressmakers'. Mrs. Kenson had sewn our dresses for as long as I could remember, and kept up with the fashions in London. While I knew an engaged young lady typically went to the City to have her wedding clothes made, I was more than happy to turn to Mrs. Kenson.

The older woman was pleased to have us in her small shop. And once she heard I was to be married, she was quick to pull out all of the latest fashion plates for Mother and me to peruse. As I had expected, Sarah had no interest in this and spent the hour searching for the specific trimmings she wanted for her ball gown.

Initially, I worried about the cost of making such a large purchase all at once. After all, I would be getting a completely new wardrobe, from morning gowns to evening dresses. Mother was quick to stop me every time I tried to suggest being more economical. "Your father and I have planned for this since you were born, Diana," she said in a low voice. "Your wedding clothes will not be as extravagant as other young ladies will have, but they will show you to great advantage."

"But so many—!" I fingered the beautiful green dimity in front of me.

Mother closed her hand around mine. "You will go to your wedding attired as a well brought up and respectable young lady ought. Think nothing of the expense. It's no worse than should be expected."

With a sigh, I nodded. "Sarah, what do you think of these?" I asked.

Sarah's sense of fashion was unparalleled, for all she disliked looking at the fashion plates. I always relied on her to know what would or wouldn't work. Her preference for simple elegance matched my own, so there were no quarrels between us on that point. When it came to colors, though, we often butted heads. She preferred blues, and I adored greens.

Coming over, my sister glanced at them. "They're nice," she said before she stepped away.

That seemed the best I could expect from Sarah. Studying the designs for a moment longer, I nodded and chose them. Mrs. Kenson checked my measurements. Promising to hire some help, she vowed to have everything I needed in a matter of weeks. She also swore to keep the news quiet until after the dinner party.

And with my wedding clothes chosen, I had to find the net lace I had envisioned for my ball gown. I also needed something to dress up the gown I intended to wear to the dinner party. I frowned at the different choices I had in front of me. Did I want lace, or silver lining? Silk cord? Chinz bordering?

"I want the Vandyked lace on my gown," Sarah said, leaning around me. "Unless you want to copy me, pick something else."

"I can choose whatever I want, Sarah," I said sharply. Vandyked lace had become popular, so I was surprised Sarah would choose it for herself as she usually wished to be more original.

"I think you both should try these pink ribbons," Mother said, reaching over to pick up a pink striped satin ribbon.

Sending a horrified look in my direction, Sarah hurried away. I finally decided on silver beading, not because Sarah had warned me away from the lace I admired but because I thought it would look better against my gown.

With our selected trimmings in hand, we returned home. When we arrived, Father met us outside and took one look at the packages we held. "Did you buy every bauble Mrs. Kenson had on hand?" he asked, his tone teasing.

"Of course not," Sarah said indignantly. "That would mean I brought home that hideous pink ribbon Mother always tries to push on me."

Father sent a wink at Mother, which made her blush. "I think you would all look wonderful in pink. In fact, I believe you should have a gown that is completely pink, Sarah."

Looking both shocked and horrified, Sarah shook her head. "You know I detest pink, Father!" She hurried away, her nose in the air.

"Your Mr. Richfield was here," Father said to me, his eyes bright with mischief. "I told him you have called the engagement off and had run away with one of the footmen."

My heart stopped. He was joking, wasn't he? "What?" I asked, my voice a high pitched squeak. "Father! You didn't!"

"No, I didn't," Father said with a laugh. He paused, and then continued, "I merely explained you were off spending every penny we had, and he should naturally expect you to continue to do the same after the wedding."

That was not any better. I closed my eyes as I covered my face with my hand. "Stop teasing the girl," Mother said chidingly, though her tone was amused. "Take your purchases inside, Diana. You will need to get to work right away if you are going to be ready."

She was right about that. And I knew I would be slowed down by the visits of my betrothed because I didn't want him to see the alterations I had planned for my gowns. As I hurried for the door, I heard Father say, "One down, and only three more to go, Mrs. Forester. Well done."

I glanced over my shoulder in time to see Father kiss Mother's cheek. Those rare moments showed the love between my parents and always warmed my heart. Such was what I hoped my marriage would be.

THERE WAS ONE PERSON I knew I had to tell before the dinner party. Every time I saw Anna, though, there were many people around, and for several days, I did not have the chance to speak a word to her in private. I was thankful that during these times, John managed to behave as he had any other time, so no one suspected anything had changed between us.

Anna, as usual, took matters into her own hands. The day before the dinner party, she arrived on the excuse she was to help me alter my gowns. In the privacy of the sitting room, she and I sat at a table with various trimmings spread out in front of us.

She had only been there for five minutes when she sent a surreptitious look at the door. "Now that we are alone, tell me all, Diana," she said. Holding a piece of ribbon against my dress, she studied the effect for a moment and then tossed it aside. "You are going to a great deal of trouble with this gown for tomorrow night, so I know there is something."

I couldn't keep my cheeks from flaming up. "I want to look my best. Besides, you did just the same when Sir Rodger courted you."

That was all I had to say. Anna's eyes lit up with excitement. "This has to do with Mr. Richfield, doesn't it!" She leaned closer and lowered her voice. "Has he proposed? Or given you a hint he intends to do so?"

"Yes, he has. Proposed, that is," I said, unable to keep a happy smile from my face. "That is why my parents arranged for the dinner party tomorrow, to announce the engagement."

Laughing, Anna reached across the table and embraced me awkwardly. "I'm so happy for you, Diana," she said when she sat back. She balled up a ribbon and threw it at my face. "Why didn't you figure out a way to tell me this before? Why wait until the day before everyone else knows?"

"Well, it was surprisingly difficult to get you alone. Your mother knows us all too well and kept us occupied every time I was at the manor." Anna's penchant for plotting mischief hadn't abated with her marriage, and I had gone along with her too many times in the past.

"You could have sent me a note!"

That was true, and I searched for a reason as to why I hadn't done so. "I've had a great deal on my mind?"

"I'll just bet you have," she said, her voice a good-natured grumble. "It's a good thing we are such good friends; otherwise I might not have forgiven you for keeping this news from me. When I think of how you were the first person outside of my family whom I told about Rodger's proposal."

Raising my eyebrow, I sent an incredulous look at her. "Be that as it may, I recall your mother arriving with the news right before you made it here to tell me. And you had only been engaged for an hour!"

"What plans do you have?" Anna asked, ignoring my response. "I want to help you choose your wedding clothes."

With a slight laugh, I shook my head. "Sorry, my friend," I said. I gestured to the beading I had tacked to my gown. "Where do you think I purchased this? Mother, Sarah, and I went just the other day to get it done."

Anna huffed in disappointment. "I will arrange your bouquet the morning of the wedding then. I will do something with you for this wedding. When are you to be married?"

"John is hoping his mother and sisters will be there, so it will be some weeks. As soon as the date is set, you will be the first person I tell."

"I would hope so."

Silence fell for a moment as I concentrated on attaching my beading to my gown. "Philip is severely disappointed, did you know?" Anna said all of a sudden. "It is the second time this year I've seen him look so crushed."

Looking up, I frowned at her. She couldn't mean her brother already knew about my betrothal. "What do you mean?"

"Do you know why he invited the Reynolds here?" Anna asked, setting aside the ribbon she had been fingering. Puzzled, I shook my head. "He believed the family to be quite wealthy and thought perhaps he would be able to convince her to marry him. He confessed it last night when I demanded to know what was wrong."

Surprised, I took a moment to consider the news. "I never thought your brother was the least bit concerned with marrying an heiress," I finally said. Such an idea would have been at odds with his proposal to me not so long ago! What had changed in the past few months? "And has he given up the pursuit of Miss Reynolds?"

"Naturally. The family is on the verge of being penniless!"

"Penniless?"

Anna nodded. "I overheard Mrs. Reynolds confiding in Mrs. Carter earlier this morning," she said, lowering her tone even more. "I have heard that Mr. Reynolds trusted the advice of a relative and lost a great deal of their money in a business venture. He only heard the news after they arrived here and their lawyer sent him a letter."

I supposed this explained Miss Reynolds' horrid mannerisms. Anna shook her head when I mentioned this. "That child would be bad-tempered whatever circumstance her family is in," she said. "But, that is why she was so furious when her jewels were lost to the highwayman. They cannot be replaced."

That did make sense, and I felt a twinge of pity for her. "Poor girl. That's terrible."

"Only you would feel sorry for that impudent girl," Anna said, sitting back. "I have no idea how I shall bear the rest of her visit with my family. She delights in setting things on their heads, with no respect for the consequences of the things she says. Do you know she made Miss Delan cry yesterday by criticizing her painting?"

"It's only a small part of me that feels sorry for her, and it is for the sake of her father. John says Mr. Reynolds is a clever man, and he is the one I feel sorry for."

Anna raised an eyebrow. "You have had no trouble in referring to your betrothed with such informality, I see," she said with a smile. "And here I thought you would be prim and proper by calling your betrothed 'Mr. Richfield' up until the day you die."

A blush heated up my cheeks, and I threw a ribbon at her. "Aren't you supposed to be helping me?" I asked, changing the subject.

"I am. Do you see anyone else here keeping you company?"

Shaking my head, I didn't see Anna moving to retaliate until all of the gown trimmings landed on my head. "Anna!"

Best friends were almost more trouble than siblings.

THE DAY OF THE DINNER party was a flurry of activity for me. I was Mother's right hand in everything. No doubt she viewed it as practice for when I would plan dinner parties in a household of my own. Sarah found a way to hide from us both, thus getting out of a great deal of work.

"I think this is the largest dinner party we have ever held here," I said as I dressed. My gown of pale green, embroidered with tiny pink flowers at the hem, had turned out well with the silver beading I had added to it. "We shall be bursting at the seams I should imagine."

"A success, then." Sarah fixed her hair at the dressing table. "I'm surprised at just how many people were invited."

"The house party at the Knighton's did increase the guest list, but of course it would have been rude not to invite everyone there," I said, struggling to fasten my gown. I gave up after several minutes of struggle. "Sarah, could you help me?"

Sighing, Sarah twisted away from the mirror and made quick work of the fastenings. She returned to the mirror. "Miss Reynolds will make herself extremely disagreeable, you know. And I cannot save you from her on every occasion."

"When have you ever had to save me?"

"More times than I care to admit." She tugged a lock of her hair free to hang along her face and admired the effect. "Well, I suppose this will have to do. It won't matter once we start to dance."

In her white nankeen gown and her hair in ringlets around her face, Sarah appeared older than what she was. She held herself with confidence, more so than I'd seen from her before. "You look lovely," I said, stepping up behind her to look in the mirror with her. "I imagine if you ever go to London, you will break many a young man's heart."

"Don't be ridiculous."

"You're right. Your sharp tongue would frighten half the dandies away!"

Spinning around, Sarah swatted at me. "Go downstairs and see to your party."

It was true I did have to check everything one final time. Reminded of this fact, I left the bedroom. Hearing voices in the drawing room, I hurried down to check the state of the dining room. Every place setting was exactly as it should be, and Cook was quick to shoo me out of the kitchen with assurances all was well.

Breathing out slowly, I walked towards the drawing room. From here on out, I had to hope everything would run smoothly. With that, I opened the door and entered. The rest of my family was there, and the Sandwoods had arrived early as they usually did.

Mr. Richfield was with them. I allowed my lips to curve in response to the delighted smile he gave me. He walked over to be by my side, reaching his hand out to take mine. "Miss Forester, you look lovely tonight," he said, bringing my hand up to his lips.

"That's Richfield for you!" Miss Sandwood said in an overdramatic way. "Charming whenever he wishes to be. Take care you don't allow him to break your heart, Miss Forester!"

Clearly, Sarah had managed to keep from telling her friend of my engagement so she could not know how foolish her words were.

"I would never intentionally break Miss Forester's heart," John said to the room as he led me away from the doorway.

I accepted a small glass of something my mother held out to me. "I fear I would have her brothers to answer to if I did!"

Both of my brothers lifted their heads, neither of them looking in the least bit intimidating. "I believe it would be Sarah you would have to watch out for if you were to break her sister's heart," Mother said with a calm smile.

Everyone's attention went to Sarah, even mine. Was that true? Would Sarah be the one to be dealt with if such an occasion were to arise? "Why shouldn't I look after my sister?" Sarah asked defensively. "Goodness knows she needs it sometimes."

"I do not!" I said in protest.

Thankfully, Mrs. Davison arrived just then. She, I knew, would be thrilled beyond words when she learned. That was why I had insisted she be included in the dinner party. Everyone from the house party arrived right behind her and the drawing room felt filled to the brim.

Somehow, John managed to stay by my side through all the greetings. There was an almost proprietary air about him. No one seemed to notice it but me, though.

The entire Reynolds family seemed to be quiet for once, which didn't surprise me now I knew more of their situation. Anna was lively, anticipating the news revealed that night. Philip Knighton, on the other hand, behaved in a brooding manner and I was shocked he had attended at all.

John escorted me to dinner, where I had made sure he sat next to me. The conversation, for once, did not center on the highwayman. It revolved around the activities the Knighton house party had enjoyed so far.

When the meal neared its end, Mother caught my eye and raised her eyebrow. I took a deep breath and nodded. Under the table, John's hand closed around mine and squeezed it gently. Mother surreptitiously nodded to Father.

Clearing his throat, Father rose. "If I could have your attention," he said, raising his voice to be heard. Slowly, everyone became quiet, their attention going to my father. "I have an announcement to make.

"This week Mr. John Richfield made an offer of marriage to my oldest daughter, Diana, and was accepted. Please join me in wishing the couple much joy."

A murmur spread down the table, and though my face felt like it was on fire, I couldn't keep from smiling. Out of the corner of my eye, I saw Miss Reynolds scowl. She took the news just as badly as I had expected, though I could feel some sympathy for her. For good reason, she had targeted my now betrothed as her choice of husband and had now lost all hope of securing him.

Just down the table, Philip stared at me in open astonishment. His gaze met mine and he shook his head. My smile faded as I tried to figure out what he meant. Before I could work it out, though, Mother stood up to lead all of the ladies out. Richfield squeezed my hand once more before letting me go. I braced myself for the congratulations I knew would come flooding my way in minutes.

"YOUR MR. RICHFIELD looks like a remarkably handsome man, Miss Forester. You are to be congratulated!"

Not so long ago I had been saying words of a similar nature to a young lady in London. And now I heard them said to me in various forms. I did not have much success in coming up with clever replies. Much like the young lady in London, all I seemed to be capable of doing was smiling happily at whoever spoke to me.

Barely ten minutes after the ladies all left the dining room, I was surprised when the door opened. "That was quick," I said to Anna as James was the first of the men to come in.

"Who would dare to keep a newly engaged man from his future bride?"

However, John wasn't among them. And neither was Mr. Knighton or Philip. I remained against the wall with Anna while the gentlemen scattered throughout the room. Sarah sat up straighter at her harp, and I frowned. She'd never been concerned with her posture when she played.

Not surprising was how Anna caught my look. "Diana, have you even been paying attention to what's been happening around you?" she asked as her husband came to join us. "You are not the only one who has had their head turned."

Sarah? Who could it possibly be? I searched the gathered gentlemen, but couldn't pick out any specific gentleman giving my sister any particular attention. She had acted strangely a few times, and now that I thought about it, each occurence had been when the gentlemen had been in our presence. Why hadn't I realized this before?

On the other hand, I did see James bending down to speak to Miss Delan. I had never seen my brother show particular interest in a young lady before, and I wasn't sure what to think of it. Miss Delan was a lovely young lady, but I didn't know her well at all. Was she worthy of James' attention?

"Careful, Diana," Anna said with a soft laugh. "You're getting a calculating look in your eye. Let your siblings have their courtships."

"Or give them as much grief as they have undoubtedly given you in the past," Sir Rodger said with a grin.

I laughed. "They have given me plenty of ideas."

Miss Reynolds stepped beside me. "You must tell me your secret, Miss Forester." I had to take a deep breath before I could face her. She, of course, had the elder Miss Carter at her side. "I underestimated you in London. You must tell us how you manage to acquire such a man as Richfield. It is obvious the unattached ladies here are in need of your wisdom."

Not a word of what she said was sincere. "I'm afraid I have no secret to share, Miss Reynolds," I said, determined to be pleasant. I would not insult a guest in my parents home. At least not if I knew I would get caught. "I am sure you have every skill you need to find yourself a husband."

"Your mother wishes to speak to you," Mr. Reynolds said to his daughter, walking up to us. The young lady opened her mouth as if to protest. "Georgina, do as I ask, please. I wish to speak to Miss Forester."

Unsure what to expect, I remained where I was as everyone else walked away. "Congratulations, my dear," Mr. Reynolds said, taking my hands in his. "Speaking as a friend of Richfield's, I can tell you that you have found yourself a good man."

"Thank you. I hope I can deserve him."

"I think you shall," he said, releasing my hands. "I trust Richfield's judgment is flawless in choosing his lifelong partner."

Embarrassed, I managed a smile. Happily, I saw John come into the room then. "Mr. Reynolds," he said, giving a respectful nod as he approached. "Miss Forester."

That formality made me smile. "Let's have some music!" Anna said loudly. "Mrs. Davison, you must play for us!"

"With pleasure, my dear Anna," Mrs. Davison said in her cheerful way. "While I may not be able to dance as I once did, my fingers are more than agile enough to provide you with the music you need to entertain yourselves."

"May I have this dance?" John asked as my brothers were put to work clearing the room for the dancing.

"Of course."

I wasn't surprised to see James ask Miss Delan to dance. But the gentleman who asked Sarah did surprise me: Mr. Ward, the gentleman we had met with Philip Knighton. He towered over my sister, being even taller than James and Will.

Speaking of Will, I spotted my younger brother cajoling Mr. Reynolds into a game of piquet. "I wonder if I should warn Mr. Reynolds not to underestimate Will," I said, looking over at John.

He laughed. "Who do you think taught me?" he asked, leaning to whisper in my ear.

My breath caught as a shiver went down my spine. Mrs. Davison began playing the introduction to a lively tune, and we all fell into lines. I felt relief and lose at the space required between Mr. Richfield and me for the dance. We stood at the head of the lines to lead the dance. It was a position I had never been in before, and it made me nervous to be in such a place of honor. I could only hope I wouldn't trip over my own feet with everyone's attention on me. To distract myself, I glanced around the room and noticed something strange.

"Is something wrong?" John asked with concern.

"Mr. Philip Knighton isn't here."

"Yes, he said he had some correspondence that could not wait."

Once again, Philip behaved in a manner that showed just how thoughtless he could be. What could possibly be so important he could not leave until tomorrow? I heaved a sigh right before the first steps of the dance began. Forcing aside the disappointment I felt over my old friend, I focused on my betrothed, smiling at him. For that moment, everything just right with the world.

Chapter Eighteen

The next morning, everyone was slow to get around. Breakfast was quiet. It wasn't until I went to the garden to get some flowers to brighten up the house some that I had an actual conversation with one of my siblings.

"So now you're officially engaged to a highwayman," Sarah said, tossing a blossom at my basket with little care. Though Mother had asked us to arrange some bouquets, I suspected it more likely she wished us to get some fresh air.

"Sarah, put the flowers in the basket, if you please," I said with a sigh, reaching over to rescue the poor bloom. "And I am not engaged to a highwayman."

"Well, you don't know, do you?" Sarah yawned and tilted her head to face the sun. "You haven't talked to him about this. You haven't asked for the truth. You don't know." She paused and then added, "Unless when you did so, you discovered I was right, and have kept this from me."

Groaning, I cut another daisy. "Oh, that," I said, striving for a careless tone. "I had quite forgotten."

"Liar."

I made a face, choosing not to argue the point. "It doesn't matter, does it? John and I are to be married."

"So it's John now, is it?"

"To me, yes. You, though, will respect propriety and refrain from addressing him in so informal a manner."

Sarah hummed a thoughtful note. "I suppose I shouldn't be surprised. After all, he was calling you 'Diana' far earlier."

Why were we talking about how I referred to my betrothed and he to me? That's right. Because I didn't want to talk about whether or not he was the highwayman. I wasn't at all sure this was a better subject.

"You know, I will miss this," I said, not even aware I would say it until it left my lips. Sarah glanced at me in confusion. "Talking to you like this about whatever is on our minds. Whenever no one else is around to overhear us."

She stared at me for a moment. "The sun is too much for you," Sarah said, looking slightly concerned. "You should put your bonnet on or go inside."

"Sarah, I'm serious." Why was it every time I said something sentimental, everyone became concerned? "For all the times we cannot get on, I want you to know I wouldn't trade you for anyone else."

It wasn't often I admitted to being even remotely fond of my sister. She had better remember this moment because it wouldn't come again. And hopefully, I would think back on it with amusement, even though she deliberately tried to provoke a fight.

It was wishful thinking on my part.

"Diana!" I got to my feet in answer to Mother's call. "Mr. Richfield is here to take you riding."

Riding? Had we made plans and I had forgotten? "He's what?" I said in my oh-so-clever way. Sarah snickered, and I had an impulse to kick her. "Riding?"

"Yes, Diana. It's what you do when you are on a horse," Sarah said. "Surely you've heard of the past-time?"

"He says he has a surprise for you," Mother said, ignoring Sarah's sarcastic statement.

That had my attention. Thrusting my basket of flowers at Sarah, I hurried towards the door. "What kind of surprise?" I asked, pulling off the apron I had been wearing to protect my gown. "Did he tell you what it is?"

"Perhaps," Mother said with a smile. He had! I could tell! "But you will not get a hint from me. Now, hurry up and get ready. It wouldn't do to keep him waiting."

It wasn't often I had an opportunity to wear a riding habit. Anna had given one to me several years ago after she'd bought a new one, and it had been altered to fit me. Sarah had spent days in a jealous fit because it was the most elegant thing in either of our wardrobes. She didn't know I intended on leaving it for her when I married. After all, I would be getting a new one in a lovely deep blue.

I tried to get changed as fast as I could but only ended up slowing myself down as I became tangled in the fabric. Finally, I was able to pin the hat on, thankful beyond words the lump had faded and no longer gave me any problems. Checking my appearance in the mirror, I nodded in satisfaction.

John was in the hall talking to Father. I allowed a smile to curve my lips as they focused on me. "That's one thing you will have to become accustomed to, Richfield," Father said, the mischief sparkling in his eyes. "Waiting for your lady to be ready."

"Father!" I knew I should expect such teasing from my father, but in front of my betrothed was embarrassing! "Please!"

"I'm sure I will manage to survive such a trial, sir," Richfield said with a laugh. He held his arm out to me. "I shall have her back to you soon."

I was surprised when Father followed us out. Our groom was holding the bridles of two horses. The large black one I dimly recalled Richfield bringing me home on. The smaller white horse next to it must be for me.

Having little horse sense, I was careful to approach the horses. "Hello, beautiful," I said to the white horse as it nudged my arm. I stroked its nose. "You are friendly, aren't you?"

"Do you like Lady Juliet?" Richfield asked, a hint of nervousness in his tone.

Glancing over at him, I laughed. "Lady Juliet? Is that a reference to Shakespeare? Yes, she's lovely. She looks like a perfect lady."

"She's yours. Lady Juliet is my gift to you."

Shocked, I stared at him. "Mine?" He'd bought me a horse? I could hardly believe it. Richfield nodded, clearly delighted to have surprised me. Impulsively, I threw my arms around him. "Thank you!"

Chuckling, he hugged me back, lifting me off my feet for a moment. Father cleared his throat loudly. "You're not married yet," he said. Face burning bright red, I jerked free of John's embrace. "You should be on your way," my father reminded, looking amused by the whole situation.

John was the one to help me up and adjusted the stirrup. I remembered to wave goodbye to Father as I rode away from home. "Where are we going?" I asked, looking over at my escort.

"You'll see."

AS IF TO CONFUSE ME, Richfield chose an aimless course across the countryside. But he didn't take into account I knew this county like the back of my hand. I recognized the orchard Mr. Davison had taken such pride in before he died. We crossed the creek at a different place but we were still headed to the east. We were drawing closer to the Knighton estate with every step we went, a fact I was not particularly pleased to think of.

The further we rode, though, I realized we were headed straight for a small estate the Knightons had purchased alongside their family estate five years ago. I held my tongue since my betrothed had wanted to surprise me with something there. Still, why would he be taking me there?

"I had a letter from my mother this morning."

Pulled out of my wonderings about what John had planned, I frowned. "Not bad news, I hope."

"She looks forward to meeting you," Richfield said quickly. He hesitated, and my concern grew. "She did express some concerns we have not known each other long. That we —I— might be rushing into this engagement without properly considering everything."

"I see."

"When she meets you, she will adore you, I am sure of it. How could she not?"

How could I not be delighted by his confidence that I would get on with his mother? "I'm looking forward to meeting her and your sisters."

"It won't be long before you will."

Clearing my throat, I sought a way to change the subject. "Oh, look! It's the Vanderson estate."

We had arrived at the front gate of the estate. "Yes, this is what I wanted to show you," Richfield said with a smile. He led the way down the lane, going through the open gate.

There were servants hard at work all along the lane leading up to the house, and they all nodded respectfully as John and I rode past them. I couldn't keep from frowning in puzzlement. The Knightons had purchased the estate but had never done anything with it. Why the sudden need for repairs?

"Do you not like the Vanderson estate?"

Was that worry in his voice? "I don't know." I paused and then tried to explain. "I mean, I do like the house. What I have seen of it. Which is only the outside. There has never been an opportunity for me to think on the matter any further than that."

A relieved smile appeared on John's face as we neared the house. It was more of a cottage, one of the more modest homes in the county. The windows were open, and I could see several maids moving inside.

"You've never been inside then?" Richfield asked as he dismounted. He moved to help me down.

"No, I haven't," I said honestly. The Vanderson house had last been occupied by the elderly and grumpy, Mr. Vanderson, who had died five years ago. His surviving relatives had promptly sold the estate to the Knightons.

"Then, let me be the first to show you," Richfield said, holding his arm out to me.

There was a slight musty smell as we walked in. The rooms were light and airy. Richfield had something positive to say about every room we entered, something to point out to me. He made sure I noticed the intricate details in the molding, and then remarked on the view from the window, though i'm not sure why he was so delighted with a view of the stableyard.

"What do you think?" he asked when we once again stood in the entrance hall.

"It's even more lovely than I had ever imagined," I said, looking around once again.

"I can't tell you how happy I am to hear that. I bought it." My heart stopped, and I brought my attention back to him. "I knew you would want to be at least within riding distance of your family. Mr. Knighton was willing to negotiate, and we completed the business last night."

So that's why he and Mr. Knighton had not joined us in the drawing room with everyone else. It took me a moment to realize exactly what he had done for me. He'd bought a house for me, not far from Mother and Father. I wouldn't be completely separated from my family when I married, but there would be enough distance for me to start the next chapter of my life. It was, quite simply, perfect.

"I—I thought you already had an estate."

"I do, but it is much smaller than this one," Richfield said, looking and sounding pleased with himself. "I knew it would make you happy to be close to your family and the investment is a sound one."

Tears welled up in my eyes as I covered my mouth with my fingers. A laugh bubbled up as my betrothed began to look concerned. "It's perfect." For the second time that day, I threw myself at him, winding my arms around his neck. "Thank you!"

My face ended up close to his, and the scent of his cologne—a tangy lemon, a far cry from the bay rum scent I'd smelled on my father— filled my senses. His pulse beat in his neck and I swallowed hard, a feeling of nervousness overtaking me. Slowly, I lifted my gaze until my eyes locked with his.

Everything else, the sound of the repairs, faded away. John's eyes shifted to my lips, and he lowered his head. For a moment, I felt his warm breath on my lips. "I would like to kiss you now," he said, his voice low.

And then, he did. His lips pressed against mine and my eyes closed. His left hand came up on my back and pulled me closer to him.

Something clattered nearby, and we broke apart. My eyes must have been as wide as saucers, and I couldn't look away from him. It took me a moment to regain my balance. I cleared my throat after several seconds.

"I should return home," I said, my voice unsteady. If I stayed here, I knew I would definitely kiss him again.

"Right," Richfield said, sounding just as off balance as I felt. "Of course. Your father warned me he would count the minutes until I returned you."

"How long did he give you before he would start a search?"

"About four hours."

That long? Odd. I would have expected Father to make it a bit more of an impossible time limit. A great deal can happen in four hours. "How long has it been?" I asked, glancing around in vain for a clock. It felt like it had been no time at all since we had arrived.

Richfield pulled his watch out. "Three hours." His eyes met mine.

I definitely needed to get back home. Mother would need to be told, and we should start planning for my new home. There was no doubt much advice I would need to take note of for running my own household, and—.

"I didn't show you the garden," Richfield said all of a sudden, interrupting my thoughts.

Any idea of returning home vanished. "I would love to see it!"

"YOUR FATHER WON'T BE angry, will he?" Richfield asked when we were finally riding back.

We were going to be at least an hour late. The garden at Vanderson Cottage had provided several little nooks where Mr. Richfield could steal a kiss. I considered the situation carefully. "No, I don't think so. But there's been no situation that can serve as a basis of comparison, so I can't be completely certain."

Richfield laughed. "You're so amusing sometimes, Diana."

Making a face, I focused on the bridge we were crossing: the place where I had been attacked. "I wish I could remember what happened here," I said softly. What was it I had picked up and then lost? I knew it was important, but my mind wasn't cooperating!

"You will. Even if you don't, I will never let anything happen to you. There hasn't been sign of the man since then, besides one last attack on Mr. Sandwood. Perhaps the search your father and every other man has made finally convinced the man he ought to take himself elsewhere."

He could speak of it so calmly. Was that the proof he wasn't the villain of the story?

"Sarah said it was you." I hadn't meant to say it. I had sworn not to think about it at all. There was no truth in it.

Richfield gave a startled laugh. "She did?" he asked. "She thought I was the highwayman? Why?"

It made me laugh to think of the whole thing. Had it only been a few weeks since Sarah had made me so furious with her wild theory? "She became suspicious when you said you were in Bath at the time of the highwayman terrorizing the gentry there. It just spiraled from there. I had such a hard time keeping her from telling people."

"The interrogations she's put me through have been because of this?"

There was a strange note in his voice, and I focused on him again to see a frown on his face. "Yes," I said slowly. "She,

Miss Sandwood, and Will were all set on proving the theory."

"Well, I suppose that explains why the Sandwoods and the Knightons felt the need to write to London about me."

My breath caught in my throat. What? "They did?" was all I could think to stay. Sarah was going to be in so much trouble when I saw her! I knew our parents were aware of it, but Miss Sandwood had obviously talked! "I—I didn't know that."

"Your sister truly believed I was the one to harm you? Why would she have thought that?"

No longer did I think it amusing. Richfield struggled to control his anger. "She said it was because you were there so fast after they found me." Maybe I wouldn't be the one to scold Sarah. John's eyes were narrowed, his forehead furrowed. He wouldn't "She didn't mean anything by it! It was just idle speculation!"

"Idle speculation?" Richfield scoffed. "Did she have no care to what 'speculation' can do to a man's reputation?"

"You weren't supposed to find out," I said before I could think better of it. I shouldn't have said a word. How this had become so negative, I didn't understand, but I had to try to smooth over the damage. I'd been incensed when Sarah had first mentioned the matter, but I'd never dreamed John would be *this* angry. "No one was! It was to go no further than Sarah and Miss Sandwood."

His gaze landed on me. "But you knew? This whole time?"

"Yes, but I did everything I could to keep her from speaking of it!"

"Did you not think I would need to know this?"

"It was just a theory! I didn't think anyone would have believed her!" I said defensively. "I didn't believe her when she told me."

"When she told you." His eyes narrowed. "But you did believe her at some point."

"No! Of course not. I tried to prove your innocence to her."

"'Tried to prove'? Then, you didn't succeed? You still accepted my offer, thinking I was a man who would purposely harm you," Richfield said, his tone a mix of disbelief and fury. "Did you imagine I would be the only man to ever offer for you? Were you so desperate to be married you would accept a man under suspicion of being a criminal?"

Desperate? Me? "Why would you ask me that?" I asked, feeling my temper rising. "I accepted you because—."

"But that's what you did, didn't you?" John said, interrupting me. "You accepted my offer despite knowing what was thought of me. Was it because of my family's wealth? Was the money worth the risk of marrying a criminal? "

Tears of anger, and not joy as they had been a few hours before, filled my eyes. It was what I had done, but not for the reasons he implied! "No," was all I could choke out. What could I say? "That is not why I accepted you."

"You believed I would hurt you?"

It was clear he was in no temper to listen to me. Or, at least, he wouldn't believe a word I said. I couldn't even think straight anymore.

Regardless of the safety of such a move, I slid out of my saddle. My skirt caught on the pommel, and I ended up hit-ting the ground. Lady Juliet was kind enough not to move as I struggled to my feet. I was sure to have bruises from that. I jerked my skirt free, ignoring the sound of cloth ripping at my actions, and began to run for my family home.

"Diana!"

He was following me. "Just go!" I said sharply, spinning to face him one last time. "I'm sorry you were hurt. I'm sorry you believe me to a fortune hunter. Think the worst of me! I cannot stop you!"

"Diana, what's wrong?" James was rushing towards me. I hadn't realized I was so close to home, but I was. "What happened?"

Tears were streaming down my face, and I made no move to brush them away. I had nothing to say to my brother, even if I didn't feel choked. Whirling back around, I ran past James. Barely slowing, I pulled the door open in my rush to get to my room.

I heard Sarah call after me, but I definitely did not want to speak to her. Throwing myself onto my bed, I buried my face in a pillow. How could Richfield think such things about me? Why had I brought the subject up? Should I have let the matter die with my engagement to him?

Never had I felt so miserable.

"Diana, Mr. Richfield has gone." Mother. It felt like it had been hours since I'd feld from John, but it could only have been a matter of minutes. Mother sat beside me on the bed, her hand on my shoulder. I twisted my head to look at her. "Your brother managed not to provoke a fight in defense of your honor. Now, dry your eyes and tell me what has happened."

"It was terrible," I said, rubbing my face. "He said such awful things." Well, I couldn't assign all the blame to him. "And it's all my fault!"

"Tell me."

Mother would help me make everything right. So I told her everything.

Chapter Nineteen

To her credit, Mother listened patiently as I poured out the whole situation to her. "It seems to me what we have here is a miscommunication," she said when I finally ran out of things to say and just sat there sniffing in what I'm sure was a pathetic way. "On both sides."

"Miscommunication?"

Firmly, she nodded. "I understand you wanted to make a clean breast of things, and if it had been bothering you so much, it was quite right of you, but simply running away as you did was not wise."

"But he wouldn't listen to me!"

"Were you listening to him?"

I paused, rubbing the side of my head. I had such a headache. "Yes, I was. He said such angry things."

"He spoke in anger, but he had reason to do so," Mother said, her tone gentle. "His reputation has been tarnished. The Sandwoods are friends of his family, and they felt the need to investigate whether he was respectable or not. That cannot be easy for a man to learn. And then to learn his betrothed has had doubts about his character as well?"

Fresh tears welled up. "But I didn't doubt his character, which I tried to explain to him. I tried to prove he was innocent. What am I to do?"

"You and he must sit down and discuss this as the rational adults you are," Mother said. Groaning, I covered my face with my hands. "Tomorrow, we dine with the Sandwoods. You can put all things straight between you then."

"I never should have listened to Sarah! Why did she have to say such ridiculous things and ruin everything?"

Perhaps it was wrong of me to blame my sister. Sighing, Mother got to her feet. "But you did listen to her, Diana, and after you were warned you not to do so. You knew better than to let her imagination affect you. Sadly, this is the consequence you must face."

I was reminded of the first argument with Richfield I had ever had. He had said I would allow my siblings to lead me into trouble and the idea had annoyed me at the time. Though, it hadn't been the trouble he could have been referring to, how right he had been! I was such a fool.

Sitting up, I rubbed my face. "Did James try to defend my honor?" I asked, remembering what Mother had said earlier.

"Your father managed to keep him from doing anything he would regret later on," Mother said with a slight smile. "Wash your face. Your father will want to talk to you once I have explained the situation to him."

That would not be an enjoyable conversation. I nodded, and Mother left the room. Pulling the pins from my hair, I took off my riding hat. Going to the water basin, I poured out some water and splashed it on my face.

"Diana?"

I forced myself to take a deep breath before I faced my sister. "Sarah," I said quietly, rubbing my face dry. Folding the towel, I replaced it on the stand.

"I overheard what you and Mother were talking about," she said slowly.

Of course, she had. And there was nothing I had to say in answer. "I know you think this is my fault," she said. She wasn't wrong, and I still had nothing to say to her. "I just want to tell you I'm sorry."

Sorry? After everything that had just happened, that she had just heard, "sorry" was all she had to say? I felt a sharp burst of anger but then felt too tired to argue with her. All I could do was stare and hope she would leave.

"Please don't look at me like that."

Still, I had nothing to say, and I shifted my gaze to the hat in my hand. "For goodness sake, Diana, say something!" Sarah said, her tone sharp.

"What do you want me to say?" I asked equally as sharp. I threw my hat at the bed and watched as it bounced to the ground.

"Tell me what you're thinking!"

DIdn't she realize that was a dangerous topic? "That would not be wise." My poor hat. It was not to blame for what had happened. I stooped to pick it up and dust it off. "I have nothing to say to you, Sarah."

Sarah stood in the doorway and stared at me for several moments. "Fine," she finally said. She spun around and slammed the door shut behind her.

What a mess this had all become! My movements slow, I changed out of my dirty riding habit into a clean gown. Inspecting my knees, I discovered bruises forming from my un-graceful dismount. I sighed again and shook my head.

It served me right.

WHEN FATHER SAT ME down in the library, all he asked was what had happened. Instantly, my composure broke, and I started crying again. It took longer to tell him than it had for Mother and I could only be grateful Father was the most patient man I had ever known. He heaved a sigh when I finally came to an end.

"Your mother told me what she has advised, and I agree with her assessment," he told me as I wiped away my tears. "You have been foolish, Diana."

"Yes, I know, sir," I said quietly, for how could I argue with my father? I hesitated. I needed to know one thing. "Mr. Richfield said Mr. Sandwood and Mr. Knighton wrote to London about him because of the rumors being spread. Is this true?"

Again, Father sighed. "They mentioned they intended to do so, though they did not give an exact reason behind it."

I covered my face with my hands. No wonder Richfield had been so furious. "I should have told him sooner."

"Diana, if you recall your mother and I advised you not to do so." Father shook his head. "Looking back, perhaps that is not the advice we ought to have given you. Still, I don't think there would have been any time he would have taken it well. The whole thing seems to have been blown out of proportion. "

With that, Father dismissed me. I left the library, astonished there was still some daylight left. I went to the drawing room and sat down at my pianoforte in the hopes some music would calm me. At least, it would give me something to focus on other than my problems.

I found the most complicated piece of music I had and set up the sheets in order. Working through the notes, I increased my tempo each time I began. Learning the piece kept me from overthinking.

"I figured this is where you would be."

Will. In the middle of the piece, I stopped playing. "Is there something you want?" I asked, straightening the music to keep from looking at him. After all, he had played a small part in this whole thing.

"Sarah thinks you hate her," Will said as he leaned against the pianoforte.

That made me look up. "She does?" I asked. My brother nodded, and I sighed. "I don't hate her, Will, but I am perilously close to it."

"I wanted to see James hit Richfield."

Of course, he had. I couldn't stop a bitter laugh from leaving my throat. "Forgive me if I say I am glad he did not hit my husband-to-be."

"Are you sure you can still call him your 'husband to be?'" Will asked, his expression holding disappointment. "From what I heard, you and he fought."

I couldn't tell if his reaction was a little-seen brotherly instinct of 'no one makes my sister angry except me' or if he only because he wanted to see a fistfight. "We may have fought, but that doesn't mean I want you or James to hit him for me," I said firmly. "We're still going to be married, you know."

"Really? Because I thought you told Richfield to leave."

My hands came down on the pianoforte keys, making a loud crash of noise. He was right. That's precisely what I had said! I dropped my head to my arms. I hadn't meant it! "What have I done?"

"James and I can kidnap him if you want."

"You will not kidnap anyone!"

Will gave an exaggerated sigh. "I just thought you should know we would. You ought to get ready for dinner, you know."

Dinner? How was I supposed to dress for dinner as if nothing had happened? And yet, I knew I would have to. Life moved on. Whatever happened, life continued at its usual pace. Sighing, I got to my feet. "Yes, I know."

I THINK I WAS THE FIRST one ready to leave the next evening. After a day of uncertainty, I was anxious to be able to talk to Richfield. I sincerely hoped he would forgive me and be willing to move past this misunderstanding.

"She's as bad as when she first came home from London," Sarah said on the ride over. "I hope when someone courts me, one of you will slap me if I ever start acting like this."

"Sarah, that is enough," Mother said immediately.

"I'll slap her!" Will said at the same moment. He lifted his hand in demonstration.

"You better not!" Sarah said, horrified at the idea.

Closing my eyes, I leaned my head against the side of the carriage. I was more than ready to be free of the small space when we arrived at the Sandwoods. The moment I stepped into the drawing room, I searched the room, reminded of when I had sought Richfield at the musical soiree in London.

And just as it had been in London, he wasn't there.

"Is Richfield not joining us?" Father asked. I was so thankful he asked the question and not me. I wasn't sure if I would have been able to find my voice to do it.

Mr. Sandwood frowned as he handed my father a filled glass. "Did you not know? Richfield had to leave us this morning. I could have sworn he said he would tell you of it. He couldn't say when he would return."

"But the Knighton ball is in a few days," I heard Sarah say in a whisper.

He had left. Just as I had told him to the day before. My heart felt like it was breaking, but I couldn't let anyone see it. Swallowing hard, I lifted my head. "Miss Sandwood, did you finish the watercolor you were working on at the picnic?" I asked. My voice was steady. Good. "I would love to see it."

There was a look of pity on Miss Sandwood's face. If there was anything I hated, it was pity. "Of course, Miss Forester," she said. "It's right over here. I will be more than happy to show you."

Through sheer force of will, I was able to admire her work and make appropriate comments on her brush strokes. I also carried on entire conversations during the meal. I don't remember what I said, but I know I kept up my end of the subject.

It wasn't until the ladies were sitting in the drawing room I found myself alone for a brief moment. I stood at the window looking out over the garden. Not for the first time, I cursed inwardly at the unfortunate lack of control I'd had over my temper. Never had it gotten me in trouble over something as important as this before.

I had finally fallen in love with a man who fit in well with my family. My dearest friend approved of the match. And I destroyed whatever good impression he had of me by not warning him of my sister's wild talk.

How would I recover from this?

I felt something wet on my cheek and realized I was crying. Wiping my face, I took a deep breath, hoping no one had noticed the crack in my composure. Somehow, I had to keep myself under control until I got home. In my room, I could cry my heart out, but not until then.

"Diana, why don't you play us that piece you have been practicing since yesterday?" Mother said, getting my attention. When I glanced over, there was compassion and understanding in her eyes.

"Yes, of course," I said, forcing a smile. "I would be happy to."

There was no doubt in my mind I would someday hate this particular piece of music. Typically, I preferred Haydn over Beethoven, but I had been playing this piece over and over all day, hoping the complex movements would distract me.

In the end, it hadn't. I was just extremely good at playing it now.

Miss Sandwood had the original sheet music I had copied, and she located it for me. "Don't worry, Miss Forester," she said in a kind voice. "You are engaged to Mr. Richfield, are you not? Then, you can with all propriety receive letters from him. I am sure that is what will happen. He will write you to explain everything."

A letter? I could not hope for that, not after the angry words we had exchanged. Taking the music from her, I set the sheets up in order. "Thank you, Miss Sandwood," I said. She walked away, shaking her head. Taking a deep breath, I began to play. At that moment, nothing mattered but performing the song flawlessly.

NO LETTER FROM MR. Richfield came for me.

Without acknowledging I was doing so, I waited for five days. I even contemplated writing to him, and had begun writing it but only crumpled the sheet in frustration before I finished. If I had, though, I had no idea how I would have addressed it. He had never told me the name of his family's estate and his rooms in London had not been owned by him.

There was nothing I could do except wait and hope he came back to me.

On the second day of waiting, Mother asked if I wanted to talk about it.

I did not.

By the third day, Father asked if I wanted to talk about it.

I had no inclination then either.

Through it all, Will didn't ask how I felt. He was extra nice to me, though, which would have been alarming if I had given it any thought. As it was, I didn't acknowledge the change in his behavior.

Every now and then, James would put his arm around my shoulders whenever he saw me, giving me a half-hearted hug. I suppose he meant to be comforting, which was on the same level as Will being sweet.

Sarah also didn't ask any questions. Then again, she was undoubtedly more aware than everyone else I was miserable. We shared the same bed, so she heard my crying each night. Though I was still angry with her, I appreciated she didn't say anything about it. She chattered more than usual, so that helped keep up the pretense. I guess in her own way my sister tried to do me a favor. Maybe she felt guilty about what had happened, and this was her way of making it up to me.

The hardest person to be around was Anna. I didn't want to tell her what had happened, because what if he came back? She was more than capable of being disagreeable if she thought it was deserved. And she never took it well when her friends were upset.

So I pretended all was fine. My heart wasn't in the alterations I had to do to my ball gown. The only reason I finished attaching the blue ribbons to the dress was due to Anna, Miss Delan, and Miss Elizabeth Carter frequently visiting. We were all working on our dresses together, and I kept my hands busy with sewing.

By the day of the ball, though, they knew something wasn't right. "Is Vanderson Cottage in such a terrible state your Mr. Richfield must spend all his time there?" Anna asked out of nowhere. "I can think of no other reason we haven't seen him among the other gentlemen of the house party."

She made a point of not looking at me. Apparently, Miss Sandwood had at long last learned not to gossip otherwise everyone would have known what had happened. "What an odd question!" Sarah said. "Diana and I haven't joined the ladies in many days, and you aren't commenting on that. Why single out poor Mr. Richfield?"

"I thought for sure we would see him here, too," Anna said stubbornly as if Sarah hadn't spoken. "After all, not too long ago you were complaining he was always underfoot."

My relief at having Sarah deflect the question shifted to annoyance, and I glanced at her. Sarah's cheeks flushed red with embarrassment. "I think maybe you should just worry about your own business, Lady Carlyle," Sarah said in a sharp tone.

Miss Delan and Miss Elizabeth gasped at the rudeness of Sarah's statement. "You're keeping something from me," Anna said, not taking offense. She was more than used to Sarah's sharp tongue. "I see how it is. I shall figure it out."

I was very much afraid she would do so. Sarah's response had only piqued Anna's curiosity, and convinced my friend that there was something to discover.

When Sarah and I were dressing, I couldn't resist saying as much. "You should not have challenged her in such a way. She would have moved on to something else if you had left it alone."

"While she is not my best friend, I do know her well, Diana." Sarah sat patiently while I arranged her hair. "She wouldn't have left without learning the truth. I have delayed it for a while."

"And what shall I say when he is not at the ball tonight?"

Sarah sighed. "Maybe he will be there."

"Wishful thinking, Sarah." I wove the last of the flowers into her hair. "There. You're ready."

"You haven't left yourself much time," Sarah said, standing up. She faced me, her eyes narrowed with suspicion. "You are going with us, Diana."

"Yes, I know," I said with little enthusiasm. I had briefly considered crying off, claiming a headache, but I knew Mother would never have allowed it. "I have left myself plenty of time to get dressed."

Sarah put her hands on her hips. "Have you? I fail to see how you will make yourself look your best in such a short period."

For the first time in several days, I allowed myself a small smile. "I don't believe anyone put you in charge of my appearance, Sarah." I was startled when Sarah pushed me into the chair in front of the dressing table. "What are you doing?"

"Sit still," Sarah said. "Someone has to make sure you look beautiful tonight, and that person is me."

Touched by her concern, I sat there and let her do what she wanted. Whenever she was determined on something, Sarah moved at a quick pace. She hummed as she worked, and grumbled to herself when a curl would not lay as she wished it. Still, Father called up several times for us to hurry up before I finished dressing.

"Whatever happens tonight, no one will say you did not look well," Sarah said when she stepped back.

I glanced down at my white gown, admiring the new blue ribbons I had added. "Of course that is the all-important objective." I arranged the shawl on my shoulders and twisted before the mirror to check my appearance.

"It is important," Sarah said, pushing me towards the door. "Father will leave without us if we don't hurry! Quickly, Diana!"

With more haste than grace, we made our way down to join the rest of the family. It was time to face all our neighbors. What would they be saying? Somehow, I would have to find the fortitude to face whatever I heard.

Chapter Twenty

Knighton Manor was lit up from within, and we could see it from miles away. For the first time, I saw my father relax. I hadn't even realized he had been tense until the moment he relaxed. "Were you worried about something, Father?" I had to ask.

"The highwayman struck again two days ago. A family who were on their way here for the Knightons' ball," Father said seriously. Silence filled our carriage. Clearly, I was not the only one who had not been aware of this. "With everyone dressing their best and wearing their jewels tonight, it was feared there would be many potential targets for the criminal."

Out of the corner of my eye, I saw Sarah sit up straighter. The only thing I could think was that Mr. Richfield had gone, so there was no conceivable way he could be even remotely be construed as the villain behind this crime. Or, I had to wonder, did she imagine it was proof he was involved because he could have returned to the area unnoticed.

Why did it even matter to me anymore? The subject had caused me more than enough grief and heartache.

Stepping out first, Father helped Mother down, and then Sarah and I. James and Will were last. The Manor appeared even more impressive against the darkening sky than it did in broad daylight. It towered in the dark sky, like I imagined a mountain would do.

"Diana, you're going to get left behind," Sarah hissed, pulling my attention from the view to her. The rest of my family was already walking towards the door. "Hurry up! I did not make you look good so that you could stand outside all evening!"

Lifting my skirt, I walked quickly to catch up. A footman relieved me of my shawl in the foyer. There were people everywhere. Mother and Father were quickly drawn into a conversation. Will and James had vanished while I gave up my shawl. How did they manage to do so with such ease?

"If I leave you, you won't try to hide?" Sarah asked, leaning close to my ear so I could hear over the din of conversation and the orchestra playing. "I want to take a turn around the room."

"There are very few places where I could do so" And I'd tried to utilize them in the past for far less important reasons than to avoid explaining where my betrothed was.

"You always manage to disappear somehow," Sarah said. A look of relief appeared on her face. "Oh, look. Here's Anna. Maybe she can keep you from running off."

She slipped off into the crowd as Anna reached me. "Finally," my friend said, linking her arm with mine. "I had begun to think you weren't coming. I have so much to tell you, Diana."

I laughed at her dramatics. "I saw you this afternoon, Anna. I hardly think you have much to tell me that is new."

"The Reynolds' are not here."

Startled, I stared at her. "What?"

Glancing around, Anna pulled me to the side of the room. It was only marginally quieter there. "It happened so fast, while I was visiting you," Anna said, babbling in her eagerness to tell me all. "Mother and Father asked them to leave. I have never been so shocked!"

"Why?" I asked, confused about why the Knightons' would ask their guests to leave on the day of the ball. It must have been something serious. "What happened?"

"Now, you must promise me you won't be angry. It was brought to our attention that Miss Reynolds has been spreading horrible rumors about you."

It was as if there were no ball happening around us as I focused on what Anna was telling me. I wasn't sure I had heard her right. I couldn't possibly have heard what I thought I'd heard. "Miss Reynolds has what?"

"She told anyone who would care to listen you were marrying Richfield for his money because your family expects you to make a brilliant match. It was only by the merest chance Mother overheard her speaking of it to Miss Carter, bragging about just how many people agreed with her!"

Mr. Richfield had asked if I were marrying him for his money. Was Miss Reynolds the source of such an idea? She must have been! Anna had warned me not to get angry, but I couldn't see how I could avoid it! "How dare she? That insufferable girl," I said, clenching my fists. "How many believed her?"

"It doesn't matter," Anna said, trying to soothe me. "She is no longer here."

"Anna. How many?"

My friend sighed, looking as though she regretted telling me. "She would not name any families specifically, but you know we have had most of the neighborhood at the Manor at one time or another in the past three weeks," she said. She hurried on with her story before I could ask for further clarification. "Mr. Reynolds was most apologetic and agreed the best thing to do would be for them to leave. He asked I give you, Richfield, and your family his most sincere apologies."

I took a deep breath, trying to untangle my feelings on learning this. On the one hand, I was furious Miss Reynolds would stoop to such a level. At the same time, I felt pity for her desperation, but I also felt honored the Knightons would take such offense at insults aimed at me.

Mainly, I felt heartbroken to know Richfield had listened to her. Even knowing her character, he had listened to Miss Reynolds' lies. Perhaps not truly believed every word she had said, but he had doubted he knew me because he'd listened to her.

But had I done any different? Struck by this thought, I paused to consider. I'd listened to Sarah, which had caused me to doubt what I knew of him because of what my sister had said. I couldn't make any judgments because I hadn't acted in any better.

"Diana, you look like you're going to cry," Anna said, looking horrified. "All will be mended soon! It doesn't matter what those families believe! Your Richfield knows the truth, and so do your friends!"

Why did she have to say that? This was no time to go into it. "Yes," I said, forcing a smile. "My friends know me."

Anna frowned as if sensing there was still something she didn't know. "Now, let's have some fun tonight," she said, linking arms with me again. "I've made Rodger swear he will dance with you."

I forced a laugh. "Of course you have."

"But not before I have had my dance," Philip Knighton said as he approached. He bowed stiffly. "Would you do me the honor, Miss Forester?"

With a mock scowl, Anna slapped her brother's arm. "Don't you think Diana will want to save the first dance for her betrothed?" she asked. "There's no need to be so formal with her, either. She's practically your sister or have your London friends made you forget everything?"

That made me flinch. Philip's impassioned proposal some months before was the one secret I'd never told Anna. I had no idea how she would have reacted to it. That he had never spoken of it to his older sister either made me think I had made the right choice. Who had he told? His parents? But they had never spoken of it.

"The music is about to begin, Anna, and I don't see Richfield," Philip said, holding his hand out to me. "Miss Forester?"

A refusal now meant I would not be dancing at all evening. "Certainly," I said, putting my hand in his. I had to have something to distract me because I was sure I would be spending most of the evening on the wall with the spinsters.

The floor had been cleared, and lines were forming for the first dance. At the head of the room, the musicians were beginning to play. "I wanted to tell you I wish you every happiness, Miss Forester," Philip said as he led me forward. "You and Richfield both have my congratulations."

"Oh. Thank you," I said, surprised by this sudden attempt at reconciliation.

"When I think of my conduct this winter, I am ashamed," he said without acknowledging my words. "I had no intention of hurting you, and hope you will forgive me."

His wording puzzled me. Hurt me? As far as I knew, the only thing damaged had been our easy friendship. "Of course I forgive you," I said as I stepped into place. After all, it would have been churlish of me to hold it against him, even though the suddenness of it all made me uneasy.

He smiled as the first steps of the dance began. Whatever his reason for apologizing right then, I decided to put it aside until I didn't have to think about each step coming next.

AS HE HAD IN THE PAST, Philip made me laugh as we danced the lively country jig. It felt good to be on somewhat easy terms with him once more, though I knew I would never have the same friendship I had once had with him. To be on speaking terms at all was a relief in itself.

"I see Richfield is not yet here," Philip said as he led me off the floor at the end of our dance. "Isn't that strange?"

It was as if he was fishing for information. I chose to ignore it. "Look, Mr. Ward is dancing with Sarah!" I said, spotting my sister being led out for the next dance.

"I honestly did not think to see Ward show any interest in a young lady," Philip said, looking a little concerned. "He's something of a rogue in London, you know."

No, I hadn't known and chose not to comment. I had learned well how idle comments could destroy someone's reputation. That didn't mean I wasn't going to keep my eye on Mr. John Ward. Just in case. I would not allow my only sister to be hurt by someone who had no serious interest in her.

Making me promise to dance with him again, Philip excused himself and went to dance with Miss Carter. I was surprised to see the young lady without anyone at her side. Then again, Miss Reynolds had been a close companion, and she hadn't exactly endeared herself to any of the other young ladies. A fact she must be regretting.

Standing on the sidelines felt worse than it ever had before. My toe began to tap in time to the music.

"You're not dancing?"

Richfield?

My breath caught in my throat, and I slowly spun around. He stood before me in his impeccable evening wear. There was a smile on his face. Something I had thought I would never see again. I opened my mouth to speak, but nothing came out. Swallowing hard, I tried again. "You're here?"

His smile broadened, and he held out his hand. "I am. Shall we join the dance?"

He had come back. After all that had been said between us, he had come back! I could not think of anything else as I put my hand in his. He led me out, and we joined the dance. I did not smile as I moved through the steps. As I danced down the line, I caught Sarah's eye, and the look of absolute shock on her face made me laugh.

"What, Miss Forester, is so funny?" Richfield asked.

I shook my head, unable to explain. How was it possible to go from feeling miserable to completely happy in a matter of moments? In any event, I didn't know, and I didn't care.

"There is someone I want you to meet," Richfield said once the dance had ended. "If you don't mind sitting a dance out."

"No, I don't mind at all," I said, struggling to show some decorum.

Smiling, Richfield put my hand on his elbow and led me through the crowd. I quickly spotted my parents. We were headed in their direction. Not recognizing the woman they were speaking to, I frowned, my curiosity piqued. "Mother," Richfield said. Oh. Oh! "I would like you to meet Miss Diana Forester, my betrothed."

"Mrs. Richfield!" I said, bobbing a curtsy. "I'm pleased to meet you finally. I didn't know you would be here tonight."

For a moment, Mrs. Richfield simply watched me, a serious expression on her face. I fidgeted, feeling sweat forming on my palms. Then, she began to smile, her expression relaxing. "I've been hearing a great deal about you, Miss Forester. I'm pleased to meet you as well."

Well, that could have gone so much worse. "Mrs. Richfield and I were just becoming acquainted," Mother said to me, smiling.

"Why don't we have a seat and have a brief chat," Mrs. Richfield said, gesturing to the chairs. "I would love to become better acquainted with my future daughter-in-law."

"I'll get you something to drink," Richfield said with a smile.

Mrs. Richfield took my hand and pulled me towards the chairs. I glanced at Mother for support. She merely nodded at me and continued speaking with Mrs. Davison. This was a conversation I would have to face on my own.

FOR TWO DANCES, I SAT and talked to the older woman. She had many questions for me, such as what education I'd had and what my interests were. I had the feeling she was studying my character. Richfield brought us both lemonade and then went to talk to Sir Rodger, presumably to give us some space. I wasn't sure whether I appreciated or was annoyed he had done so.

"Miss Forester, I believe this is our dance."

Startled, I lifted my head to see Philip, holding his hand out. I hadn't even heard him approach. I didn't remember promising him a second dance. Refusing would mean I wouldn't be able to dance with John again. Unable to see a way out, I glanced over at my companion. Mrs. Richfield nodded, smiling pleasantly. "I look forward to speaking to you more when we have time to ourselves," she said.

Smiling my thanks, I stood up. "Until later, Mrs. Richfield," I said. I took Philip's arm as I walked back to the dancing.

"So that was Mrs. Richfield," Philip said in an offhand way. I could have kicked myself. Good manners meant I should have introduced him to her and I hoped my failure wouldn't leave a bad impression on her. "Her daughters are two charming ladies."

Richfield's sisters were here as well? "I will have to meet them," I said, resisting the urge to search the crowd. I wouldn't have recognized them, and they were not the only strangers at the ball.

Philip shook his head as he led me out onto the dance floor. Down the line, Richfield watched me with a smile. He was partnered with Anna for the dance. I felt a little sorry for him because the look on Anna's face said she intended on getting every bit of information she could, however she could.

The music began, and I curtsied. When Philip took my hands in his for the next step, I noticed something I hadn't seen when I danced with him earlier. "You're wearing your family ring?" I asked. I had often teased him about before, since he wasn't fond of the large gold piece of jewelry. It even had a family crest on the surface. It had sealed the letters of at least five Knighton generations before Philip was given it.

To my surprise, Philip stumbled. He'd never missed a step while dancing since he was fifteen and first learned how to dance like a gentleman! "Father likes it when I wear the stupid thing," he said as he regained his footing.

Laughing, I glanced down at his hands and then I was the one who missed a step. *His ring.* Time seemed to slow as I remembered kneeling down by the bridge and picking up the glinting piece of gold. I remembered rubbing at the mud that had been caked on the surface, thinking I'd seen the roaring lion before. I had seen it on Philip's hand half a dozen times before!

I also remembered hearing someone behind me. I'd thought it was one of my siblings, having somehow come around. I'd turned to see who it was a show them what I had found, but before I could, something struck my head. And when I woke, the ring had been gone.

It wouldn't have made sense for the highwayman to attack me just to get back a ring that would have been easy to trace. But if it identified who he was...

Philip Knighton? My friend, the young man who had asked to marry me, was the highwayman?

Chapter Twenty-One

I felt as though I couldn't breathe. It couldn't be true, but I knew I was right. Everything fell into place perfectly. He had returned for his ring knowing it would identify him, and he hadn't been robbed by the highwayman. But when he arrived, I had been in his way. How could he have done it, though? To our friends and neighbors?

"You look pale, Miss Forester," Philip was saying. He put his arm around my waist and pushed me forcefully away from the dance. Several people were looking at us with frowns. We must have disrupted the dance. "Let's get you some fresh air."

Before I could object or even think what to do, he pushed me out of the crowd. In the empty servants' hallway he guided me into, I jerked free. I refused to go a step further without some kind of explanation. "Philip, what did you do? What have you done?"

"I don't know what you're thinking—," Philip said, holding his hands up.

"I'm thinking —no, I remember— how I found your signet ring at the creek," I said, pointing at his hand. He flushed and hid his hand behind his back. "It was you, all this time. You stopped all those carriages and robbed all those people How could you? Philip, those are our neighbors. Our friends! And you stole from them?"

With a frustrated groan, Philip grabbed my arms. "Hold still for a minute before you start screaming, Diana. I have a perfectly good explanation—."

"There is no reason good enough for what you have done!" I said as I struggled. "Let go of me, Philip!"

"Would you just keep your voice down and listen to me?" Philip asked, tightening his grip. No one grabbed me without coming to regret it. Angrily, I kicked his shin. Yelping, he let go of my arms and jumped backward, grabbing at his injured limb. "What was that for? That hurt, Diana!"

What did he think it was for? He had robbed my friends and neighbors and hit me over the head. Now he was because I kicked him when he wouldn't let me go? Did he not see what he had done was wrong? And he wanted to explain it to me as if it would make everything better?

Maybe I should have been afraid. After all, he'd already proven he would hurt me to keep his identity protected. However, I was too angry with him to have room for fear.

"I'm telling your father," I said, straightening to my shoulders. Mr. Knighton would deal with this, and I would go back to the ball. I'd apologize to John for having ever wondered he was the highwayman. I spun to do as I said.

"Just listen to me for one minute, Diana!" Philip said, jumping forward and grabbing my arm.

"You're hurting me!"

"Diana!" Sarah came rushing to my side. "Philip Knighton, let her go this instant! Diana, are you well? What has happened?"

Immediately, Philip jerked away as a strong arm came around my shoulders. *John.* "Is there a problem?" my betrothed asked, his voice sounding strangled. I glanced up at him and noted the way his brow was furrowed. "Sarah and I were both concerned when you left the dance looking so pale, Diana."

I took a deep breath. There was only one course of action. "Sarah, please go find Mr. Knighton," I said, keeping my eyes on my once friend. "I think he will want to know his son is the highwayman."

The arm around my shoulders tightened protectively as Sarah gasped. "Philip?" my sister said in shock. "No!"

Philip said nothing and dropped his gaze to the floor. "I think you should do as your sister asked, Miss Sarah," John said gravely. "Diana would not make such an accusation without cause. Mr. Knighton should be here, and your father as well."

For a moment, Sarah didn't move. I realized too late what she intended to do when she stepped forward. "Sarah!" I said, stretching my hand out in vain to stop her. Sarah brought her hand up and slapped Philip. He said nothing as she glared at him, only put his hand against his now reddened cheek. I flinched in sympathy.

"You should be ashamed of yourself, Philip Knighton! After you swore to love my sister, you would hurt her?" Sarah snapped before she spun on her heel. "I'll be back."

"You're unharmed?" John asked, keeping his arm around my shoulder.

What a question. "As well as can be expected," I said with a sigh.

WE STOOD THERE FOR several minutes before Mr. Knighton, my father, and Anna came rushing in with Sarah right behind them. "Philip, what is this about?" Mr. Knighton asked, looking concerned. "Miss Sarah there was something we needed to know. Is there a problem?"

Even at his father's direct question, Philip didn't say anything. He was going to make me say it, and I wanted to hate him for it. "He's the highwayman," I said, forcing the condemning words out. "I know from the ring on his hand. I found it at the bridge. He must have dropped it and returned for it when he saw it was in my hand."

"Diana, are you sure? This isn't something to be taken lightly," Father asked, his expression serious. I nodded in answer, not trusting my voice.

"Don't be ridiculous!" Mr. Knighton said, stepping to his son. "Philip, what do you have to say in answer to this? Tell them there's not a shred of truth to this wild story."

Still, his son kept his silence, and Mr. Knighton moved back, reeling in shock. "Philip, our friends!" Anna said, her hands flying to her mouth. "How could you!"

"I needed funds!" Philip finally said, his tone sharp. He wouldn't look at any of us. "I had built up debts in London. I only stole from people with money. They could replace what they lost!"

I immediately thought of the Reynolds' and their recent loss of funds. No wonder he had invited them in the first place. His disappointment must have been great when he learned. How many of the other guests had he robbed before the ball today?

"Why did you not come to me?" Mr. Knighton asked, his tone anguished. "Why did you not trust me to help?"

"And tell you how much I had gambled? I couldn't disappoint you! I wanted to find my own way out of the mess. You weren't supposed to find out about any of this!"

Mr. Knighton put his hand on his face. Father focused on me. "Richfield, I think you should take Diana and Lady Anna back to the rest of the guests," he said. His eyes narrowed. "Sarah, I thought I told you to stay with your mother!"

Flushing, Sarah hurried for the door. John moved his hand from my shoulders to my waist and escorted me out of the hallway. "If Papa doesn't kill him, I will," Anna said as she followed us. "No. I will scream and shout at him and then I will kill him!"

"No, you won't," I said tiredly.

"Lady Anna, may I suggest you find your husband?" Richfield said.

"Yes, of course. He will be livid when he hears of this. He's warned Philip about the races countless times."

Anna stormed off, intent on finding Sir Rodger. "Perhaps I should have let her calm down first," John said in some concern, watching her weave her way through the crowd.

"She won't say a word to anyone if that's what you're worried about," I said. "She's protective of her family and friends if you hadn't realized that. She does know when to keep quiet about something. She would never breathe a word of this to anyone."

"It's not that I'm afraid she will say something, but any-one who looks at her right now can tell she is furious," John said as he faced me. "And you look like as though you are about to faint. Do you need to sit down?"

Sitting down sounded wonderful at that moment. I nod-ded, and he guided me to two empty seats. He bent over me. "Is there anything else I can get you?" he asked.

"You could sit down, so I don't have to look so far up," I said with a smile. Looking rueful, he did so. For a moment, we just watched the other dancers. Then, it came to me we needed to clear up what had happened the last time we were together. Now was as good a time as any. "I'm sorry for not telling you what Sarah said."

"Peacemaker," John said with a soft chuckle. He then sighed. "I'm sorry I called you a fortune hunter."

I had to smile at that. "I shouldn't have let Sarah's wild stories affect me. I knew you were not the highwayman. Sarah accused me of being blinded to the truth because I kept insisting she was wrong."

"Did you honestly have a hard time keeping her and Will from trying to prove I was the highwayman?"

"Oh, you have no idea," I said with a laugh. "I was con-vinced they had elaborate plans and I had to watch them all the time. Then Sarah admitted they simply liked watching me worry over nothing and there were no plans. I had wor-ried for no reason."

John laughed, drawing looks our way. "Yes, I can imagine you did."

"Don't laugh! I was a complete wreck the entire time. I'm surprised I was even able to put a sentence together."

"No one would have been able to tell," Richfield said, patting my hand. "I suppose you know where I got the idea about you being a fortune hunter."

"Anna told me, yes. Can we agree to not listen to other people's gossip from now on? It appears to have a bad effect on us."

"I think that sounds like a wise decision. I suppose it is something your mother said?"

"Well, she may have said something similar, but the words are my own."

He nodded. "My mother likes you."

Did she? That was a relief and a surprise. What had happened to her being concerned about it being too soon and all of that? One meeting and I had changed her mind? "I'm glad," I managed to say. I cleared my throat, struggling for composure. "I like her as well."

"My sisters are anxious to meet you," Richfield said, glancing at the dance floor. "They have a bit more interest in dancing than meeting their future sister, though, so you will have to meet them properly when you come to tea tomorrow."

"Am I coming to tea tomorrow?"

"Our mothers arranged it."

The current dance came to an end. In the absence of music, the conversations around us increased. "Diana, what did Sarah mean when she said Knighton loved you?" John asked abruptly.

Groaning, I covered my face with my hand. "He asked for my hand in marriage over the winter. I had to tell him

I wouldn't marry him. Tonight was the first time we've exchanged civil words. Or any words at all."

"Why did you refuse?"

Why were we having this conversation now? I hadn't wanted to have it at all. "Because he was like a brother to me and not at all the man I envisioned myself spending the rest of my life with," I said a little bitterly. I still couldn't believe what he had done. And for money?

John took my hand and squeezed it. "You'll forgive him," he said confidently.

"Not any time soon. My head hurt for days, you know."

He laughed again. "And of course, you're not one to hold a grudge at all."

My smile faded as I went back to thinking about what had just happened. "What will happen to him?" I asked. I hadn't thought about it before, but highwaymen were generally hung for their crimes, weren't they? Had I just condemned a friend to death by hanging?

"Don't worry yourself over it," John said, seeming to sense my sudden panic. "I doubt there will be any real punishment. I imagine the items will be returned anonymously. Or perhaps compensated in the same way. No one will ever find out about it."

Perhaps it wasn't justice that the son of the gentry would get off where another man might be punished with his life, but I did feel relief. "I only hope he appreciates what his father will do for him," I said softly.

"The waltz," was announced loudly, sending a minor ripple of astonishment through the room.

"Oh, Avonton society won't recover from this," I said lightly with a laugh. Only a few brave souls were stepping out onto the dance floor, Anna and her husband being at the forefront. "Though I'm not surprised the Knightons would attempt to bring the latest style of dance to the country."

"Only an attempt?" John asked as he rose from his seat. He kept my hand firmly caught in his as he made a low bow. "Would you do me the great honor of dancing, Miss Forester?"

Startled, I stared up at him. "You cannot be serious! Waltzing by the pond, out of sight of everyone, is one thing but in front of every acquaintance I have—! It isn't done!"

Smiling, John tugged on my hand before bringing it up to his lips. "I took you for a forward thinker, Miss Forester. We cannot allow Lady Anna to have all the fun, can we? You know she will think you sadly faint-hearted if you do not."

What would Mother think? I opened my mouth to protest more, but couldn't find the words. Richfield pulled me to my feet. I'm sure my cheeks were a shade of red that had never been seen on a lady's face as he led me to the floor. Anna's smile was proud and excited but did nothing to hide the pain in her eyes.

"Everyone is staring at us," I whispered as the music began. I made my curtsey, determined not to look like a fool.

"Let them," John said, bowing. "After this, you won't have a choice but to marry me, Miss Forester."

"Is this your evil plan? To ruin my reputation completely, so I have no other choice? I might begin thinking you are a villain of a different sort."

We linked hands as the dance began. "You have found me out," John said as he circled. "I beg you, do not tell your sister. I fear she would give me the same treatment she gave poor Philip Knighton."

I was sure he was right on that point. "Then you shall always have to behave yourself." My cheeks flushed again. Flirting did not come easily to me.

He laughed at me. There was a sudden shriek, and the dance came to a stop as the musicians stopped playing. "Highwayman! The highwayman was staring at us through the window!"

Other ladies began screaming, and all the men rushed towards the windows. Anna stood with a shocked look on her face. I glanced around and couldn't find one specific person. "Will." I exchanged looks with my betrothed as we spoke at the same time. I added, "I'm going to kill him. Where does he get these ideas of his?"

"With your father occupied, perhaps we should find your brother?" John asked.

Out of the corner of my eye, I could see Mother already moving across the hall. She seemed to have remembered what I had not: that when Will became bored at large gatherings, he tended to cause trouble. "I think Mother has it in hand," I said with a small laugh.

"I see she does. Should I feel sorry for Will?"

"Yes."

"Will I be in trouble for giving him the idea in the first place?" John asked.

I lifted my gaze to his in shock. "You gave him the idea?" He shrugged in response, and I shook my head. "Yes, you will be in a great deal of trouble. And not just with my mother."

"Then no. I did not give him the idea."

"Liar."

Laughing, John offered his arm and escorted me away from the dance floor. A different dance was beginning, ladies pulling their partners away from the windows. It was just a typical evening in my life, it seemed.

I wouldn't have had it any other way.

Epilogue

Four weeks passed in a flurry of activity. Mrs. Richfield and her two daughters, Katherine and Emma, had settled in Vanderson Cottage until the wedding. They were more than happy to help with the planning, and I believed we would be fast friends in no time.

Invitations were sent out, and my entire family did come for the wedding. The look on my husband to be's face when he met my family is one I will never forget. He hadn't believed me when I had warned him about the number of Foresters there were.

On a beautiful Friday morning, I became Mrs. John Richfield. The gold band on my left hand felt strange, but I knew I would become accustomed to it. I couldn't keep from smiling as I walked out of the church, my hand in John's.

Philip Knighton had left his family home the day after the ball. We didn't hear any more about the highwayman, and the whole matter was quickly forgotten by everyone who did not know the truth.

As I had expected, Will was severely disappointed to have been left out of the capture of the highwayman. I fully believed he would pull some prank on my wedding day in retaliation, and had charged Emma Richfield to keep an eye on him. She thought he was adorable, and he used all his skills to keep her as far from himself as possible. Given that Emma was only a year older than Will, I thought it fitting he should be intent on avoiding her.

I hadn't forgotten my sister's interest in Mr. Ward and had asked Richfield to look into it. He could find nothing against the man, but we both agreed to keep an eye on the situation. Mr. Ward was invited to our wedding, and Sarah had used every strategy to be by his side whenever she could.

The wedding breakfast was loud with conversation and music. I was more than ready for the silence of the carriage ride to Vanderson Cottage.

"You are unusually quiet, Mrs. Richfield," my husband said, taking my hand in his.

"I'm just taking it all in."

Smiling back, he leaned over and kissed me. I wrapped my arms around his neck and pulled him closer. Married life was definitely going to agree with me.

Acknowledgements

This book would not be what it is today without the help of a few other people. A huge thank you to Carissa Dillon for editing and polishing up my book better than I'd ever hoped for. Thank you to my sister for being my first reader, and my mom for being my first critic. I'm thankful to my writer's group for always supporting me. And, of course, I can't forget about my lovely followers on Wattpad for being with me from the beginning.

You all rock!

Also Available By Bethany Swafford

My Hands Hold My Story

For fans of A Knight of Silence and Read My Lips comes a YA historical western full of grit and heart...

In 1874, Ivy Steele's deafness is more than a handicap. It's a disease. Surrounded by a family that doesn't understand her, she's learned to cope and find solace where she can. Then, the unexpected happens. Her aunt dies, and her uncle sends her away to rejoin her father's family in Montana.

Left to fend for herself, after the companion hired to escort her abandons her, sixteen-year-old Ivy faces continual hardship and danger. Several men see an unaccompanied Ivy as a flower ripe for the picking, and things only get worse when masked men hold up their stagecoach.

Barely scraping through, Ivy makes it to Montana with her nerves shaken and what little money she has in her boot. Expecting a peaceful if not affectionate welcome, Ivy finds herself in greater hardship than she's ever known.

Surrounded by a stepfamily that hates her, and flung into a life where hearing is vital, Ivy finds solace in a handsome cowboy named Remy. But things with her new family are not what they seem. And Ivy is about to find out that the danger she faced on the journey west, has followed her to Montana...

Bethany Swafford dazzles with her stunning young adult debut, introducing a strong heroine, the hardships of frontier life, shocking twists, and a slow-burning romance that will leave you wanting more.

Third place winner of the 2018 Rosemary Award

Available in paperback and ebook form from all retailers.

Emily's Choice

EIGHTEEN-YEAR-OLD EMILY Lawrence believes life to be simple and that the only challenge she faces is convincing her cousin and companion, Rosalind, to have more courage. This belief changes when Mr. Adrian Williams moves into the neighboring estate. Emily's father forbids her from having anything to do with the man, but when an unexpected illness throws her into Mr. Williams company, Emily finds that obeying her father is more difficult than she imagined.

Emily struggles to understand why her father is so insistent on the matter. What happened eight years ago, when the Williams left the estate? Is it a coincidence that Emily's mother died at the exact same time?

Available as an ebook and in print.

Coming Soon

Not My Idea (A Gentleman of Misfortune, Book One)

"*L*ucas, you must return home."

Twenty-two year old Lucas Bywood abandons his Grand Tour in response to those words from his father. Everything is not well at home and he finds himself in a bit of a fix. A little warning that his father had made tentative arrangements for his marriage would have been nice but Luke really wishes it had been anyone other than the young lady chosen. After all, Phoebe Ramsey had always been an annoyance and any time they had spent together had resulted in physical injuries for one of them.

Just when Luke thinks he's escaped that particular future, he finds himself courting a young woman he doesn't want, a furious best friend who wants a duel to satisfy honor, and the responsibility of finding who and why someone had caused an accident for his mother.

This was not his idea of what the summer was going to be like.

Keeping the Past (The Lady's Maid Trilogy,

Book One)

IMPELLED BY A NASTY rumor that implicates her late father and brother as traitors to the Crown, Juliet Sinclair embarks on a course to save her family name. Relying on her five year absence from society to keep her identity safe, she assumes the name of Julie Nelson and takes on the unlikely position as a lady's maid.

Just what has she gotten herself into? Why is Mr. Oswyn Harper constantly on hand? Will Juliet's heart be tempted once more by her former beau, Mr. Henry Bladen?

There's no doubt that Juliet's adventure is only just beginning.

Don't miss out!

Visit the website below and you can sign up to receive emails whenever Bethany Swafford publishes a new book. There's no charge and no obligation.

https://books2read.com/r/B-A-LHKF-QRIV

BOOKS 2 READ

Connecting independent readers to independent writers.

About the Author

For as long as she can remember, Bethany Swafford has loved reading books. That love of words extended to writing as she grew older and when it became more difficult to find a 'clean' book, she determined to write her own. Among her favorite authors are Jane Austen, Sir Arthur Conan Doyle, and Georgette Heyer. When she doesn't have a pen to paper (or fingertips to a laptop keyboard), she can be found with a book in hand.

To get notified about new releases and any news, sign up to Bethany's Newsletter here: https://bit.ly/2Hg7KJw

Read more at https://bethanyswaffordauthor.wordpress.com/.